Left Horse Black

S. J. Reisner

Left Horse Black

Sorcerers' Twilight Book One

S. J. Reisner

Darkerwood Publishing Group
United States of America

Discounts are available for bulk orders of this title. Contact Darkerwood Publishing Group by e-mail at:

darkerwoodpublishing@gmail.com

or visit us at

http://www.ofs-demonolatry.org/darkerwood/

Left Horse Black - First printed in Hardcover in 2005 by ArcheBooks

Library of Congress in Publication Data:
Reisner, S. J.
      Left Horse Black
      ISBN 978-0-9669788-7-2
      First Trade Paperback Edition
      I. Fiction II. Fantasy

Cover Art © 2006 by Steven Lafitte

Dedication

For my sister, Connie, who spent countless hours going over my manuscript, encouraged me to go after my dreams, and whose valuable insight helped Tnasha and Aragel find their way.

The West Ocean Mainlands

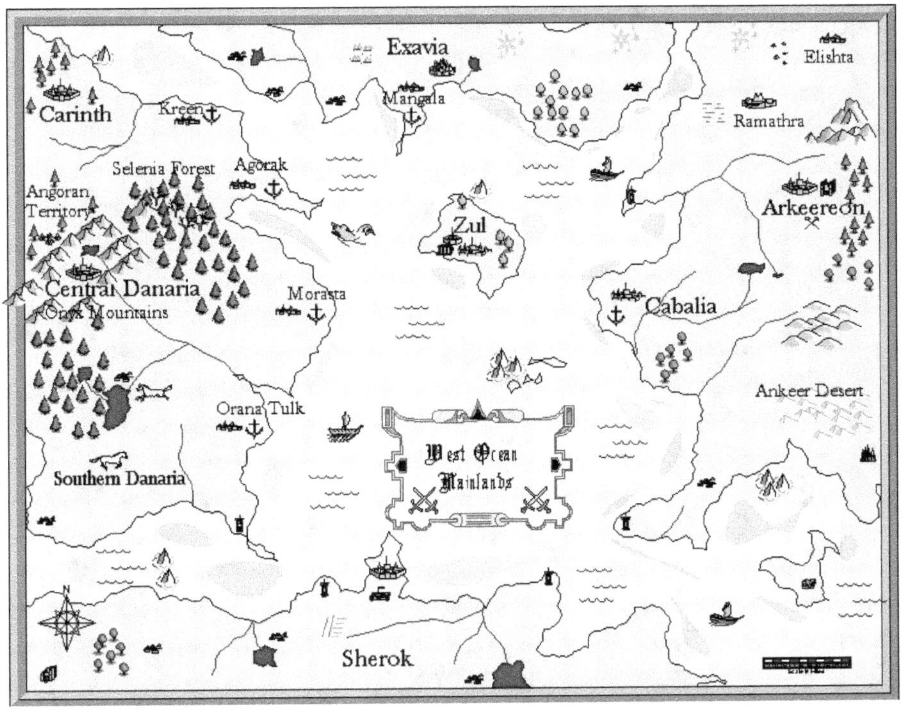

CHAPTER 1

Aragel woke with a start and sat up in his bed. The heavy oak door across the hall from his own slammed shut with such force, that his own door shook on its hinges in sympathetic response. Night's shadows enveloped the chamber, and he could vaguely make out the outline of his sparsely furnished room, a cedar clothes chest, a plain chair, and an old oak table. With reluctance, he pulled back the thick, maroon quilts covering him, and with hesitation, touched his bare feet to the cold floor. Pausing, he stood, feeling the cold sink into the arches of his feet and slide up the rest of his body. The fire in the hearth had long since extinguished, and nothing remained save for a few orange coals that offered little heat. Aragel picked up a gray silk dressing gown from the chair and hastily wrapped it around himself. Once his feet touched the rug underfoot, the chill retreated. Very distant, he could hear the sound of low, but frantic voices filter beneath his door. He furrowed his dark brow in puzzlement, then hurried to the door to see if his ear could lend better purchase to what was happening outside.

Prince Hermond had arrived the day before, and took the usually empty room across from Aragel's own. The Exavian prince visited more frequently now that his marriage to Princess Serena drew near. The low grumble of men's voices still resounded faintly from the room across the hall. Aragel slipped his hand over the door's cold, brass latch and sprung it open with a click that seemed to echo endlessly through the hallway. He winced as if wincing could make opening the door quieter. The commotion in the adjacent room grew louder as he stepped from his room. Keeping himself hidden in the dank shadows of the pitch corridors, he listened carefully to the voices drifting luminously from the Exavian prince's chamber.

Prince Hermond had a visitor. That much was clear. Aragel could make out the prince's overly lilting accent more rightly than he could the other, but he did not recognize the affluent, and somewhat chiding speech of the man with whom Hermond spoke. A cold chill made its way up his spine, causing the soft dark hairs on the back of his neck to stand straight up. After adjusting his ear to the sounds, he could finally make out the words.

"It is simple, Prince Hermond," the unfamiliar voice toned, resolute and sure. "You wanted power and I have given you the means by which to gain it. Sherok is an easy attainment. Danaria and Carinth will not be as easy."

Aragel shoved his back into the wall as if to become one with it. Prince Hermond moved closer to the door, his voice sharper and clearer now.

"Darak is not the problem. What about young Prince Aragel? With Darak gone..." his words trailed off.

Aragel's eyes widened in horror and he could feel his hands, as if being controlled by some unseen force, pressing against the wall; chaffing against the rough stone.

"We cannot have him running about either, can we?" said the stranger without hesitation.

Prince Hermond remained silent for a moment. "Of course, Your Eminence," he finally said.

Aragel had heard enough. With his deepest fears realized and manifested, the young prince darted back to his room and grabbed the chair that sat near the window. Since Hermond's room had once been used for storage, the door opened outward instead of inward, so as quiet as he could manage, he brought the chair into the hallway and carefully propped it against Prince Hermond's chamber door. He secured it beneath the doorknob, shoving it firmly in place so whoever was in there with Hermond could not get out. Once he was sure it would hold, he bolted down the hallway to the spiraling stairs leading to the main hall. As he hurried along, the dancing shadows from the torchlight jumped at him. Once again, he felt the hairs on his neck stand on end, but he did not chance a glance back. He kept himself focused upon reaching his destination - the king's quarters.

When he reached the heavy oak door ornate with ironwork, he knocked lightly. No guards greeted him as he hoped; nor had he seen any. The long halls remained tomb-like and empty. Likely, the guards were in other parts of the castle patrolling the more obscure corridors. That was the drawback to having a part time, voluntary military.

From the king's room, no response came.

Aragel opened the door and slipped inside, being careful to close the door firmly behind him. The foyer was dark, but a faint light from the sleeping chamber led Aragel past the dark outlines of the room's contents to the king's bedside. He took a deep breath and gently shook his uncle by the shoulder.

"Uncle Darak?"

The king mumbled something inaudible and rolled over to face Aragel, opening his weary gray eyes ever so slightly. "Aragel?" King Darak yawned and closed his eyes again.

"Please wake up. I've just heard something you should know about."

King Darak let out another yawn, lifted himself up, and leaned over to light the lantern on the bedside table. "What is it at this hour?" He seemed annoyed. Darak was a sturdy man. His many years revealed fine lines in his forehead. His deep gray eyes boasted years of wisdom and knowledge. A graying full beard covered the lower half of his face and his once thick, dark hair now stood streaked with gray, receding slightly.

"Prince Hermond has a visitor," Aragel said, then added quickly, "They're planning to kill us!"

The king's reaction was not what Aragel had hoped for, and certainly not what he expected. The king let out a laugh.

"That's nonsense, boy. You must have been dreaming."

"But Uncle, I was *not* dreaming. I was awake as I am now. I heard him talking to someone in his room, just now. I know I wasn't dreaming!" Aragel could not believe this.

"Aragel, I assure you it was nothing more than a dream. At this hour, no one in Sherok is lucid. If you're concerned, perhaps you should find one of the soldiers, take him with you, and knock on Hermond's door."

The king studied his nephew for a moment. Aragel shifted uncomfortably in his gaze wondering if Darak was noting their resemblance as he was. His hair was thick and dark, and fell to his shoulders. He bore the same sturdy stature, and broad shoulders. Just recently, fine hairs had begun to emerge from Aragel's chin and upper lip, though the king had not made mention of it, for which Aragel was thankful.

"And do what?" Aragel threw his hands up in disbelief. "Ask him to introduce us? I've barricaded them in the room with a chair."

King Darak sat up suddenly, startled. His face bore the look of a stern father, something Aragel had not seen in years. "You did what? With whom was he speaking?"

Aragel shrugged his shoulders. "I'm not sure. But the man had a distinct accent. One I've never heard before. Hermond called him *Your Eminence*, I fear for both our safety, uncle. I know I have no evidence yet, no proof. But we cannot risk the safety of Sherok. I think you and I should take several guards and go to the room!" The young prince began struggling for breath, wheezing.

"Fine. I'll agree to that." The king put a reassuring hand on his nephew's shoulder in attempt to calm him. When the wheezing subsided, Darak stood and reached for his clothes. "Wake commander Corigerg and gather some soldiers. I'll be with you in a moment." He sighed and shook his head as Aragel left.

Commander Corigerg and two guards stood patiently outside the king's chambers when Darak finally emerged. Aragel stood at the far end of the hallway with his head cocked attempting to hear any far off noises. Together, the men hurried toward the southeast tower.

As they approached the stairwell, Hermond met them. He came from the direction of the courtyard. Hermond's long, pointed nose gave him away as Exavian. The blonde hair and crystal blue eyes, along with his pale flesh and thin bony build further set him apart from the muscular, tan skinned, dark haired residents of Sherok.

"What are all of you doing up at this hour?" Hermond's gaze darted suspiciously at the king, Aragel, and the armed men flanking them.

"We were just going to ask you that same question." Darak smiled at Hermond kindly, and then raised an eyebrow at Aragel. "Just getting in?"

Hermond paused a few stairs ahead of them. "I was checking on my mare. She seemed to be acting strangely earlier and I wanted to make sure she was not coming down with colic. So I walked her for more than an hour. Her bloodline makes her more susceptible to such ailments."

Aragel nodded with disbelief clear on his face. "She's fine then?"

Hermond started back up the stairs. "It seems so. Though I do have one of the stable boys watching after her while I try to get some sleep."

"We should probably come with you then. It has come to our attention there may be intruders in your room," King Darak told him.

The Exavian prince stopped again, and turned around, feigning surprise. "Intruders? Really?"

Aragel rolled his eyes. "I *heard* people talking in there," he said, his voice overly laden with caution.

Drawing his sword, Hermond, the soldiers and Commander Corigerg moved quickly up the stairwell with Aragel and King Darak lagging behind.

When they reached the door Aragel gasped in disbelief. The chair still stood wedged beneath the doorknob. Hermond pulled the chair away and opened the door, careful to stay behind it. The soldiers rushed in ahead of him. Inside, the room was dark and cold. Hermond lit a wall torch and the bedside lantern as the soldiers made their way around the room, searching for the alleged intruders.

Hermond chuckled and scanned the room. "Hmm. Nothing is out of place. I think perhaps young Prince Aragel was having a dream."

"But *you* were in here with someone called *Your Eminence*!" Aragel protested. He narrowed his eyes and glared at the foreign prince.

"*I* was out with my mare most of the evening," Hermond said in what seemed gentle mockery.

"But I heard everything, your plot to kill my uncle and me. I know I wasn't asleep." Aragel drew a deep breath and searched Hermond's face for evidence of dishonesty.

"What?" Prince Hermond looked at Aragel confused. "You and your uncle are family to me. I would never do anything like that!" He put his hand on Aragel's shoulder, "You had a dream. Were I in your position I may have done the same thing. Sometimes dreams can seem very real."

King Darak took a deep breath. "Aragel, it is obvious no one has been in this room all night."

Aragel looked down at his feet in attempt to avert the eyes staring him down. Vanquished, he found his voice. "I suppose you're right. Maybe it was a dream. I'm sorry I woke everyone for nothing."

King Darak patted Hermond on the shoulder and bade him goodnight. He turned and left with the soldiers behind him. Commander Corigerg stayed behind a moment longer and gave Aragel a sympathetic look then glanced at Hermond with angry, dark eyes. He quickly turned his attention back to Aragel, "Would you like me to post some guards at your door, Prince Aragel?"

"No. After all, dreams can't hurt me, right?"

"No, I suppose not." Commander Corigerg's gaze fell on the open window, and then moved to the hearth where a faint glow of several small burning embers remained. Aragel had been following the commander's shift in attention and realized that the room did not seem as cold as it should have. With a sly backward glance in Hermond's direction, and a quick warning glance at Aragel, the commander retreated from the foreign prince's chambers.

After Corigerg had gone, Aragel turned to Hermond. "Well good night, Hermond."

"Sleep well, Aragel," he said with a sly grin.

Aragel picked up his chair from the hallway and retreated to his own room, closing the door gently behind him. Once inside, he turned the lock then took the chair back to its spot by the window. He sat and drew his knees to his chest. He often used this chair for thinking. He knew what he heard. He had *not* been dreaming. Somehow, Hermond had managed to leave the room and replace the chair in the time it took Aragel to gather his uncle and the soldiers.

He decided he would not be too hasty and would wait for sunrise to talk to Commander Corigerg. Corigerg was the only commanding officer in the Sherokean military. He was much more suspicious about people than King Darak. The commander had given him a look that said, "I believe you," had he not? Or was that a dream too? Nonetheless, it was clear to him that his uncle had no intention of doing anything. Darak was fond of Hermond. Sometimes Aragel felt like his uncle paid more attention to Hermond than to him. Hermond had pulled the wool over the king's eyes. Or Darak simply did not trust Aragel's judgment of the Exavian prince. Either way, something had to be done.

As the sun rose in the east, a thick mass of fog withdrew to the ocean. For the first time in his life, Aragel was truly frightened.

He found himself drifting in and out of restless sleep as the sun lifted high into the morning sky. His dreams took him back to his childhood, to when he was four. At that age, he was a spice merchant's son living in the city of Kreen. His parents stood tall above him, placing amber-colored jars of spices on the highest shelves.

His mother's smooth, dark face and beautiful brown eyes looked down on him, soft and loving. "You put these spices on the lower shelf, Aragel," she said. She smiled at him, encouraging him to place the spices on the lower shelf.

Pride overwhelmed him. "All right Momma." Carefully, four-year-old Aragel put the jars on the lower shelf making sure they were even and straight.

"What wonderful work you do!" She caught him in a hug.

Then the dream changed, moving forward two years. The images frightened him. Her pale face and deep sunken eyes stared out at him. Everything about her was lifeless. He woke, shivering and sweating, with his heart beating wildly in his chest. Both his parents died that year. The plague, Gloxorthia, the same illness that killed Queen Aubrey, killed them as well. Once their bodies had been buried deep in the ground, Darak had relatives put young Aragel in a carriage that brought him here, to Sherok, as King Darak's ward.

Aragel shook the visions of death from his mind, breathed a sigh of relief and looked around. Uncle Darak had given him the tower room on his sixteenth birthday. He liked the small chamber. Smiling, he recalled the argument he and his cousin, Serena, had about it.

"But I need a sewing room, father!" She stomped one small, leather clad foot impatiently.

"Your chambers are large enough." Darak's calm, even tone was a trait Aragel admired. He never seemed to overreact to anything. Aragel often tried to mimic it, though he thought he failed miserably.

When the argument was over, Aragel won the room through gender as Darak reasoned the young Prince was almost a man and needed his privacy. For that privacy alone, Aragel was grateful. He endured many years of Serena's mothering, even though she was a mere year older.

And now she was marrying the gat-toothed Exavian Prince, Hermond. An assassin. Across the hall in the visitor's quarters, not a sound surfaced, and the tower rooms stood bathed in silence. The young prince's gaze shifted to the door, searching the light seeping underneath for shadows passing by. Those shadows grew dimmer as the sun rose higher into the sky, reaching into his window in golden beams of light.

After Garik Darak, the king's son, was assassinated, the

king prepared Aragel's training for his eventual rise to Sherok's throne. Someone had to be king, and Aragel's royal bloodline put him next in line for the monarchy. He lifted an eyebrow at the idea and chuckled to himself.

"I suppose I should get used to people wanting to kill me," he whispered aloud, allowing his gaze to fall on the fields far below him.

The horrible vision of his mother resurfaced, rearing its ugly head from the deep recesses of his memory. She gulped, sucking in air as she tried to take her last breaths. A deep rattle emerged from her chest… He shook the memory from his mind and tried to focus on something else.

He closed his eyes. Exhaustion overwhelmed him. Darak had lied about his only son's assassination. Aragel remembered it clearly now as if someone suddenly pulled back a black veil. Garik had *left*. He and Darak had an argument. Garik threw his responsibilities aside, abandoned his right to the throne, and ran away - without Darak's knowledge or permission. The last words he remembered his cousin speaking were, "I need more than a seaside farming community." Aragel had been very young when it happened, hiding in one of the empty stalls in the stable, watching his cousin stride off, leaving Commander Corigerg agape.

Becoming heir to the throne happened so suddenly. He was ten when he found out.

"You are going to be a king, boy! It is an opportunity few men have. You will be one of those privileged few."

Aragel remembered Darak's words. Ten-years-old and wide-eyed, he recalled his response. "Can I tell people what to do?"

Darak laughed and nodded. "Of course, but you cannot rule with a heavy hand, my boy. You must be sympathetic to the needs of your people, strong in negotiation, and firm, but yielding with your allies."

"I don't think I can do all of that."

"You will learn."

"How?"

Darak's gray eyes softened. "I will teach you."

Since then, Aragel often looked forward to the task. He loved Sherok, unlike his predecessor, and could not imagine living anywhere else. Sherok was his whole world now. Had he stayed in Kreen he would have been nothing more than a dead spice merchant's son. Now that he was older, he spent his days studying treaties and trade agreements. He was educated in courtly behaviors and well versed in the Danarian, Carinthian, Exavian, and the Arkeeronish languages. Up until now, his training for the monarchy had proceeded faultlessly.

Aragel opened his eyes suddenly and stared out the window, inhaling the cool, humid morning air. Mornings were so quiet. Sherok was a peace loving country. With its economy built solely on crop exportation and fish markets, they were a simple people void of opulent luxuries and finery.

Scrunching his nose in thought, he remembered last year's harvest. All of Sherok, even the aristocracy took to the fields to help bring in the crops. It was some of the hardest work he ever engaged in. But afterward, he and Darak spent a week partaking in the festivities. That alone made the hard work worthwhile. He had never felt such a strong sense of community among people of various social classes before.

In Sherok, the summers were warm and not too hot, while the winters remained mild. Year round, bouts of heavy rain crossed the continent making the climate ideal for producing large, bountiful crops. Sherok was, in fact, the largest exporter and provider of fresh fruits and vegetables in the West Ocean Mainlands.

There was one drawback as he saw it, however. The insects that flourished in Sherok were larger than on any other continent. Perhaps the worst economical drawback was in crop failure due to insect invasion, the nastiest of these being locusts that grew larger than a grown man's foot. With his eyes cast on a freshly plowed and seeded field in the distance, he felt his lips turn upward in a smile, remembering the first time he dined on battered, fried locusts and fire ants covered in a thick, sugar icing. He laughed to himself and felt his eyelids growing heavy.

All of these memories led to one simple thought. Sherok was his home and he was determined not to let anything happen to it.

Aragel's mind finally settled on the situation at hand. He needed to have a plan, just in case. Because Sherok's military consisted of part time and volunteer soldiers, it would be necessary for Aragel to put together reinforcements to protect his country and his throne. Four years ago, Sherok signed a peace treaty with Danaria; home to the West Ocean Mainlands' largest armies. Even if Hermond had no intention of war, a reinforcement of Danarian soldiers to guard his family might foil the prince's ill intentions. But he decided to wait until he could talk to Commander Corigerg just in case the commander had a better idea.

Still huddled in the chair, drifting in and out of sleep, he heard a rustle in front of him, and he jumped as if suddenly recalling the events from the night before. He rubbed the residue of sleep from his eyes and stood. Near the large arched window stood a man dressed in black.

Aragel swallowed hard and cleared his throat, trying to find his voice, but the stranger spoke first.

"Hello Aragel," the man said in perfect Sherokean.

Aragel cleared his throat again and lowered his voice. A poor attempt to sound more menacing. "Who are you and what are you doing here?" he asked, noting that his voice quivered with the anxiety consuming him. His mind raced furiously. Had this been the same man he heard Prince Hermond speaking to only hours earlier? No, he decided quickly; the accent was wrong.

"You might say I'm an old friend of the family. It has been some time since I last saw you. You were a young child back then. Maybe six?" The man crinkled his brow as if studying what he saw.

"What do you think you're doing in here?" Aragel's eyes darted to the door. His mind raced back to the lecture Commander Corigerg was always giving him. "Assassin's are everywhere, boy," he had said. Aragel never really took the old warlord seriously - until now. Until last night. Sherok did not have enemies. It seemed Prince Hermond had not wasted time.

The man pulled down the hood of his cloak. His

Sherokean features took Aragel by surprise. His thin, lithe stature, high cheekbones and fine long dark hair mimicked Princess Serena's, while his angular jaw and gray eyes resembled those of King Darak. His chin boasted a thin beard, the result of having gone several days unshaven. In all plausibility, it seemed that he and the stranger before him could certainly be related. Unsure, Aragel paused. Was this a relative? Then a small thought crossed the young prince's mind. He pursed his lips. *Garik?* Aragel narrowed his eyes. If it was Garik, and King Darak discovered him, he would surely be tried for treason. After ten years, the king was still upset about Garik's unexpected disappearance. It was still a sensitive subject. One that few people dared to discuss with the king.

He considered grabbing his sword, but decided it would be better to wait and see what happened. To get to the sword he would have to dart past the stranger. It was too risky. Perhaps even hasty. He casually moved across the room closer to his sword, trying not to be too obvious, just in case the stranger was working for Hermond.

"I do not know you. You certainly don't act like a friend," Aragel said sharply. "Friends generally use the front door."

The man took a step toward him. "You do not remember me?" His Sherokean was faultless and laden with the dialect of Sherok's more aristocratic inhabitants.

Aragel remembered his training for situations like this. Now, in an actual instance, the training seemed impractical. "No. Besides, if I knew you I expect you would at least knock before entering a room. How do I know you are not here to kill me? Who are you, really?"

The man shook his head. "If I wanted to kill you, I would have done it already. What would you think if I told you I was someone from your distant past?" the man paused, searching Aragel's eyes for some sign of recognition. "I'm sorry to have startled you. I need to talk to you. It's important. I need to know about Prince Hermond's business here."

"You don't get it, do you? Get out! Even if you are someone from my past, why should I want anything to do with you?" Aragel felt fear swell in the pit of his stomach. The reality of the night before slapped him hard across the face, and his knees quivered. He could hear muffled footsteps ascending the upper stairs from the hallway. He began wheezing.

The man held up his hands in retreat and glanced nervously toward the door. "I'll come back later when the castle quiets down, but you musn't tell anyone I was here."

Aragel gasped for a breath of air. "What do you mean not tell anyone? Out!"

The man turned back to the window and put one leather-clad foot on the ledge, "Promise me."

The lock rattled, clicked, and the door opened. Serena poked her head into the room with the castle's master key in her hand. "Aragel, why is this door locked?"

Serena was a petite, thin young woman. Her ebony hair fell well below her waist and her soft brown eyes, delicate features, and high cheekbones showed impeccable breeding. Many said she was the mirror image of the late Queen Aubrey.

He turned to Serena, startled. Attempting to calm his wheezing he closed his eyes and took several deep, measured breaths. "Do we have a visitor to the castle?" he finally asked her, pointing to the corner.

Serena lifted her eyebrows, puzzled. She gave him a worried look. "There is no one in this tower other than you and Prince Hermond. Please do not leave your door locked anymore. It worries me. Perhaps you should see the physician today. You have dark circles beneath your eyes."

Aragel turned to the corner. The man was gone.

"I didn't sleep well," he said, not having to feign sleepiness. He yawned. In reality, the yawn felt more like a sigh of relief rather than a reminder of a sleepless night.

"I think Commander Corigerg has done some damage to your pea-sized brain making you play soldier out in the sun all day. It's no wonder you've been having strange dreams and difficulty catching your breath. Now get yourself together and come down to eat," she admonished him in the stern, motherly voice Aragel most resented.

After Serena left, he looked around the room in

disbelief. Nothing seemed out of place. His bed, covered with rumpled quilts, lay untouched. The deep purple tapestry still hung flat against the cold wall. The maroon rugs on the floor had no stray dirt on them. Yet he knew he had seen the man, Garik; he had actually talked to him.

Maybe Serena was right. Listening to Commander Corigerg for hours beneath the glare of the sun was beginning to wear on him. His intrepid venture the night before could have also induced some kind of a hallucination. Nonetheless, he told himself he would talk to Commander Corigerg about Prince Hermond. He decided he would catch the commander after the midmorning meal, before he started his daily activities. He made his way down the corridor to the stairs. All the while, the haunting words, "Promise me," lingered in his mind like a bad dream.

Upon reaching the dining hall, Aragel found that everyone had arrived before him. Commander Corigerg sat to the left of the king, wearing a faded purple tunic and gray leggings, the same thing he wore to every meal. Commander Corigerg was a thick man. His muscular arms and sturdy legs boasted his many years as a weapons master and warrior. His once dark hair had turned almost completely white, and his skin was thick and tanned, weathered from exposure to the elements. His eyes were deep brown, almost black, and alluded to a fierce, yet reserved spirit.

Prince Hermond sat next to Serena with a half-cocked smile on his face. "Did you sleep well, Prince Aragel?"

Aragel remained calm even though he wanted to panic. "No, thank you. I kept waking up all night, which is why I've gone and under-slept half my day away." He sat down at the table and examined the room before him. A room he had seen every day for the last ten years. It seemed different today.

The large, cold room before him had always made him feel uncomfortable. The family escutcheons that hung on the walls bore the same deep shades of maroon and purple that colored his own room. The ceiling of the room vaulted high above them. Gray pillars stood at each of the four-corners along with an armed guard. "For safety, boy. It's common sense," the commander had told him once. Aragel stifled a private snicker. Safety was so important that people were climbing into his window at mid-morning.

"Oh. I told the servants to keep you away from sugar. That could have something to do with your nightmares," Serena said with a quick, angelic smile. Hermond nodded in agreement to appease her. His eyes passed over Aragel with the stealth of a thief, plotting and cold.

"Good." Aragel noticed the genuine concern on Serena's face. He was not in the mood to listen to her theories.

Serena smiled again and before he could stop her, she called across the table to her father. "Father, perhaps we should have the physician look into Aragel's sleep problem. I'm somewhat concerned about his shortness of breath as well."

The king looked over to Aragel, who shrugged his shoulders. "I don't think it is anything serious, Serena. Perhaps we should let it be." The king paused long enough to take a sip of wine from a plain metal goblet. "Where are those servants? I expect the meal to be here by the time I sit down. I am a very busy man."

Serena shrugged meekly, stood, and went to the kitchen with her pink skirts trailing behind her. Aragel sat back in his chair and took a drink from the cup of water in front of him. It was warm and bitter. With a look of disgust, he set the cup back on the table. His mind descended into thought again.

I will tell the commander I would like to talk to him after the meal about a private matter, he thought. *You cannot do that*, his reason told him. *The prince will suspect something. He will impose himself to accompany us. He is as scared as I am. He knows I know his plans.* Aragel's thoughts of doom subsided when he heard his name.

"Maybe you should send Aragel to Cabalia. After all, the boy knows about the corn trade as much as anyone," the commander was saying.

Prince Hermond agreed. "He can come with me on my ship and we will drop him off."

Aragel could feel his eyes widen beyond his control. "Cabalia?" The mere thought of traveling anywhere with Prince

Hermond threw his stomach into dancing spirals. The nausea gripping his stomach began its ascension to his throat. He gulped.

"No. It's much too dangerous for him to be cavorting around the world," the king said, tugging thoughtfully at his gray streaked beard.

Aragel breathed a sigh of relief.

"But, Majesty, the boy needs to travel. He needs to see the world. How else do you expect him to become a man when he's never seen the outside world?" Prince Hermond's argument was laden with caution.

King Darak waved a hand in annoyance and shook his head. "No. It's unheard of. These foreign cities are crawling with assassins. I have no other heirs and therefore I cannot risk Aragel's safety. I will go myself."

"I suppose you're right. My ship could let you off. I have a shipment of goods, textiles actually, going to Cabalia. Perhaps I should stay here and assist Aragel in watching over things while you are away." Hermond narrowed his eyes.

Commander Corigerg sat back in the chair, his dark eyes darting wildly from the foreign prince to the king. "Perhaps I should go in your place, Majesty."

Prince Hermond feigned shock. "You do not trust Aragel, yourself and I to watch over things, commander?"

The commander took a drink from the cup in front of him. "Forgive me. It is not a matter of trust, Prince Hermond. I'm merely considering the king's convenience."

Aragel exchanged a brief knowing glance with the commander. Corigerg knew something was wrong, too. Even then, it was doubtful Corigerg would do anything without the king's approval.

"Commander Corigerg, I really need to talk to you after the meal," Aragel started. He had to bring it up now or the risk the chance that the commander would not have time later.

Commander Corigerg nodded. "Yes, Prince Aragel. That would be fine."

"What is it?" the King asked. By the way the king fidgeted with his cloth napkin, Aragel could tell he was still perturbed with Hermond.

"It's about my..." he paused, "my archery lesson the other day." Aragel met his uncle's gaze with a half-hearted, brief smile.

Prince Hermond lifted his cup. "The last time a young man came to me with that it was about women!"

The king chuckled lightly.

Aragel lifted an eyebrow. "No."

"Don't be embarrassed, Aragel! Why don't you and I go riding though the vineyards this afternoon and discuss it, man to man." Hermond smiled and narrowed his eyes, turning to the commander. "Of course, I don't want to overstep you if you would prefer to talk to him, commander. I was just thinking it would give me a chance to get to know Aragel better. After all, we are soon to be related."

Darak nodded in concurrence. "I agree."

Aragel jumped from his seat, which sent a spoon crashing to the floor, startling everyone at the table. "But *that's not it*. I have to talk to Commander Corigerg!" His eyes plead with his uncle.

Hermond was visibly unsettled now.

To save himself Aragel quickly came up with an excuse. "My arm has been giving me some trouble when I'm lining up on my target. My wrist hurts. I was thinking maybe I'm holding my bow wrong. Maybe I should start wrapping my wrist beneath the guard...or something." He paused, wanting to crawl beneath the table. To disappear. The excuse sounded so contrived he was sure it gave rise to suspicion.

"All right. After we eat you can go with the commander." King Darak shrugged and gave the commander a suspicious look. He knew it was not like Aragel to lose his demeanor so quickly. Whatever the issue, it was clear to all of them that Aragel had no intention of sharing it openly.

Serena returned to the room with the servants following her closely. They carried large platters filled with steaming meats, thick sliced cheese, and warm breads.

Aragel did not eat much. He choked down the meat and cheese with a few swallows of goat's milk and shot Serena a warning glance with dark, overcast eyes. This, however, did not stop her. Again, the motherly smile appeared on her lips. She looked innocent with her long dark curls and flawless skin. But Aragel knew better.

"So, Aragel, did eating make you feel better? You were very tired when I came to get you."

"I'm fine. Would you please stop babying me?"

Serena's brown eyes widened in surprise, "You are terribly defensive and ill-tempered this morning."

Both the commander and the king turned their attention to Aragel, confused.

"Are you sure you're feeling well, my boy?" the commander asked. His weathered forehead crinkled with uncertainty.

"No, I mean yes," he said, then tried to explain. "No. I was simply humoring my cousin. It's nothing."

The king rose from his chair nodding. "You probably did not get enough sleep. I have affairs to deal with. I'll be in my study." He paused and turned to Hermond. "I trust you can find your way around the castle, Prince Hermond?"

Hermond, with a mouthful of food, lifted his glass and nodded.

"Good." With that, the king strode from the room.

Commander Corigerg stood soon after with Aragel close at his heels, Hermond's curious gaze following them from the room. When they reached the commander's private quarters Aragel closed the door behind him after checking the corridor to make sure no one had followed.

"There is something going on and I don't like it," Corigerg started. It seemed that talking so candidly made Corigerg uncomfortable most of the time. But today it did not. He sat down in the maroon upholstered chair behind a plain pine desk and leaned toward Aragel waiting for a response.

"I know *what* I heard and I know *who* I heard. It *was* Prince Hermond. I don't know how he got out of that room without moving the chair. But he did, though I can't prove it. If my uncle won't do anything, I will. "

Commander Corigerg reacted more readily than Aragel

18

expected. He stood, and wrung his hands. "I agree. A room that small would not have been as warm with an open window. There were remnants of burning coal in the fire. It does not add up. Your uncle likes Hermond. Darak has a kind heart and trusting ways. I've had word that Hermond is in trouble with other authorities. Though I must admit, I never anticipated he would have plans to assassinate the king, or you. While we cannot prove he is planning such treachery, we cannot take risks either."

Aragel sat down in the plain cross frame chair across from him. "If he kills my uncle and me..."

The commander's brown eyes went wide, increasing the appearance of the thick wrinkled folds in his forehead. "He becomes King of Sherok. But *that* is *not* going to happen."

It was a terrible revelation that neither of them wanted to believe. Corigerg searched Aragel's eyes for a deeper understanding of the full ramifications of such an act.

"I'm concerned and afraid," Aragel said, finding solace in admitting his fear. "You know I would never tell you lies, don't you?"

Corigerg nodded once. "I know you would not tell tales, Prince Aragel." He stopped, took a deep breath, then leaned forward, and looked Aragel straight in the eyes. "When you were a boy, do you remember when you broke the bridle? You were using it to hang from a low tree branch. You immediately brought it to me and admitted what you had done. Since then I have trusted everything you have ever told me to be truth. Tell me what happened again, from the beginning."

Aragel once again recounted the events from the night before. The commander listened intently. When Aragel finished the commander stood. "I do not think you were dreaming, Aragel. Assassins are everywhere, boy! Everywhere! And your uncle will not even consider the prince's possible ill intentions."

"There's more," Aragel told him. "This morning there was a man in my room. He spoke perfect Sherokean and claimed to be someone from my past. I thought he might be my cousin, Garik. The resemblance was striking. He wanted to ask me questions, but he never had a chance because Serena interrupted. She used her key to get in and he went out the window. I considered he could have been someone working for Hermond, but I dismissed the idea because I recognized him. What should I do about *that*?"

Corigerg gasped and sat back down in the chair, looking at the floor as if contemplating a response. The old man knew things. Things he would never tell the king; and things he did not intend on sharing with Aragel. Aragel sensed it. He could tell because the commander's eyes narrowed and he leaned in to Aragel, and lowered his voice. "I would not worry about that. Say nothing to no one about seeing him. Not your uncle, not Serena. If it was your cousin, which I think it may have been, perhaps he can help. It is Hermond you will need to be careful of. I would not put anything past Hermond."

"How can we know my cousin is not working for Hermond?" Aragel asked. He was confused, and sure the commander would have at least considered the possibility of his cousin being an assassin.

The commander bit his lip then shook his head. "No. Call it a gut feeling, my boy. If your cousin was working for Hermond, you and I would not be having this conversation. You would be dead already."

"All right." Aragel fought back the unsettled feeling in his stomach; shocked the commander was so sure of Garik's motives.

Quickly, the commander inscribed something on a piece of paper, folded it, and impressed it with his wax seal. "Here is what we will do. You are going to Danaria. I know nothing about this, do you understand? The less I know, the safer you will be. Take this letter to the warlord General Termark O'Schoitt. You will not return to Sherok with the legions he will send. You will stay in Danaria with the sorcerers, where you'll be safe."

"Legions? Sorcerers?" Aragel hesitated. He knew it would come down to this. Then another frightening thought emerged. "What if my uncle disowns me?"

Corigerg gave the young prince a startled look. "Why would he disown you?"

"He disowned Garik for running away."

"You're not running away. You are protecting your kingdom. Not deserting your future throne."

Aragel sighed deeply, realizing Corigerg was probably right. Though legions seemed a little premature, and sorcerers? Sorcerers made Aragel nervous only because he had never met one. Nevertheless, he had heard plenty of tales. He took the letter from Corigerg and put it down the front of his tunic.

"I'll get ready and leave before sunrise." He stood to leave.

"Be careful, Aragel. Assassins are everywhere, boy." Suddenly the warning seemed more urgent. More realistic.

Aragel let out a deep breath. He did not know what he should worry about more. Hermond or his cousin. Or sorcerers. Or legions of Danarian soldiers. Things were getting complicated, and the fate of Sherok weighed heavy on his shoulders. Though he was apprehensive of the burden he was handed, Aragel hurried from the room, leaving the commander behind him. He retreated to his chambers for the remainder of the day in order to prepare for his journey. As long as Prince Hermond was in Sherok, no good would come of it.

CHAPTER 2

Shadon Longbowe followed Prince Hermond from the port at Menegala, to the Agorak Peninsula and finally to the main port at Sherok. He was tired, but he pressed on knowing the prince had a plan. While he was not sure what it was exactly, he knew it was something urgent, especially since the prince had embarked with three of his fastest war ships to the southern ocean. He had left the war ships further up the coast on the Danarian-Carinth continent. It was doubtful that King Darak, or any other Sherokean for that matter, were any the wiser since the prince had arrived on a well-disguised, Exavian merchant ship. However, Shadon knew something was amiss. He could sense it and he did not like it.

His concerns aside, he had his own reasons for following Prince Hermond here. Rumors out of Kreen insisted the prince had an illegal shipment of ale leaving Sherok en route to Morasta or Orana Tulk, where it would be distributed into the Danarian black market. That alone was job enough for Shadon, and Danaria paid him handsomely for spying. Danarian customs officials would catch the shipment and impose yet another heavy fine on the prince for violating international trade agreements.

Shadon gained passage to Sherok with the help of his friend, Captain Adarack Vogman, aboard an unassuming, small freighter ship called the *Narassa*. Careful to hide his own dark

Sherokean features beneath the cowl-hooded cloak he wore, he kept his head down when any Sherokean passed him too closely. Further still, when required to speak to a Sherokean, he mumbled with a thick Danarian accent to hide the perfect dialect of his natural Sherokean tongue. He was not welcome here.

A falling out with the king years earlier had him banished from the city indefinitely. Undoubtedly his description was well known, even now, years later. It was, perhaps, one of the most formidable events in recent Sherokean history next to the Kersian attack on the city, and the crop failure seven years prior to that. Nonetheless, he was set on the idea that, if he had reason to, he would warn the Sherokean monarchy even if it meant his life. Exavia, the coldest continent in the western world, would never have sent war ships unless they had plans to use them.

Now, he stood on the Narassa's deck, peering inland at the dark outline of the castle contemplating his next move. With nothing left to do, he bided his time - watching and waiting. After several hours, he stepped from the Sherokean dock where the *Narassa* was moored. Captain Adarack followed closely behind.

"I'll be in the tavern, just north of the castle," the captain was saying.

Shadon did not acknowledge the captain's comment. He was too busy thinking about his visit to his cousin earlier that morning.

"Would you prefer me to do it?" Adarack asked. "I can walk right into that castle, request an audience with the king, and come right out with it. Or perhaps I could talk to the boy. Hmm?"

Shadon turned to the dark haired man, his friend for more than ten years. "No. He looked scared, Adarack. He thought I was there to kill him, and almost accepted the fact. He didn't even fight it. No calling for guards, nothing. He knows something and I have a bad feeling about this. There is more going on here than we know."

"I have to wonder if this has something to do with Exavia's new alliance."

Shadon lifted an eyebrow. Exavians had a reputation for being underhanded when it came to trade negotiations and their choice of allies. "What alliance?"

"I thought you would be the first to know, surely..."

"No." Shadon's mind raced through all of the information he had recently acquired. None of it suggested any such alliance. "I did not know this."

"Exavia opened trade negotiations with Zul last month. I heard this from the captain of an Exavian merchant ship in Morasta a week ago. It seemed harmless enough, a peace treaty driven by the exchange of commodities. Though seeing Hermond here creates suspicion. Or perhaps I'm simply a paranoid old man." A tense grin appeared on the captain's normally sober face.

Shadon felt his stomach turn. He pulled his dark hair away from his face and tied it up with a strand of leather. "This is becoming more interesting with every moment, Adarack." Shadon rubbed his eyes. He could feel a headache coming on. His jaw tightened and the feeling in his gut turned sour.

Adarack put a calloused, heavy hand on Shadon's bony shoulder. "You'd best be careful. I'll be here if you need me."

They walked through the fisherman's ports, toward the inner buildings of the small city. The weathered, broken down buildings that stood closely together on the narrow streets left Sherok uninviting for those used to cleaner, larger cities. The coastline stretched for leagues in either direction, in some areas rocky, while in others the water lapped up to smooth white sand beaches that backed up to tall, rocky cliffs.

Shadon stopped and looked around. Fishermen pulled large barrels of the day's catch from their ships and lined them along the docks. Large fishing nets were hung over the sides of their respective ships for the night, while others were hung on posts along the docks for repair. At dusk, many of the sailors headed toward the taverns and inns of the inner city.

Sherok was a peaceful kingdom, staying neutral to the rest of the world's affairs in most cases. Though the violent marauding of the Kersian's did not spread this far south, even the poorest farmer and mariner bore a weapon, just in case.

It had happened before. Shadon remembered. He was merely eight when three large ships full of Kersian legions came ashore and slaughtered more than half of Sherok's meager population. The castle had withheld the siege with a handful of soldiers and young Lord Aithian, who was visiting the king in the aftermath of Queen Aubrey's unexpected death from Gloxorthia. It was Lord Aithian, son of Luithian and keeper of the powers of water and serpent, who had saved Sherok that day. Shadon did not see the hierarch sorcerer invoke the hurricane that swept the Kersians into the ocean. Nor did he see the great serpent conjured from the depths of the sea killing those Kersians who traveled farther inland to avoid the wrath of the serpent god. Shadon had been below, in the castle's dungeons, where the king had sent him with his sister, and the servants for their own safety. Since then, all of Sherok's male inhabitants, lords and servants alike, were provided weapons and training, all compliments of the monarch as long as each agreed to fight for Sherok if the Kersian's ever came back.

Thus, the true voluntary military of Sherok came to be. Prior to the military, King Darak had employed a hundred men for castle and city security and had appointed the best of his fighting men, Grag Corigerg, as their commander. As far as Shadon knew, the commander was still the appointed head of Sherok's understaffed military. It was this inactivity that he hoped would help him to retrieve information from the castle without consequence. The Sherokeans were not warriors and knew nothing of devising battle strategy or organizing defense efforts. They were farmers and fishermen. Nothing more. Shadon smiled, knowing he had the advantage over King Darak.

"I need to find some more equipment and get to work," he told Adarack.

The captain nodded. "You need to be at the tavern before the sun rises in the morning. I smell a hurricane." Adarack, bent down to rub his big toes on both feet through his black, knee-high boots. He gazed out to the ocean, noting the thick mass of black fog that crept inland, hovering over the frightfully calm water. The storm was leagues away yet. He licked a finger and held it up to test the current direction of the air.

"How do you know?" It was merely another obstacle for Shadon. His concern showed itself in the deep worry lines at the corners of his eyes.

Adarack smiled with reassurance and stood. "I just know. I've been a ship's captain a long time, Shadon. Aside from that, my toes ache before a hurricane."

Shadon sighed deeply and shook his head. "Can we avoid it?"

"If we leave in the morning, early, we may be able to steer around it. At worst, we'll get the gale winds and high waters. If we stay here and it hits the northern side of the continent, this port will take heavy damage. My ship and cargo will parish. We have a better chance going around it and trying to miss it altogether," he explained.

Shadon nodded in understanding. "I'll be there if I can."

"Aya, I'll see you then." The men parted ways. Adarack headed to the tavern, and Shadon to the merchant's pavilion to obtain needed supplies.

●

The sight of the castle of Sherok brought back memories. They flooded into Shadon's mind like a swollen river impregnated with heavy rain. He slid his long, thin fingers through the length of his tied back black hair, unknotting the tangles. He headed around the city and to the south side of the castle, taking the long way, through several wheat fields. It was easy to remain unseen, ducking into the evening shadows between the rows of newly planted crop. The cry of locusts echoed out from the deepest reaches of the fields. He noted the damage the ravenous insects were doing to the seedlings already. If something was not done, many of the fields would be ruined before the harvest.

He wondered about Serena. He gave her up when he gave up his father. He had disowned them and they him, and now cursed himself for doing so. He had betrayed his family, and now needed to warn them. Or at least retrieve more information. Oh how he hated this. It hurt to be so close to the castle and to be so unwelcome at the same time. Maybe he would run into Serena. He had almost revealed himself earlier, but she would not have understood. She was sure to be angry with him for abandoning her. She probably would not remember him anyway. She was only a small child when he left. He sighed as he closed in toward the high battlement walls of his childhood home. They loomed before him, thrusting high into the sky, its gray-taloned towers with banners of plum color, whipping in a soft breeze from the south inlet.

The tall tree, abundant with new leaves, stood high above the castle walls only several yards from the castle wall itself. It did not surprise him to see it still there after ten years. He had climbed it the evening before, and made himself a watch-post in the highest branches. He had spent most of the morning there as well. Again, he climbed the tree. Lithe and quick, he found himself adjacent Aragel's window in little time. From his earlier observance, he noted that the soldiers on duty passed every half hour on their patrol atop the battlement walls. As with the tree, it did not surprise him that a ground patrol passed only twice a day: once at daybreak and the second at the setting of the sun. The Sherokeons did not concern themselves with high security and tedious safety details such as the tree. Again, he mused at how trusting and peace loving they were.

He settled into his position and watched the soldiers with amusement. *They still haven't noticed my grappling hook and gray rope*, he thought. The rope was still and unmoving, painted gray as the castle walls, camouflaged well for its purpose. He would use it later, fleeing for his life if need be.

The daylight faded fast as the sun set against the pale pink skies in the west, casting orange ripples in its descent. The castle was dark except for the candles and torches lit to fight the oncoming darkness. Aragel's room glowed with the flicker of candlelight. The colors of the fields and flowers were soon lost to black night as the crickets began singing their haunting melodies to the moon. Shadon watched as the evening patrol rounded the corner of the castle on horseback. They rode the path beneath the tree and finally turned to the other side of the castle. He relaxed then. And waited. Finally, Aragel's room fell dark, and Shadon could see nothing.

After a short time staring into the black window, Shadon decided to make his move. The wind picked up. He waited for the castle guards to make their way to the tower, high above him on the battlement walls, and then climbed down the tree once they had gone. He reached the rope and climbed, as quickly and quietly as his training allowed. Upon reaching the sill, he climbed into the window, slowing the swing of the rope only gradually with his hand. Much to his surprise, his cousin was awake, jamming a few final things into a leather satchel.

Aragel went to his swords and picked up a short sword from where it lay on the bed. He studied it as if trying to decide whether or not to take it. The grip of the weapon was covered in soft black leather, and the pommel and hilt were adorned with intricate engravings of dragons. The blade itself was made of fine steel and bore identical engravings.

The young prince smiled and put the sword into the scabbard on his belt. He looked around as if trying to remember if he had forgotten anything.

"Going somewhere?" Shadon asked from the corner by the window.

Aragel jumped and turned toward the voice. Shadon, dressed in black, emerged from the shadows.

"You again?"

"Yes. You forgot several things." Shadon ambled toward the chair.

"You shouldn't be in here." Aragel took a step backward and looked around nervously.

"The name's Shadon. You know, if you're going to sneak away, you'll need a grappling hook and about two hundred feet of rope."

"Your name is not Shadon."

"It is right now, as far as both of us are concerned."

"Fine. So what will I need the rope for?"

"To climb down the side of the tower." Shadon sat down in the chair and leaned back casually.

"Why would I want to do that?"

"Why don't you tell me? You don't mean to imply that you really thought you could sneak out of here without being seen?"

"Maybe I could. What do you care? What are you doing here? Come to make amends? Why have you changed your name?"

"Whoa, slow down. To answer your first question, I'm just trying to be helpful. Idiocy aside, you're still family. Second question, my business is really not entirely your business just yet. Next, I think you know why I'm here. It certainly isn't to make amends. Lastly, my change in identity is none of your concern."

Aragel shook his head and rolled his eyes. "How did you get in here?"

"I told you. A grappling hook and rope. The guards don't patrol this side of the castle much, or have you noticed? I've been watching them for a few days. Now, I think the question is how are *you* going to get out? There are about twenty guards between here and the front gate. There are four patrolling the walls every half hour. I've been watching them from that large tree over there," he said, pointing out the window. He turned back to Aragel. "Only an idiot would leave that tree where it is, then again, the king has never been one for intelligence. How about you? I bet you don't have any money either."

"I have six shinder and two keldin." Aragel set his jaw, grinding his teeth. He kicked at the rug and bit his tongue. No one had ever spoken to him that way.

"Okay, so you're not as daft as I thought. It's a good thing stupidity is not hereditary. Eh? You know, I could let you use my rope to get down."

"What makes you think I'm running away?" Aragel sounded shocked. "Is arrogance your way of dealing with the painful emotions of being ostracized?"

Shadon's mind raced with the possible situations that would cause Aragel to leave. He narrowed his eyes. Shadon took the running away statement as an invitation to find out more, and decided to ignore the arrogance comment altogether.

"Did I say you were running away? You said it, not me.

Besides, do I look like an idiot? I ran away a few times when I was about your age." Shadon chuckled at the boy's slip of tongue.

"How do I know I can trust you?" Aragel whispered, glancing back at the door as if he half expected shadows to pass over the light seeping in from the crevice between the door and the floor. He picked up his satchel and hoisted it over his shoulder.

"Rule number one. Don't trust anyone, not even me." Shadon paused, then added cautiously, "And certainly not Prince Hermond." He studied Aragel's reaction, noticing the boy winced at the mention of the Exavian prince.

Again, Shadon climbed to the sill of the tall arched window. He knew then, that if Aragel was leaving because of Hermond, it had to be worse than he thought. Exavia in trade negotiations with Zul. *Kersian Sorcerers*, he thought.

"You know about Hermond?" Aragel asked. He searched the outline of Shadon's face for an answer.

"Why else would he leave three war ships ported just north of here? A welcoming committee? What's going on?" It seemed like a good time to ask.

"You're a spy!" Aragel cried triumphantly. "Commander Corigerg knew all along! So who are you working for?"

Shadon shook his head and held a finger up to his lips. "Shhh. We're wasting time talking about this here. Let's get out of here first and finish this conversation someplace else. If the king catches me here..."

Aragel nodded in agreement and followed with his pack. He looked out the window, down at the ground, then at the grappling hook with its long line of gray rope. He inhaled deeply, then swallowed hard. "I'm not so sure this is a good idea. If I can't trust you, why should I come with you?"

"Because you want to get out of here without being seen and I have the means. Besides, I have a feeling we are both going after the same thing. You'll be fine. Now give me the pack and tie your hair up with this piece of leather so it stays out of your face." Shadon was grateful for his current situation. He would not have to drag information out of anyone unwillingly after all. At the same time, it also proved his suspicions were correct. Hermond was up to no good.

With some reluctance, Aragel gave Shadon the pack then took the piece of leather and tied back his shoulder-length hair.

"First we'll throw the pack down. Just clothes in here?" Shadon did not wait for an answer and threw the pack out the window.

Aragel nodded and watched the pack fall to the ground far below. "I, I don't know." he looked out the window again and gulped at the lump in his throat. It never occurred to him, until now, that he was afraid of heights.

"Too late. The pack is down there and you're up here. Explain that, with that nosey prince listening in to everything." Without waiting for a response, Shadon started down the rope.

Aragel leaned out the window. "How do I know you won't kill me when we get to the bottom? How do I know you're not working for *him*?" Aragel asked.

"I would have killed you already. I told you that yesterday. Remember?"

"But if I can't trust you..."

"Can we discuss this later? I'm hanging two hundred feet from the ground." Shadon rolled his eyes. *Great, the boy is afraid of falling, what's next? I knew this was too easy*, he thought.

Aragel took a deep breath and put one leg over the side of the window. Not wanting his uncle to disown him, he paused long enough to drop the note he had written. He anticipated Serena would find it, and hoped she would take it directly to his uncle without hesitation. He turned his attention back to the window when he heard Shadon's voice.

"Now grab hold of the rope and swing your other leg over."

With great reluctance, Aragel did as he was told. Finally, he found himself hanging off the rope. High above him he noticed the grappling hook secured on the sill of the storage room window just below the crown of the tower. He took a deep breath and turned his head to ask Shadon what to do next.

"Don't look down! Put your feet on the wall, lean back, and climb down slowly one hand after the other," Shadon whispered. He hurried ahead hoping Aragel would not let go and fall on him.

Shadon noticed Aragel's breathing become more rapid as his face slowly faded pale. The boy's hands were sweaty, clutching the rope tightly between pale white knuckles.

Shadon reached the ground first, stood, and watched Aragel with amusement. Aragel had his eyes squeezed shut. "You go any farther you're going to plant your hind end into the ground." He chuckled.

Aragel opened his eyes and realized that he was almost sitting on the ground. The tower loomed high above them. Shadon leaned up against the tree, watching him with curious interest. Aragel stood and leaned over with his hands on his knees feeling his breath catch in his chest. The bile rose in his throat. He heaved, wiped the corners of his mouth, took another deep breath, and shook his head. Rubbing his hands on his pants, he wiped off the sweat.

"That wasn't so bad," Shadon said with a smile.

"It was nothing." Aragel brushed himself off and grabbed his pack. "Well thank you for helping me. I'll be on my way now."

"Wait! Do you know where you're going? Once the sun is up, someone will know you're gone. The soldiers will be combing the city for you. Besides, we had a deal. I help you if you give me information. What is Prince Hermond doing on this side of the world?"

Aragel stopped and looked at Shadon, then turned and started to walk away, down the dirt path that led through the fields, toward the city. *Assassins are everywhere, boy.*

"I have a proposition for you," Shadon yelled after him. He knew he was either going to have to talk fast or resort to taking his cousin by force.

Aragel spun around. "Will you be quiet? Someone will hear us!"

"Listen," Shadon whispered, "I have a friend, a ship

captain. He runs a merchant ship that will be going to Danaria. His ship leaves this morning, and you could be on it. Of course, you'll have to hide your identity, but you'll be out to sea before anyone has a chance to catch you. You *are* going to Danaria, right?"

"As a matter of fact I am, but even a spy wouldn't know that!" Aragel glared at him. "And you expect me to hide my identity. Like you? I'm not so sure you are my cousin. Any person related to me would not abandon his own birth-given name."

Shadon winced. "Fair enough. I probably deserved that. I just figured if *I* was leaving home because of Hermond, I *might* be going to Danaria for reinforcements. You now know Hermond has war ships up the coast, but you still haven't told me why he's here."

"He's marrying Serena. Do you know what that means? It means all he has to do is kill my uncle and me and Exavia inherits Sherok. Since you abandoned your responsibilities and left it to me, that is. Is that what you wanted to hear? Now I'm vulnerable, I've told you everything I know, so kill me." Aragel started to walk away again.

Shadon ran after him, grabbing his arm. "Look, I'm sorry you feel I'm a traitor. I'm sorry I left you with a responsibility you're obviously more suited to than I am. Or maybe you think I'm here to claim what was once mine? I assure you I do *not* want your job as heir to Sherok. I'm here because it's my job to watch criminals like Prince Hermond. So now I need to know – did you hear Hermond say he was going to eliminate you and the King?"

"Eliminate?" Aragel laughed at his cousin's formal choice of words. "Yes. Late last night when Hermond was talking to someone." Aragel pulled his arm away, but Shadon grabbed it again.

"Who? Who was he talking to?"

Aragel shrugged his shoulders. "I don't know. If I knew, I would have said so. Someone called 'Your Eminence'. Now can I leave, please?"

Shadon paused and squeezed his eyes closed. The stakes

were high and the young prince was right. Going to Danaria for reinforcements was their only hope. "Let me take you to Danaria. I know people. The right people. Generals, warlords and high commanders in the horde. I have the means, but we have to go now."

Aragel contemplated the idea for a few moments remembering Corigerg's note, which was nestled safely in an inner pocket inside his tunic. Patting his chest he assured himself the note was still there. He finally concurred with a quick nod. "All right, but no surprises or I'll slit your throat." He stopped. "Do you know General O'Schoitt?

Shadon smiled. "Yeah." He looked at what Aragel wore and took in a deep sigh. His clothes alone would attract too much attention. Shadon then looked at the pack and the sword. *Pack will pass, the sword will too, long as he keeps it sheathed.* "Give me your tunic quick."

Aragel took off the tunic with reluctance, and handed it to him. The note for the general... He started to panic, feeling his breath become faster and shallower.

Shadon rubbed the tunic into the dirt and handed it back to him. "Put it on. You would have attracted too much attention in something clean."

Taking the tunic, he felt for the note and breathed a sigh of relief. It was still there. He hastily put the tunic back on.

Together they crept away from the castle, down the dirt path and through the sparse trees. The strong smell of wet spring manure lingered in the humid air after them.

CHAPTER 3

Tnasha fen Schoitt sat in the narrow stair well of the castle tower on a small sill. From the precisely cut crevices of the window, she could see far into the center of central Danaria. The tops of trees canopied roads and rivers. The only other buildings emerging from the trees of the forest city stood the other castles with their high towers and fortifications, side by side with the high spires of the city's temples. Down there, it was undoubtedly loud with clanking metal, hooves, and voices, but up here, the world seemed silent. Here, she could see the mountains more clearly. They surrounded the whole of Danaria. Far above, the deep blue sky stretched forever with few clouds to cover the sun's merciless rays. It was hot up here. She thought about climbing to the top of the tower and quickly dismissed the idea. Tnasha was much too afraid of the tower, and the dizzying climb up the uneven stone spiral staircase had already put her stomach in knots. Aside from that, the crowning pinnacle stood out from the tower wall by a foot's length, and for drainage, the extra foot contained mere metal grates that one could see through - all the way to the ground far below. She closed her eyes and inhaled the thin, hot air.

Her thoughts drifted to the nightmares. When she was younger, Tnasha's nightmares were always the same. From her window, she watched terrified as horsemen bearing gold-colored long swords and adorned in silver plated armor, raced through the streets of Danaria, killing everyone in their wake. Many fell beneath the hooves of the Kersian's horses and lay dead in the wake of the onslaught. At the sight of this horror, Tnasha would flee and hide in the corner behind an oak chest, listening to the people scream, covering her ears to their death cries. The wretched sounds of swords slicing into flesh, carried by the acrid scent of smoldering blood, lifted to her window. And then she heard confusion and screaming from within the castle walls, and in the main corridors far beneath her. Heavy footsteps ascended the stairs and her door flew open. She trembled and held her breath, as tears streaked down her face. A man entered the room as if looking for something, then left abruptly upon hearing the shout of someone below.

Once everything fell silent, save for the sound of fire devouring the city, she would stand and move cautiously down the stairwell of the castle only to find her family slain. She remembered the blood most of all. Her father had fallen over her mother as if to protect her, but it had been too late. One of the gold plated swords still protruded from his back. She sobbed and screamed with uncontrolled fear, feeling lost and empty. And when it was over, Tnasha would wake still sobbing and screaming, only to find herself surrounded by the candlelit faces of the very people she had found slain moments before.

As the years went by, the dreams became more vivid and changed. More clearly now, she could see the Kersian High Priest preaching his sermon to a multitude of people whose faces remained blurred. She was there, too. The high priest held her firmly over a pit of fire while the scent of scorched flesh rose from the flames, permeating the air. There were others waiting to die as she did. At the last moment, before being tossed into the fiery chasm, she heard the battle cries. Faceless people quickly ascended the stairs. They wielded weapons of war. The dream stopped there.

The sun had risen further now. She was late. Tnasha stood carefully, hanging on to the rough stone wall for support and began making her way steadily down the steep stone stairs. About half way down the tower, she emerged onto the walkway of the battlement walls and crossed to the adjoining tower. The stairs there were a foot's length wider and certainly not as steep. Finally, she emerged from the tower into the garden courtyard below. She looked back up at the towers shielding her eyes from the sun. Sometimes all it took to take her mind off things was the dizzying climb to the watchtowers. A grander scale helped her put everything into perspective.

Danaria was a militant society whose stratocratic government was ruled by an advising council of ex-soldiers and the high liege general, who was, essentially, a warlord elected by the people every three years. Danaria's military was not offensive, but rather defensive. Because Danaria boasted a larger population of people, sorcerers, who had mana running through their veins, and because the Kersian factions wanted that mana, they waged war on Danaria every chance they had.

Aside from the Kersian threat, Danaria was a quiet country. The people were spiritual and worshipped the ancient gods. Here, the high priestesses were entitled to sit in on the high council, along with the men, in spiritual advisement to the rulers of the country. In this, Danaria was unique to any other land in the West Ocean Mainlands. Men and women worked side by side in every line of work, including the military. Danaria' prime resources, not surprisingly, consisted of mining, metallurgy, and horses. Almost everything else, from leather to grain, was imported or brought in from the lowlands of southern Danaria.

Now that it was warmer, the battles were more frequent. The Kersians attacked daily with their need for horses, mana, and sacrifices urging them on.

The biggest problem for the Kersians was their nomadic way of life. The only territory they had managed to claim for themselves was a small island nestled in the heart of the Western Ocean, called Zul. It was rumored that several small Kersian cities existed, dotted across the continents of the West Ocean Mainlands, but none of them had been found. Not that Tnasha knew of. The one thing that held the Kersian society together was found on Zul- a grand temple to a nameless tyrant; a patriarchal god whom the Kersians believed was the highest source of power. Tnasha shuddered at the thought. The Kersian god frightened her. For any god who demanded sacrifice and destruction in the name of power was, in her opinion, the embodiment of evil.

The Kersian beliefs did not bother the rest of the civilized world, nor did their nomadic tribes, nor their wandering priests, nor their religious intolerance and Neolithic ways. It was the fact that they kidnapped and sacrificed women and children five holy days a year. That they were greedy and wanted mana and would do anything to obtain it. That they survived by stealing horses and crops all because they claimed their god sanctioned their actions, absolving them of all guilt and responsibility. But not all of them were so terrible. As with any society built around a religion the Kersians boasted their fair share, or perhaps more than their share, of zealots whose fanaticism drove them to the ghastly deeds and acts abhorred by their neighbors. Danaria was, perhaps, one of their most formidable adversaries.

Since the fighting began many centuries before, the act of war had become a sport for both sides. Each military even employed scorekeepers to tally the dead once the battlefields cleared. Tnasha found it repulsive, but realized it was necessary. Danaria's militant ways were a requirement to ensure the freedom and safety of thousands of people, many who were sorcerers. The military was all she had ever known. Her father and his father and his father's father before him, and on down the bloodline for thirty generations or more were all soldiers. Every last one of them warlords, and each having served their own terms as the high liege general of Danaria's Sirus Horde. Now, her father, an uncle, and her grandfather sat on the advising council.

Tnasha stifled a nervous giggle. She was the first female in her line to become a soldier. As an only child, did her father expect her to become a warlord? A high liege general? He certainly acted that way. And now, every mid-morning, she was to meet her father for a bout in the stable arena. She wished the morning would be chilly, but it was no use. Wishing did not change the fact that the sun bore down on her with such force she wished she had worn something lighter.

Tnasha quickly strode through the garden, heading toward the stables. Without warning, and not a second too soon, Tnasha's cousin, Anetta, in a whirl of pink mana, hurried up behind her.

"Good morning!" Anetta called out in a shrill voice making Tnasha's dark auburn hair stand on end.

Tnasha turned to her cousin and managed a fake smile. "Good morning, Anetta."

Tnasha was not like the other females in her family. She had no male suitors and no interest in acquiring any. Her first and foremost worries were her horses, her weapons, and her commanding officers. Not necessarily in that order. Anetta was the last person she wanted to see first thing in the morning. The women of Tnasha's family were forever attempting to persuade her into a more feminine role befitting the daughter of an aristocratic warlord.

"You have missed the morning meal yet again," Anetta started, her tone chiding and superior. "We were hoping you would join us. We invited Lord Amalc. You really ought to meet him. He's fond of you, you know."

Tnasha started to walk away. Anetta followed.

Tnasha turned to her with indifference. "I wasn't hungry. Besides, I promised my father I'd meet him."

Anetta hurried alongside. "But what about Lord Amalc? You are going to die an old maid with your indifference," she said in a flat voice. She smoothed imaginary wrinkles from her lavender, silk dress and neatly set her collar as straight as she could manage as she walked.

Tnasha stopped at a bench along the path and sat down, toying with the silver and turquoise amulet she wore. She said nothing. What Anetta said was true and it did bother her, a little. Nothing could change the fact that she was nineteen and almost an old maid. Nervously she twisted the amulet on its chain, fidgeting. It was a habit that showed itself any time Tnasha was uncomfortable in a situation. The amulet itself was a gift from the Sorcerer Kalath. It was a constant reminder that she was a fifth generation sorceress.

Being a fifth generation sorceress was a position she

gladly did not speak of. The generations were marked first through fifth for a reason. Fifth-Gens, as they were commonly called, had stronger mana than other generations. They were usually incapable of bearing children, and had a high mortality rate because if left imbalanced, their mana would implode, slowly killing them.

Tnasha was an exception. Her mana was considered anomalous because it boasted a stronger energy than the average Fifth-Gen. As a result, Tnasha's mother had gone barren soon after giving birth to her.

So, Tnasha was reclusive when she was off duty. When she went into the city streets people would gawk at her, entranced by her mana. Not that sorcery or mana was uncommon, or even unacceptable, but rather the whole concept of sorcery intimidated her. And the people of Danaria seemed to think a sorceress with such mana should be adept in parlor tricks at least. Tnasha could not seem to grasp the necessary skills. Of course, she could not hide her mana without extreme effort, either. If she had the strength and resolve, she would have. Her mana was a bright violet light that radiated two to three feet around her body in all directions. But only the other sorcerers could see it, just as she could see theirs. For Lord Amalc, it would be a great prize to obtain a Fifth-Gen wife. Undoubtedly Tnasha's own children, if she were able to have them, would be born with the mana. Lord Amalc could start his own family sect, and secure a new position on the family sect council.

"I've heard, from many sources, that Lord Amalc has more keldin and shinder than our entire family, among other things," Anetta was saying. There was a hint of hope in her voice. Her chosen words screamed for an argument. An argument Tnasha was not interested in pursuing.

Tnasha realized she could avoid it no longer and turned to her copper-haired cousin, leaning in close. "I am tired of everyone trying to run my life, including you. I know you mean well, but for the last time, I'm not interested in Lord Amalc and his alleged wealth, nor any other *fitting* catch."

Anetta raised an eyebrow and pursed her full, red painted lips. "I'm only concerned for your happiness, Tnasha."

Tnasha nodded. *Right!* Everyone was only interested in her happiness. Or at least that's what they said. She sometimes wondered if they were in a hurry to marry her off, and be rid of her.

"I have to go." She stood.

"But Tnasha, we really ought to discuss this..." Anetta called after her.

Tnasha stopped. "I don't care to discuss it," she called back over her shoulder.

Anetta offered no reply.

Without looking back, Exasperated, Tnasha shook her head and hurried along. She was even later now. But she expected more of her female cousins would show themselves before the day was over, attempting to convince her that Lord Amalc was, indeed, a viable marriage partner.

One down and three more to go, she thought.

The morning light shifted suddenly as several small light gray clouds slipped over the mountains, shielding parts of the valley. She reached the practice arena without incident only to spot the golden mana of the triplets on the far side, watching the swordsmanship session. Two soldiers parried on the other side. Her father, bathed in the familiar maroon light of his own mana, stood in the center of the arena. She took a deep breath, groaned, and squinted in an attempt to block out some sunlight.

"You're late!"

Tnasha looked at her father somewhat startled, shook her head, and glanced at the triplets one final time before giving him her full attention.

Her father's gaze drifted to the three young women, all dressed in courtly gowns made of Carinth silk, unfitting for their current surroundings. "Ignore them. If raiders ever marauded this city and the castle was left open to attack, they would be the first to die." He turned to his daughter. "*You* would survive."

Tnasha stood shocked for a brief moment. Her father did not usually compliment her so highly. Only a year ago she had felt small and insignificant beneath his shadow, but recently the glares of disappointment and looks of disapproval had vanished. She knew then that the time spent practicing by herself, making the sword an extension of her body and soul, was paying off in the way she had so desperately hoped it would. The *ritual* undoubtedly helped as well. She nodded in agreement and without word readied herself.

Her father wasted no time in starting the practice. He always told her that if she practiced daily, even though she had already ranked into the Sirus Horde, she would become better. He shared his hopes that one day she would go undefeated on the battlefield or in the games. It was what any father would have wanted for his son.

Her father took his stance. "Remember that this is not a body contact fight. The object here is to gain control of the weapon you wield. Better yet, gain control of *my* weapon. The rules are, as always, you cut me, I cut you," he reminded her firmly.

On his first attempt, her father swung low. With precision, she stopped his blade with her own. Her father smiled and nodded in approval. Tnasha felt a warm feeling deep in the pit of her stomach. She was improving. Again, he brought his blade down, this time to her left side. Then suddenly, he brought it back and went for her lower right leg. She blocked this as well, but somewhat clumsier than the previous block. They continued with parries and blocks for the rest of the practice.

The cry of steel ripping into steel echoed off the high castle walls well into the afternoon. Tnasha found herself exhausted and thirsty, and made her way to the kitchens in high spirits. When she reached the large, hot room she found Margore, her eldest male cousin, sitting by the baking ovens, staring into them pensively. His dark brown hair stood disheveled and he was unshaven. Green mana framed his well-chiseled jaw and sturdy, tall frame. He merely glanced up at her approach.

Being short, Tnasha stretched on the tips of her toes, reached and took a flask of mead from a high shelf. She fanned herself. "What's wrong with you and why are you sitting in here? It's hot as southern Arkeereon in here, isn't it?" she asked him, taking a long drink.

"Can I ask you something? Candidly?" He lifted his gaze to meet hers and stood.

"I'm assuming we're taking it out of the kitchens where no one will hear?"

"We'll go to the garden," he said, looking around to see if any of the servants had heard. They were busy with their work, preparing for the evening meal. Not one of them turned to watch the two leave.

Once in the garden, amidst the flourishing colors of newly planted spring flowers, Margore stopped and turned to her. "I can't do it. I simply cannot!"

Tnasha stood confused for a moment then realized what he was talking about. Their previous evening's conversation regarding the Lady Briana had gone nowhere. "What have you come up with?"

Margore took a deep breath and held up his hand. "How about, you have the most entrancing eyes I ever did see."

Tnasha choked back a laugh. "That's trite."

He sat down and let his green eyes bore into the stone of the garden wall. Then his eyes lit up and he jumped up from where he sat. "All right. What if I said, no rose equals your beauty."

A slow smile spread across Tnasha's lips and her dark brown eyes showed amusement. "Really, Margore. That's even worse than the last." She moved over to the garden bench and sat down.

Margore whirled about suddenly. "I've got it! It was prophesied that you and I would meet during the dark winter. Hot spring?" He stopped and waited for her response.

Tnasha shook her head. "Come now! No woman in her right mind would fall for something like that. Let alone Lady Briana. Prophecy my foot. Dark winters, ha! You're hopeless." She laughed, and playfully swatted at him with her hand. Of all her cousins, Margore was her favorite. Nikodemus and Martiga, Margore's twin, fell closely behind in the ranking. They had been her childhood playmates, and best friends.

"Well," he whined, "I don't know what to say."

Tnasha rolled her eyes. "You can be such a child. Why

don't you try talking to her?" She shrugged her shoulders. She could feel the sweat from her morning parry drying into a thin film on her skin.

He sat next to her and stretched his legs out in front of him, revealing a small hole just above the knee in his black leggings. Margore often dressed for comfort rather than appearance. "It's not easy."

"Of course it is. Pretend I'm Briana."

"All right. What do I say?"

"An appropriate thing to say would be, good day to you, Lady Briana. So say it."

Margore rolled his eyes, lifted an eyebrow and methodically said the words as if he were reading them from a dull book. "Good day to you, Lady Briana."

"And to you, Lord Margore."

"Um."

"Pretend that it is a lovely day. What would you say?"

"Uh, nice day. Isn't it?"

Tnasha groaned, and with exaggeration fell backward from the bench into the empty bed of soil behind her. She sat up on her elbows, her legs still propped on the bench. "No! Why not say, it's a lovely day. Would you like to accompany me for a walk?"

"But what if it's a dreary day?"

"By Natyis! Why is it that you have to make everything so difficult? All you want to do is to become acquainted with her."

Margore smiled, his cheeks hinting the crimson that crept into them. "So maybe I'll ask her what she thinks about the treaties between Danaria and Exavia."

"Much better. Go on."

"No. That's idiocy."

"Why?" Tnasha knew the conversation was going nowhere. Margore seemed destined to be bashful no matter how hard she tried. She was the only female he felt comfortable discussing women with, and she knew it. Laughing at the thought, she mused at her own lack of suitors. Was she qualified to give him advice on such matters?

"What if she doesn't care? What if we have conflicting opinions and she hates me?" His eyes averted to the ground.

Tnasha lifted herself from the ground and brushed herself off. "Perhaps you should be honest and tell her that you like her. Rejected or not, you'll know for sure if she likes you as well. Your other alternative is to ask Anetta and the triplets what they think. I'm sure they'd love to meddle in your personal affairs. They would gladly deliver your message of affection for Briana if they knew."

He rested his head in his hand and sighed deep. "Thanks."

The conversation had ended. "I'm going to bathe. I'll see you at the evening meal?"

He nodded and managed a weak smile.

She put her hand on his shoulder. "And Margore?"

Margore looked up in question.

"Be sure, whatever you do, wear a pair of leggings without the wear of comfort," she said, pointing to the small hole.

He smiled and stuck his finger in it.

Tnasha left the garden and started toward her chambers. It was time for the *ritual*. When she reached her room, she slid the door lock firmly into place so Anetta or the others could not barge in, uninvited. After peeling off her clothes, she slipped into a light muslin gown, and then unlocked a small chest buried behind the stacks of books in the corner. From inside the chest, she pulled out a red glass bottle and lifted it to the light from the window.

"Sherokean Red," she whispered with a smile.

She reached beneath the black fabric hiding the contents of the chest once more and pulled out a thin, delicate spoon made of fine silver. With both items in hand, she sat on the floor cross-legged and pulled the cork from the bottle. Once open, the contents of the bottle spilled its fragrance into the air. It smelt as fresh and earthy as any plowed field after a spring rain. She dipped the spoon into it, retrieving a small mound of the red clay. Then delicately, with as much grace as any lady, she lifted the spoon to her lips and inserted it into her mouth.

She savored every granule of earth and with contentment, dipped the spoon a second time.

Since she had discovered the ritual, the earth magic had never failed her. Laile, god of earth and steel, ensured her victory in all battles. So far, Liale had kept her alive so she had not failed at all. At least that's how she reasoned it.

Each time she embarked in her ritual, she felt renewed and strong. And each time, her belief in the power the ritual gave her grew even more resolute. It was the only sorcery she felt comfortable practicing because it did not require the use of mana.

She rarely held the ritual before parrying with her father. She believed it would protect her from much needed defeat. *For education's purpose*, she often thought.

"Thank you Liale for this, the stability of earth. Please grant me strength in times of peril so that I shall not fail."

With the prayer complete, she put the items away with care, and called one of the serving maids to draw her bath. She entered the bathing room and closed the door behind her. Smooth stone walls surrounded a floor of marble tile. Unlit torches jutted ceiling-ward on either side of the door and tub. At the room's east end stood a long wooden bench. Several cast iron hooks protruded the wall above the bench. The south wall housed a hearth with a large pot. The floor to the right harbored earthenware jugs the color of red sandstone. When they were full, it ensured there was enough water for bathing. The maids filled them twice daily.

For one bath, they usually filled the cauldron six times to boiling. But today they did not bother heating the water. It took four serving maids to lift the cauldrons with a pole, and carefully pour the water into the large trough-like tub. Molded of wood and lined with tiles of fired clay, the tub was sealed with natural plant leaf extracts and glues to keep it from leaking. A wooden tub cover stood against a wall. Normally it kept the water warm until all six cauldrons-full were added. At that point, the bath was ready. Now, four stout bathing maids stood in waiting with soap and towels.

She undressed, placed her muslin gown on a hook, and

stepped into the cool water. The bathing room was her retreat from the rest of the world. When she had finished, the maids helped her from the water, and wrapped her in linen towels.

As she dried off, the women set back to work and, bucket by bucket, the water from the tub was poured out the window to cascade onto the moisture loving gardens below.

A harsh knock from the other side of the door pulled her from her humble retreat.

"Who is it?" Irritation laced her voice.

"Tnasha, may I come in?" came the male voice from the other side.

"No! I'm naked if you don't mind."

"Uh, that's okay. Can I come in anyway?" the voice asked, laden with caution.

She could not place the familiar voice right off. *Whoever it is, he's awfully presumptuous,* she thought. Tnasha pulled the door open making sure the cloth fully covered her. On the other side stood her friend, Kolgern Starkweather dressed for battle, with an awkward grin on his face. His eyes slid over her.

"You're a swine, Kolgern!"

His eyes widened with amusement. "How was I to know you'd be bathing at this hour? It's well after noon. Most *normal* people bathe in the evening or early morning."

"What do you want?" Tnasha set her jaw.

His eyes settled on her lower legs. "I never knew you had such nice legs..."

"Kolgern! Why are you here?" She found herself half tempted to slap him.

As if reading her mind, he laughed and moved back a few steps. "Hold on now. I was only joking. Um, I was sent to come and get you."

"By whom?"

"Commander O'Mally is assembling our legion. Alena is waiting in the stables. Because," he paused as if he had lost his thought. "The Kersians have taken Warlord Kyran's daughter. She's human and defenseless."

Tnasha sat on the bench and rubbed some water from

her arm. "You're so tactful when sharing news. So tell me, how did they manage *that*?"

Kolgern shrugged his shoulders. "I suppose they came into the city and took her. And then they set the castle on fire."

"Right in front of everyone? Just came in and took her then set the castle aflame?" she asked, the disbelief clear on her face. Why had she not heard about this sooner?

"Uh huh. That's what I heard." He yawned and looked around the bathing room, then added as an afterthought, "They did put the fire out."

"That's ridiculous. Not even the Kersians are that dense. And you, you're quite calm about this. When did this happen?" She could feel the tension renew itself in her shoulder muscles.

"Only a short while ago. No sense in getting upset about it. We'll get her back." Kolgern stepped out the door with nonchalance. "So are you coming?"

"Do I have a choice?"

"No."

"Then let me put some clothes on. I'll meet you down at the stables."

"I'll saddle your horse for you."

"You're such a gentleman," she said, shutting the door behind him.

CHAPTER 4

After a few minutes of walking, Shadon and Aragel reached the edge of the city. Shadon pulled Aragel to the side of a run down, wooden slat building.

"We are going to go through the alleys so you aren't caught. Stay close."

Aragel nodded in silence, following Shadon through the dark, narrow alley, painfully aware of every breath and every footstep. Several volunteer patrol soldiers passed them on the main roadway and Shadon put his back flat against the wall. Aragel followed suit and held his breath. The soldiers moved on, having not seen them.

"Now we have to make a run for it. When I say *go*, I want you to run across the main road into the alley on the other side." Shadon's voice trembled slightly. He was nervous.

Aragel looked across to the other alley. Even though it was a few paces off, it seemed like a mile.

"Go!" Shadon said, pushing Aragel forward.

Aragel ran as quietly and quickly as he could. When he reached the other side, he put his back up against the wall and waited for Shadon. Seconds later, Shadon was there. He grabbed Aragel's arm and they ran. The sound of their footfalls sliced into the silence and echoed off the buildings.

"I think those soldiers spotted me, come on." He bolted forward, knowing that the soldiers would be wary of such odd behavior.

They kept going, making their way through the narrow streets and even narrower alleys, trying to avoid the patrol soldiers. Behind them, they heard the sound of galloping horses. Shod hooves pounded the cracked and decaying cobblestone streets.

"They went that way," shouted one the soldiers.

Suddenly, Shadon stopped in front of a tavern. The sign that hung outside announced to all of its patrons that the place was called the Thirsty Sailor. The wood of the building was weathered, dry, and graying.

"The captain I told you about should be in here," he said, pulling Aragel into the torch-lit entrance with a sharp jerk.

The tavern was empty, except for an old man who went table to table cleaning up the mess from a busy night. The stale air, smelling of strong warm ale, suffocated them.

The old man glanced up, "What do you want, lads? Food? I've already closed for the evening."

Shadon noticed the man had poor eyesight by the way he squinted at them. His normal tone of voice changed, and he adopted a Danarian accent. "No, my good man. We've come to see Captain Adarack Vogman. I'm his first mate, Shadon."

"Adarack never introduced us. I've known all the Captain's traveling companions over the last three years," said the tavern owner as he continued his work. He did not seem to recognize Aragel as the prince.

"This is my first trip to Sherok on Adarack's ship," Shadon said with a forced grin.

"And the lad?" The man asked as he glanced at Aragel through squinted eyes.

Shadon smiled politely. "One of our deck hands. Aaron. Could you tell Adarack we're here?"

The man nodded, then called over his shoulder. "Adarack! Shadon's here to see ya!"

Adarack poked his dark head around the back doorway. "Shadon! Have you finished getting our supplies replenished?" He paused, noticing Aragel, "I'll be out shortly."

Shadon motioned for Aragel to sit. They chose a small,

three-legged table near the door. Shadon cracked his knuckles impatiently for what seemed like hours, and glanced from Aragel to the door repeatedly. After a few minutes, Adarack stepped out from the back room clutching a small bag of coins. Undoubtedly, he had been gambling.

"Finished with business?" He asked, nodding toward Aragel.

"Yes. Meet our new deck hand. Aaron. He needs a job and wishes to go to Danaria. He's strong and he'll work." Shadon lifted an eyebrow then narrowed his eyes. He hoped Adarack would notice the look as a sign to play along. Now was not the time to reveal identities with the nosey keeper just steps away.

"I see," said Adarack cautiously. "You want to be a deck hand, eh?"

"Yes sir." Aragel glanced nervously from Shadon to the captain, to the tavern keeper.

"What's your name again, boy?"

"Uh, Aaron, sir?" Aragel hoped the obvious pause and questioning tone of voice would not give away the subterfuge.

"Hmm. Have you ever been on a ship, Aaron?"

Aragel's voice cracked as he adopted a more common accent. "No sir, but I learn quickly."

"What about your parents?" the captain asked. Shadon shook his head.

"I'm an orphan sir," Aragel said evenly. He did not want to sound too eager in his attempt to go along with the lie.

Adarack put his hands on the table and leaned in. "Good. It's time to go then. I've got a shipload of goods that will be ruined if we don't hurry. There is a storm heading this way."

Shadon stood and pulled Adarack by the sleeve to the side of the room. "We've got about four armed soldiers after us."

Adarack said nothing for a moment, confused. "Why?" he finally asked.

"They saw us running. Chances are they thought we were up to no good. We can't let them find Prince Aragel," Shadon said in a whisper as the sound of hooves approached the tavern.

"Perhaps if you had not acted suspiciously this would *not* be a problem." Adarack pushed Shadon and Aragel toward the back of the tavern. He paused long enough to bid farewell to the tavern keeper. "Davin, thank you. I hope to see you soon." His attention and feet followed Shadon and the boy. "Quickly! Out the back."

They hurried out the back of the tavern and headed toward the docks as the morning fog slowly lifted. Approaching the docks, the brackish smell of fish and the ocean assaulted their noses. The boy gasped for air as he ran. A sour look adorned his face.

Shadon again shook his head. *I always get the good ones. Not only is my cousin lacking common sense, but he's a debutante no less. My luck,* he thought.

Reaching the third pier, they slowed their pace. Shadon looked back realizing the soldiers no longer trailed them. Aragel looked around at the nets hanging from long lines of rope and at the barrels full of fish.

"There she is, my lovely lass," the Captain said proudly as if he were seeing her for the first time. His gaze fell upon the water in attempt to locate the storm.

Aragel pulled his attention away from the nets, barrels, and long piers. He stared at the ship the Captain proudly pointed out, in awe. The ship was bigger than he had expected with four masts and a high stern. The crew was busy loading the last crates of Adarack's shipment.

"What do you call her?" asked Aragel.

"She is called the *Narassa*. She is one of the fastest freight ships on the ocean, lad." Captain Adarack Vogman put his hand on Aragel's shoulder.

"The sun is rising," Shadon still wore a worrisome expression that drew out the angular features of his jaw and the lines around his eyes. Now they faced a new challenge - the storm.

Aragel looked to the east and saw the sun's first rays of light rising against the gray water and dense fog. He turned to Shadon with obvious concern. Without words, they hurried to board the *Narassa*.

Once aboard ship, Aragel seemed relieved. He let out a deep sigh, taking in his surroundings. Men bustled about their work in a hurry to leave the port at Sherok. The great expanse of ocean stood before them. He inhaled the moist salty air as the ship rocked gently with the tide, and leaned over the side of *Narassa* to gaze into the water below. His stomach lurched and gurgled with upset. He could not swim.

"Lift the anchor," called the captain. There was a rumble of chains, and with a sucking, upward splash, the anchor emerged from the water's murky depth.

"You all right? You look sick," said Shadon from behind him.

Aragel's face went pale. His skin turned cold and clammy. Adarack approached them, leaning on the railing. He was not a big man, but he had a booming voice and his dark abundant facial hair made him look intimidating.

"Is the boy already sick?"

"Eya, I'll go and get him some bread and weak ale to calm his stomach."

Once Shadon had left for the galley, Adarack spoke. "You know lad, I remember when I was your age. When I turned seventeen, my father, who was a ship captain before me, insisted that I travel with him. But you see, I wanted to be a warrior. I wanted to make others fall on their knees before me as I held a sword to their throats. The sword, to me, was all powerful. But do you know what happened, lad?"

Aragel gave Captain Adarack a blank stare. He wondered how this man could tell him mariner's tales when he was about to heave. Yet, he figured the captain was going to tell him the story no matter what, so he did not protest. "Uh, no?"

"Well, I will tell you what happened. I found myself on my father's ship. One day there was a great hurricane! The ship, called *Tesil*, began rocking with the hard waves! And the rain crashed down! And the wind howled and roared! The ship tossed to-and-fro and back and forth. Men ran everywhere, adjusting sails, steering the rudder, all to keep the ship on course and away from the eye of the great storm! I realized that day, that the greatest battle a man could ever win, boy, was a battle against the sea! That is when I decided to devote my life to the ocean. I tell you this because you too will see one of these great storms. So prepare yourself for the greatest battle you will ever come across!" Captain Adarack smiled triumphantly.

Aragel stared at him slack-jawed. He was exhausted. The captain had told him the story because they were heading into a storm. *The hurricane.* His stomach churned and he felt the remnants of bitter fluids make their way up his throat. He heaved deep and dry, but nothing. The sour taste coating his tongue encouraged the gag reflex to continue. He fell to his knees, just before he blacked out.

CHAPTER 5

The castle came alive with confusion that morning. Worried servants and soldiers searched in futility. For Serena, the morning had been like a surreal dream. She was the first to discover Aragel missing from his room. It seemed odd to her that he would be awake before she called him to the morning meal. She recalled how she searched every corner, laughing at herself when she realized how tempted she was to look beneath the bed. A folded scrap of parchment sat on the floor near the window. Aragel could be so messy at times. She shook her head, reached down, picked it up, and placed it in the pocket of her dress without looking at it. Worried, she returned to the hall and summoned one of the soldiers.

"It seems Prince Aragel woke early this morning. Would you see if you could find him outside? The morning meal will be ready shortly."

She had been so calm, not even considering that the piece of paper in her dress pocket explained everything. After instructing the maids in their morning duties, she found herself walking through the castle. A sick feeling pierced her stomach. That was when she suspected something was not right.

It was not long before a confused soldier approached her. "Princess, we cannot find Prince Aragel anywhere. Should we put together search parties?"

Her mouth went dry. "Did you check the stables?

Perhaps he went for a ride."

The soldier looked around nervously. There was concern in his eyes. He was worried, too, and he could not hide it. "His horse is in the stables. None of the stable hands have seen him. Maybe he is somewhere here in the castle?"

Serena shook her head. "I have been through every room. Continue looking. Have the maids begin another search of the castle. I will inform my father and the commander."

Now, with more than one soldier searching outside, and the servants searching every corner of the castle, Serena's thoughts traveled back to the chaos surrounding her brother's disappearance years ago. It was no wonder the fear she felt now seemed so familiar. She shoved her hands in her dress pockets, sighed, and pulled out the piece of paper. Unfolding it carefully, she read the words, her eyes widenening. As she hurried toward her father's private chambers, she practiced how the words "Aragel is missing" would fall from her mouth. Worse, how would she explain that he had run away because of a dream?

●

King Darak had not slept since Aragel woke him two nights prior. The previous night the storms of the hurricane struck with sudden heavy rains, and whipping winds. The majority of damage, luckily, was further up the coast. The king was tired, but he knew he had to stay awake to coordinate the rebuilding of several docks *and* the search for his insurgent nephew. His thoughts wandered to his son. He had told everyone that assassins murdered him. A tear came to his eye whenever he thought about Garik Darak. That *cursed* boy, he thought. *If only I had not been such a terrible father.* He knew his son had run away because of him. *And now, Aragel.* Who knew what caused Aragel to run. The king cursed himself. If only he had listened to Aragel. Done something to curb his fears. But the signs were there. The boy's theories unsettled Darak, but they could not possibly be true. Exavia favored Sherok and traded heavily with them. Hermond would do nothing to damage that relationship, and his marriage to Serena would only solidify the alliance between both kingdoms. *Solidify*? Darak scowled at the word. He wondered then if Aragel was right.

Commander Corigerg knocked heavily on the thick wooden door of the King's study. Darak sighed mournfully then cleared his throat. "Enter!"

"Majesty," the commander began as he hurried toward Darak.

The king noticed irritation in the commander's voice and sat back in his chair.

"I think we need to discuss Prince Hermond. I just overheard him tell Serena's maids to prepare to move up the wedding date."

"What? The wedding is not for six months yet!" King Darak felt the anger swell in the pit of his stomach. It seemed every time there was a problem several others converged along with it, creating chaos. Chaos required equal attention given to every problem at the same time.

"It seemed a strange request to me," whispered the commander. "I found it suspicious, which is why I am bringing it to Your Majesty."

Darak rose from his chair and began pacing, taking long, even strides. "This is all I need," he shouted, "Does he know Aragel is missing yet?"

"I don't think so," the commander said. He looked down at his feet. Darak knew then that the commander was lying. Rarely did the commander lie unless he had good reason. That reason was usually Garik. Darak knew that Garik and the commander had been close, and the commander had kept in constant contact with Garik all these years.

"Good. See to it that he does not find out. It is none of Exavia's affair that my nephew is missing."

"I fail to agree with you, Majesty," came a calm, dignified voice from the hallway. The prince stepped inside the room. He was a hideous man in some respects. The prince normally would not have been considered ugly except for one feature handed down from one royal Exavian generation to the next. His nose. It was long, pointed, and upturned slightly with wide nostrils, which made him resemble a swine. Darak smiled lightly, remembering how Aragel insisted once that Hermond was a hog-nosed idiot. The thought of grandchildren resembling swine had caused him sleepless nights. He shook his head at the thought.

"Prince Hermond. The commander tells me that you have decided to hurry your wedding plans. And now, you enter my private study without a formal invitation," said the king, mimicking the prince's dignified tone.

"Forgive me, Your Majesty. I meant no disrespect, of course," said the prince. "We can discuss the wedding plans later. I can go out and search for Aragel now if you like."

Darak narrowed his eyes. "Serena is looking now. She probably panicked without good reason. He's probably out with the horses or wandering the fields."

"Very well. Then we shall discuss wedding plans." Hermond paused and held up a finger. "I have something, I'll be right back." With a sly grin, he turned on his heel and left.

"What an insolent and arrogant ass," hissed Darak. He pulled the commander closer to him. "Corigerg, I want you to keep an eye on Prince Hermond. Perhaps I was too hasty to dismiss my nephew's suspicions because now I have a feeling that my future son-in-law is up to something. We will discuss it more, later. Place more guards in the castle and search the castle grounds for anyone peculiar!"

The commander left the room in haste to carry out his orders. Darak reclaimed his chair. *If the prince finds Aragel before I do*, he thought, *he could order him killed and then...*

A horrible thought occurred to the king. He did not say it aloud for fear that saying the words would make it come true. What if Hermond had already killed Aragel? A simple grave dug into the rich soil in such humidity would not be discovered until harvest. Within a short time, all traces of a body could be destroyed, leaving mere bones beneath the soil. He shuddered.

Hermond entered the room again interrupting the king's thoughts. He carried with him an open bottle of fine Akeeronish wine and two goblets. "Your Majesty, will you join me for a drink?"

"I suppose," Darak said in an unsteady voice. Once

again, the prince had failed to knock. That irritated Darak more than anything. He took a full goblet from the prince's pale thin hand. In one gulp, he drained the cup. Now, it seemed, Aragel's delusions were rubbing off on him.

Hermond poured him another goblet full. "How are the crops fairing this year?"

"We will not know until late summer. However, the locusts have started early this year and are already doing some mild damage to the young plants and some seedlings. I suspect, come harvest, some of the crops will not be as plentiful this year." Darak remained calm. The prince's petty conversation and avoidance of the topic of the wedding only made Darak more wary.

Hermond sensed Darak's annoyance. "The wedding plans seem underway. I wanted to move the wedding ahead because I can no longer bear to be without Serena. I love her more than anything."

The prince's insipid remarks made Darak's stomach turn. "Serena has seen to every detail. I doubt she will object. Though you could have consulted me before making that decision. I cannot change certain plans on a whim, Hermond. I will have to get word to some of our relatives in Kreen. I know they would like to attend the wedding. If you continue moving the date..." He tried to fight it, but he knew his response was curt.

King Darak was not feeling well. Drinking wine in the morning, on an empty stomach, did not agree with him. It was the likely reason he felt so tired after drinking a mere two goblets full. Suddenly, he felt as though a fever was coming on. Then chills and the fever again. He had not been sick in years. But he was also sixty-five. Tired and aging, he was bound to start feeling the wear of time. He decided then to take a nap later in the morning. Exhausted with all the worry, it was no wonder he was not himself. Hermond sat at the table across from him staring into his own goblet as if he had something else he wanted to say.

Darak made no attempt to ask him what he was thinking about. Extending the conversation with Hermond seemed moot, with all the pointless bantering and nonsense, sometimes for hours. Darak never really listened to him. To be completely honest with himself, he had to admit he only tolerated Hermond for Serena's sake. In the beginning, when he first made the arrangement of Serena's marriage, he had every confidence that if anything were to happen to him, Serena would be well cared for and Aragel would take care of Sherok. He sighed and stretched, then rubbed his eyes. He did not want Hermond to suspect his exhaustion. It would only give the prince more cause to push his will on the king. Today, Hermond seemed like a cat, sly and agile. Finding an older, weaker animal, the prince would surely pounce and devour his prey.

Aragel suspected Hermond had motives. Darak did, too, but not to the extent that his nephew envisioned them. Hermond wanted better trade agreements, and perhaps grains and vegetables below the market value. Darak laughed at the idea that Prince Hermond, or the Exavian monarchy, were looking in Sherok for wealth and prestige. They had that at home. Exavia was a far wealthier country than Sherok would ever be despite its long, cold winters and short, cool summers.

Aragel's fantasy of Hermond wanting to kill them was nothing more than the boy's own paranoia and imagination. Or was it? A dull pain sunk deep into Darak's middle. He was hungry.

Serena entered the room in a whirl of blue silk. She waited until she had her father's attention. Feeling slightly guilty for not mentioning it earlier, she decided to share the note with him. As hard as she tried to find a way, there was no easy way to say it. "Well, I can honestly say that I have looked everywhere. Three times. Aragel is nowhere to be found!"

The king gazed at her with stoicism.

Hermond cocked his head to one side. "Perhaps he is in the stables. I doubt he's missing. He should come in and join us in a glass of wine."

"He's nowhere. I have had the entire castle, stables, and courtyards searched. Three times," she repeated. "We have also searched the surrounding fields. Three times. He's not here. His horse is here, but he isn't."

King Darak said nothing and stared at the flask of Arkeeronish wine sitting on the table between himself and the prince. The label was hand scribed; the mark of a good wine. His eyes traveled across the table to Hermond's goblet. It was still three quarters full.

Hermond chuckled. "Maybe he does have a young lady outside the castle."

"Not likely." Serena sat down heavily in the empty chair next to Hermond. She finally found a way to break the news. "You know what I think?"

King Darak raised an eyebrow.

"I think," she continued, "that he's run off. Just like Garik. Run off to chase a fantasy. I'm tired of this. First my brother and now my cousin. I cannot understand boys. When we find him, I've a right mind to put him across my knee."

"He's not a child, Serena. I'm sure he will turn up. Aragel has shown no desire to leave us, and he's rarely insolent. He has an active imagination, surely," Darak told her with exaggerated confidence. He believed it no more than she did. He turned his attention back to Hermond and the wine. At least the prince had good taste in wine, but no palate for it since he had barely touched it.

Hermond took one of Serena's delicate hands. "He has not run off. He is simply missing. Perhaps he went for a walk in the city and lost himself in one of the shops."

Serena pulled away from him and slipped her hand inside her dress pocket. She pulled out a small folded piece of parchment, handing it to her father. "That could explain this. I found it in his room, on the floor by the window when I went into his room the third time. At first, I thought nothing of it, but when I finally pulled it from my pocket and read it… well, my suspicions are founded after all."

Darak unfolded the piece of paper carefully, shielding it from Hermond's snooping eyes. He read:

Have gone to Danaria for reinforcement soldiers. I shall be back. Please take care and be well guarded, uncle. Aragel.

He breathed a sigh of relief. Aragel was fine. "Why didn't you tell me about the note earlier?"

"I... I only found it a short while ago," she said.

With a raised eyebrow, he refolded the paper and stood with his hands visibly trembling. He knew his daughter well enough to know she was lying as well. He looked down at his shaking hands. It took a sheer force of will for him to get them to stop.

"Serena, have Commander Corigerg meet me in my chambers immediately."

Serena all but ran from the room in obedience. Hermond jumped up. "Is something wrong? Can I be of any help, Your Majesty?"

Darak sucked in a deep breath, startled at the wheezing noise that emerged from his throat. He knew then why Hermond was not drinking. "No. You have already done so much, Hermond. So much that Aragel is off to gather reinforcements."

"Reinforcements?" echoed Hermond. His light eyes clouded then, and his eager expression went sour.

"For some reason, Hermond, he thinks you want to kill him." Darak smiled wryly. Aragel was a lot smarter than Darak had given him credit for.

Hermond let out a nervous laugh. "Kill him? Where would he get an idea like that? From a dream?"

"I don't know, Hermond. I simply don't know," Darak lied. "Do you have any idea what may have given him that impression?"

The Prince immediately took a defensive posture. "Nothing except his imagination. Where did he go to get reinforcements?"

Darak scratched his beard with a quivering hand as the poisoned wine saturated his body. "Danaria."

The king smiled. There was no sense in hiding the information from Hermond. Aragel would be in Danaria long before Hermond had time to do anything about it. The entire Exavian army was no match for three Danarian legions of Sirus soldiers. They were professional warriors. Their aristocracy and high council were made up of warlords.

"Don't worry. Danaria won't take him seriously," Hermond said casually, then added, "If he makes it that far."

"The Danarians will come. I assure you. I signed a defense treaty with them last spring. You may have fooled me Hermond, but Aragel heard everything." He struggled for breath. "You will not get away with this..." As if a hand tightened down on his vocal cords and chest, Darak's words trailed off enveloping him in darkness.

Just before he fell into a heap, dead, on the cold stone floor he heard Hermond let out a nervous laugh and say, "Nonsense. Your reign is over old man, and Aragel will never make it to Danaria, I'll make sure of that."

●

Hermond waited for a moment then leaned down beside the dead king, checking his pulse to make sure he was, indeed, dead. It was only after he was sure Darak was beyond resuscitation that he stood and shouted as loud as he could, "Hurry, someone call the physician, I think the king has suffered a heart attack!"

As if hearing their calling, clouds of locusts descended on Sherok like a black plague from the heavens.

CHAPTER 6

Tnasha was not so sure the ambush would work. In the manner Commander O'Mally presented it, it all seemed so simple. But it wouldn't be and she knew it. The Kersians were not a foolish people. After all, they knew Danaria's military, the Sirus Horde, was after them for they *had* taken the daughter of the Warlord Kyran. Taken her right from under their noses in the *mid of day* just as Kolgern had said. Then they set the castle aflame with oil and torches. They could not have expected their activities to go unnoticed.

Tnasha stepped away from the others and peered into the forest. The foliage was dense enough to cover them and the day had gone gray with light cloud cover, leaving enough shadow for stealth moving. It would be nightfall before too long. She took in a deep breath of pine-scented air.

Kolgern stepped up behind her. "Umm, it won't work," he whispered so the others could not hear.

"I know." She turned to him with a deep sigh. "It's another plan that blatantly states, attack from the sides! Doesn't he realize that the *sides* will be fortified with soldiers?"

Kolgern chuckled, knowing her snide sense of humor. He pulled his hand absentmindedly through his blonde hair. "What would you propose?"

Tnasha looked up to the canopies of the highest trees, their branches thick with spring green and blue leaves. She smiled, noticing the bow slung over his shoulder. If she could save Kyran's daughter, she would win respect. She would not fail.

"How many bolts do you have?" she asked.

"Hmph." Kolgern looked at her through a cloud of confusion, which immediately dissipated when he realized what she intended. "You can't be serious. You don't expect me to..."

"Just pull Alena away from the others. We'll need her, too." With a brief backwards glance she moved further into the forest away from the legion's encampment.

Her plan had to work. It was a plan even her father would approve of. She was sure of it. It was also her good fortune she saw fit to do the ritual. She felt strong and infallible. While she waited, she thought about the Kersians and their intentions in taking the girl. This was not the first time a young woman had been abducted from Danaria. The Kersians used them as ritual sacrifices to their no-name god. But mostly, she thought they did it to antagonize battle. War remained a sport for them. It always had been. For the soldiers of Danaria's hordes, war defined their way of life. The gods could not have chosen two better adversaries.

Footsteps from behind her brought her attention back to the battle plan. It was Kolgern leading Alena to the clearing.

Once her friends assembled themselves, Tnasha explained herself. "We're light. We can climb further into the branches. The trees are close enough to where we can get from one to another."

Alena, the youngest of the three, only eighteen years, spoke first. "What if a branch breaks beneath one of us? I hate trees." She fidgeted with the string of her bow, rolling it between her thumb and forefinger.

"Test it first by stepping on it while holding onto the tree's trunk," Kolgern said as if stating something that should have been obvious. The continuous sighs erupting from his chest told Tnasha he was not as sure as she was. He stood with his arms crossed over his chest. Sheer boredom adorned his face. It was the same expression he wore to every battle. She often wondered if the look of boredom was a mask he used to hide his fear, or if he was genuinely bored.

As she faced her friends, it seemed to her that no one, anywhere, had thought of such an ingenious strategy. In truth, she was scared to death. Not necessarily afraid of this particular battle, but of battle in general. Outwardly, she poised herself as the fearless warrior, but inside, her stomach twisted violently with the anxiety consuming her. It was what her father deemed a leader's guise - stolid and unmovable on the outside with enough confidence to supply a legion. Inwardly, however, a leader's feelings were completely his own. Tnasha put a hand to her throbbing head. Anxiety always gave her a headache. She wondered if she should do another quick ritual to quell her fear. She shoved the idea aside. There wasn't enough time.

"The object is to get to the edge of the Kersian camp in the surrounding trees," she explained. "Then we'll merely fire on them from three sides."

"Who should we set aim on first?" Alena asked, chewing at her lip.

"The high priests-" Tnasha stopped mid-sentence and fell to her knees, motioning the others to do the same. Their confusion was evident, but they hastily did as she instructed.

"Fen Schoitt! Starkweather! We're taking position." The voice of Commander O'Mally bellowed out at them like the crack of a whip. Within minutes, the stocky, gruff commander entered the small clearing. "There will be plenty of time to pray later."

Kolgern stood from where he sat and faced the commander. "The god, Liale, of earth and steel has spoken!" His voice quivered with the religious zeal of a fanatic. While he may not have known why he went along with Tnasha's plan, he gave it a try anyway. If caught, the worst punishment they could get would be a reprimand and reassignment to guard duty.

The commander was taken aback for a moment, then turned to Tnasha who immediately set to playing along with Kolgern's sudden outburst.

"Yes, Liale," she murmured softly.

Alena stood to speak, but the Commander hushed her, holding up his hand. "She's gone into an elemental trance. I've heard about this happening to Fifth-Gens on rare occasion."

Alena managed to stifle the giggle that tumbled from the back of her throat and hid herself behind the tall, lanky frame of Kolgern. She masked it as a cough, covering her mouth with her stout square hands.

Tnasha took slowly to opening her dark eyes, pretending she needed time to adjust to the dim light of the forest. "Liale told me what we must do," she said, her gaze cast in the distance.

Commander O'Mally's curious eyes bore into her, proof of his eagerness to know what the gods had said. His expression softened.

"Liale has granted us his protection as long as we place bowmen in the trees. And those bowmen must be us," she said, soft and matter-of-fact.

"Yes, yes we can do this, Lord Liale," O'Mally agreed, throwing his voice to the trees. The commander's eyes darted around him as if he expected to see the earth elemental materialize before his very eyes. "But you should be careful. The forest around here is newer and the trees aren't as sturdy as they could be. Their roots are shallow."

"We will handle it, commander," Kolgern said with a brief salute.

"Very well." They knew O'Mally, who attended the temple regularly, would not question the authority of the gods. Especially an elemental. The commander turned on his heel and left, still searching the forest for the ethereal presence of Liale.

Once he was gone, Alena fell into a fit uncontrollable laughter. Kolgern merely shook his head while Tnasha sighed over their good fortune.

Kolgern shook his head again. "This better work. You need a bow, private."

"Yes, lieutenant," Tnasha shot back.

"This better work or we'll all be decommissioned."

Alena put her hand on Kolgern's arm, still laughing. "You're over-reacting, Kolgern. That won't happen. O'Mally likes us. The worst he'll give us is a reprimand and guard duty for three months."

Kolgern groaned.

Tnasha returned with a bow and a quiver full of arrows. "All right, I'll take the west side of the camp. Alena, you take the south. And Kolgern gets the north side."

They parted, going their separate ways.

Moving through the trees was simple enough. With ease, Tnasha made her way from branch to branch, tree to tree, and soon found herself in a tall tree overlooking the Kersian campsite. The tree's thick foliage hid her well enough. She could barely see into the encampment. The sky slowly shifted into pale crimson darkness. She lifted her bow and loaded the bolt with ease. It was upon bringing the bowstring back that it happened. The sound of splitting wood rang out from beneath her as the branch ripped away from the main trunk of the tree. She fell to the ground with a heavy thud and cried out as pain shot through her wrist and ankle. *Test the branch*, she thought, remembering Kolgern's advice to Alena. But it was too late. The world faded black around her and she slipped into oblivion.

The battle cries and clanking of swords ripping into flesh and steel woke her long enough for her to realize she had been captured. A thump, like the sound of a pumpkin hitting wood, sounded above her head. She looked up to see a body lying there. The ground on which she lay was cold and damp, smelling strongly of horse dung and urine. The foul scent drove upright into a sitting position. Movement shot sharp pains through the broken bones she had sustained from the fall. She realized her hands were bound behind her. Her wrist was broken. It felt numb and swollen. Her head throbbed in time with galloping horses and the slicing of axes, and bodies falling onto the forest floor. It was indeed a bloody battle. Immediately she concentrated on hiding her mana. If there were any Kersian sorcerers about, it would give them more than enough incentive to keep her guarded more heavily. Exhaustion was eminent.

Across from her sat a young girl no older than sixteen. Kyran's daughter was striking, with long, curly blond hair that fell well below her shoulders. Her face was smooth and round, her skin pale and flawless. She screamed at every slice and hack. Her eyes widened in horror each time she saw a soldier of the Sirus fall.

"Father!" the girl screamed hysterically.

With every bit of strength Tnasha had, her right wrist practically useless, she tried to wriggle free from her restraints, but her swollen wrist ached painfully. From behind, Tnasha was hoisted to her feet. Faceless Kersian captors dragged them, struggling, through the darkness, and lifted them to the backs of waiting horses. They were led away at a full gallop, making haste to move deeper into the Selenia Forest before the battle overtook them. Once they were far enough away, the Kersian soldiers lit torches to fight the darkness.

She could have kicked herself. While they rode on into the black night, she went over the plan in her head. It seemed perfect. But it was obviously flawed. She had not accounted for the trees being so dry. Not only were they shallow rooted as the commander had pointed out, but their branches were simply not sturdy enough to support much weight. A good commander would have known this. O'Mally was a good commander. That was the only reason he had not been the one to suggest an attack from above. She understood that now.

Then there was the ritual. There had been no time for a second one. Without the ritual, she should have known she would fail. She entrusted one would be enough. Tnasha closed her eyes and tried not to think about it, but the pain from her injuries burned and throbbed. In her own mind her inner voice could find nothing better to do than criticize. Deep down, from somewhere in the dark recesses of her mind, a small voice cried out, *they can't beat you.* Tnasha was stubborn. She decided then that she would escape. If her escape plan did not work out for her, if she was going to die, she would take her captors with her. With these thoughts came hope flickering dimly in the darkness. Tnasha concentrated on that flame of hope and found solace.

After what seemed a long span of trotting and cantering, the horses slowed to an even walk. Tnasha hung on with her thighs, using her resolve for strength. It was stupid to be riding so recklessly in the darkness. But then the Kersians did not care about their horses. After all, most of them were stolen. If one horse was injured, they would simply steal another. Tnasha said nothing, trying hard to pretend her broken bones did not hurt. She wondered if there was another camp nearby, or if the Kersians intended on taking them to one of the alleged Kersian cities. For the most part, she was thankful the Kersians had gagged the screaming girl. It gave her room to think clearly. There had to be a way out. The soil from her ritual felt heavy in her stomach and she realized she had not eaten since the night before.

In the distance, she thought she could see light and the outline of several buildings crowded into a large clearing. When they finally came upon it, she realized it was just as she had suspected. The buildings were made of slat wood and mud. Having seen the wear of years the wood was peeling and dry, while the clay on most of them needed repair. At the center of the small village, a temple rose far above the highest trees with two sets of stone stairs on either side of a pit. Her dreams flooded back to her. The fiery pit, the priest, and his servants. The people. She cringed.

The Kersian soldiers reined the horses to a stop in front of a small cottage that stood away from the others, having been well kept and painted a deep reddish-brown. Undoubtedly a dye made from wild hibiscus and clay from the depths of the forest floor. She thought of the clay and wondered what it tasted like. Her stomach growled. Now, she was grateful she had done the first ritual. Perhaps this was Liale's way of testing her. Suddenly, both she and the girl found themselves pulled from their horses and set on their feet. Tnasha stumbled and started to fall, but one of the soldiers steadied her so she could stand. Her mana was no longer visible, though she feared her resolve would diminish, allowing the mana to flow freely.

A man dressed in black woolen robes stepped from the cottage with a pleased look on his face. "Well, well. What have you brought me, General Luig?" A crimson mana sheen encompassed his body. A Kersian sorcerer.

Tnasha's heart skipped a beat.

The commanding officer stepped forward obediently.

"We have brought you the girl as you requested, sire."

The priest eyed both Tnasha and the girl curiously. "Which one of them is Kyran's daughter and who is the other?"

The officer placed a gauntlet-clad hand on the young girl's shoulder. "This is the daughter of the Warlord Kyran. The other is a prisoner, sire. A Danarian soldier."

"Very well. Bring the girl into my home," he turned around and paused, waving a hand absently. "Do with the prisoner what you will."

Tnasha's dark brown eyes widened and she glanced at the soldiers on either side. Both smiled knowingly at her. She shook her head. *Open your mouth and speak,* she scolded herself.

"Wait. I'm not going anywhere with these two," she called out arrogantly. "I'm not leaving that defenseless girl with the likes of you, either." The guard who held her placed a hold on her injured wrist and squeezed. She winced in pain, trying desperately to keep a calm expression.

The priest turned from the open doorway of the cottage and glared at her. "Loyalty to your own will get you nowhere here," he said with a malicious grin.

"And I suppose leaving me to your soldiers will? Either way, you intend to kill me. I'd rather die fighting for the girl's safety."

"Of course you would. Such chivalry coming from a woman." He smiled in pleasant mockery then motioned her to the door. "But if you insist, come in. I will extend my hospitality to you."

Tnasha pulled away from the guard and hobbled on her good, but sore leg, into the cottage behind him. While the outside of his home seemed humble, the priest lived extravagantly. Tapestries of spun silk, embroidered with golden thread, hung on the walls. The furnishings were made of oak and gold and the servants had placed golden goblets filled with red wine on the table. The priest pulled a knife from his belt and proceeded to cut the restraining ropes from their wrists. The girl immediately pulled the gag from her mouth and began sobbing softly.

"Those injuries look painful," he said, inspecting Tnasha.

She pulled her hand in front of her and examined her swollen wrist. It would have to be reset if she ever wanted to use it again. For the first time, she realized how vulnerable she was without her weapons. She lost them either when she fell, or the Kersians had taken them from her upon her capture. She was not sure which. She had no recollection of those few hours she lay unconscious.

The priest took two of the goblets from the tray and offered one to the girl. She shook her head and backed up against the wall. "Come now, dear. I'm not going to hurt you."

"Of course you're not." Tnasha leaned forward and took the second glass from his other hand, feeling the tingling sensation of his crimson mana brushing her skin. She drew back in discomfort and sat in one of the velvet-covered chairs. It felt good to take the weight off her leg. "Take it," she said to the girl motioning her to sit. If the Kersian was going to kill them, there seemed no sense in refusing good wine.

"I'm glad to see you are making yourself comfortable," the priest said. He sat down in the chair next to her and leaned on the arm rest. "So, what are your names?"

"I'm Lynae," Tnasha lied. She glanced casually at the general who leaned against the far wall. If they knew she was the daughter of the Warlord O'Schoitt, she was sure to be slain immediately or used as bait so they could capture her father. Danarian warlords were renowned for the large prices on their heads for having killed so many of the Kersians' beloved priests. She fought to keep her mana hidden. Had the sorcerer noticed it she would be brought before more Kersian sorcerers, perhaps to be used as a sacrifice, or subjected to an even worse fate. She shuddered. From what she had heard, they believed that sacrificing sorcerers gave them more mana. She smiled at the thought. *Impossible*, she told herself.

With a questioning gaze, the priest turned his attention to the girl, prompting her to answer him. She said nothing.

"Tell him what your name is," Tnasha said in a calm, reassuring voice. She did not know the girl's name either.

Commander O'Mally never bothered to brief them on details. Petty soldiers were only given the basic information they needed to fight the enemy. She would need the girl's name once she found a way to escape. She did not intend on leaving her with *them.*

"Rassia," the girl whispered, her voice quivering.

The priest smiled. He seemed to enjoy that she feared him. "Well then, it is only polite to tell you who *I* am. *I* am Morvack, a high priest of the Kersian people. Ordained by Administrator Gavgal of Zul, himself."

"So you're his henchman?" Tnasha did not bother hiding her obvious disgust. She smiled at his arrogance.

"I *prefer advisor.*" Morvack narrowed his eyes. "Why is it that you are not afraid of me, Lynae?"

"Should I be?"

He laughed and dismissed the question with a wave of his hand. "I think it's time for all of us to get some rest. Wouldn't you agree? I'd offer you food, but it is customary that the sacrifice fast before the ceremony. Tomorrow is going to be a big day for all of us."

Not if I can help it, Tnasha thought. "You're going to sacrifice me as well? I'm no warlord's daughter. Just a petty soldier."

Morvack narrowed his eyes. "You are a sacrifice all the same. I have no use for you otherwise."

"Oh, well then you could just as well let me go."

Morvack laughed. "And risk that you will lead your armies back here?"

"To Arkeereon's pits with that. If you let me go, I'd go home."

"You do not lie well, Lynae. You will be a sacrifice and that is the end of it. Our god will be pleased with the addition."

"You expect me to accept death?"

"I expect nothing. You should feel privileged."

Tnasha's eyes widened. "Privileged? How do you figure?"

"By sacrificing yourself, you will be purified."

She pursed her lips. "Purified? But I'm not sacrificing

myself with my consent. You are sacrificing me against my will."

Morvack shook his head. "Take them to their room, will you, general?"

The general stepped forward. "Yes, sire. Gladly."

Tnasha and Rassia soon found themselves in a small room in the far back of the cottage. Within the dark interior, three dingy white cots stood adjacent one another. Two windows looked out over the small village. One on each side of the room. Not even a hearth was present to take the chill off the cool night air. Amidst the darkness, Tnasha waited for the rest of the cottage to fall silent except for Rassia's soft sobs from the other side of the room.

"Rassia," she whispered into the blackness. The sobbing fell silent. "I want you to get up and look out the window over there. I'll check this one."

Rassia's dark figure got up from the cot and went to the window, peering out with caution. "There is a soldier over here, standing by the trees," she whispered, her voice cracking.

Tnasha looked out the window on her side noting the same thing. "There's one over here, too. Is he looking at the cottage?"

"No, he's facing the trees."

Tnasha hobbled back to her cot and sat down. She did not know how they were going to get out of this. Her body ached horribly from head to toe. Even if they could distract the guards, there was no way she would be able to move quickly enough to ensure the girl's safety. She leaned down and touched her swollen ankle. The pain from the light pressure shot through her calf forcing a small whimper from her lips. Rassia moved to Tnasha's cot and sat next to her.

"There's no way we'll get out of here," came Rassia's small voice.

Tnasha knew there was only one thing she could do. "There's no way *I* am going to get out of here. But we can still get you out."

Rassia sat quietly and wiped the remnant of tears from her cheeks. "How?" she finally asked.

Tnasha turned to her. "I'll try to distract both of the guards. If I can get them away from at least one of the windows, then you could slip out."

"Where would I go?" Rassia was terrified of being alone. Hearing the fear in her own voice brought more tears to her eyes.

Tnasha closed her eyes, trying to remember the surrounding area. She had tried to memorize the shadows on their way into the village. "If I get them to come to this window, you could escape from the other and go directly into the forest. It is dark enough that you would likely go unseen."

"What about you?" Again, Rassia began weeping softly. Tnasha took a deep breath. "I'm injured. I would merely make it harder for you to get away. Either I'll manage," she paused, "or I'll die." Her thoughts went to Liale and she prayed silently, hoping he was listening.

Rassia wrung her hands against the pale blue cotton dress she wore. "Maybe if I bandage your wrist and ankle?"

"That's probably a good idea either way. Regardless, I could not move fast enough. I'm in pain and doubt I could run or even limp along without drawing attention. I would be easily caught."

Rassia nodded in understanding and wiped more tears from her cheeks. "All right. Let me do it." A new found determination rose in her voice. "And I promise, the first soldiers of the Sirus I see, I will tell them you are here."

Tnasha perked up suddenly. "Horses."

"What?"

"Horses. Look out that window and see if you can see any horses." She stood and limped to the closest window while Rassia went to the other. From what she could tell, there were no horses on this side of the cottage. Undoubtedly they were all corralled or stabled nearby. They were probably heavily guarded as well.

"There are none over here," said Rassia, somewhat disappointed.

Tnasha's heart sank. Her dreams came back to her and she shuddered. Turning back to the cot, she sat down with a heavy sigh. Now was not the time to bring them up. They were too terrifying to think about. She could only imagine how Rassia would react. "That's my luck. We have no choice but to go with the first plan."

Rassia leaned down and pulled at a small tear in her dress. She pulled at it until the thin blue fabric ripped and wound around, then tore free from the bottom half. Tnasha stood, turned the cot over, and with her good hand, she gently pried off the small pieces of wood that served as legs. She winced with each loud noise, pausing to listen for footsteps from beyond the door or windows. "These will have to do." Tnasha handed her the too thick, square wooden pieces.

"If they were any thicker it would be a problem." Rassia took them and shook her head. With only the soft glow of moonlight and the light from far off torches to work by, she began bandaging Tnasha's ankle and wrist. Cautiously, she set two pieces of wood on either side of the ankle then wrapped the cloth around them firmly. "This isn't going to work all that well."

"It's better than nothing," whispered Tnasha through clenched teeth. Her temples began to pound from the pain and she felt light-headed.

Once done with the ankle, Rassia stood. "There. Now give me your wrist."

Tnasha held out her wrist and closed her eyes as if it would lessen the pain. It did not. Rassia bandaged the wrist as quickly as she could. The bandage was bulky and thick from the supporting wood, but it was sturdy. It took a few minutes before the pain subsided and went numb.

When she finished, Rassia stood and went over to the other cot. "What shall we do now?"

"First, you must open that window. Then, pretend you're sleeping. When I tap on the wall, check to see if it's clear, then climb out the window as quickly as you can," Tnasha said softly.

Obediently, Rassia went over to the window, opening it. Then she returned to the cot and lay down.

With a grunt of pain, Tnasha stood and hobbled to the window near her cot. She opened it. "Psst. Hello."

The guard turned to her. "What do you think you're doing?" he called.

"Shhhh!" she cautioned. "Come here for a moment."

He approached the window with his sword drawn. His outburst brought three other men running. "Get back in there and close that window."

Tnasha smiled at him sweetly. "I wasn't trying to escape. I wouldn't get very far, you should know that."

"I wouldn't trust you..." he started.

The second soldier cut him off. "Did you ever think that maybe she wants something?" He nudged at his friend and smiled, moving closer to Tnasha. They were a motley crew. Dirty and unshaven, they smelled heavily of sweat, dirt, and horses.

"You're the cleverest of the group, aren't you?" Tnasha asked, playing up her charm. "Come closer."

The third soldier raised his thick eyebrows. Bits of food from a previous meal still clung to his graying beard. "Where's your little friend?"

Tnasha moved aside so that they could see into the window. "She's sleeping."

The bearded man smiled lustfully, grabbed her good wrist, and pressed it to his lips.

With an abrupt jerk, she pulled away. "I'm a sacrifice, remember?" she said through clenched teeth. It was all she could do to keep from slapping him. She quickly recovered her smile.

The other two men moved in closer. The first reached in and touched her neck. "Perhaps Morvack will reconsider and give you to us." His hand moved across the lower extremity of her bare neck.

She playfully shoved his hand away. "Morvack and I have an agreement. I am to be sacrificed." With her uninjured hand, she tapped on the wall, then leaned forward. Squeezing her eyes shut, she held her breath, and planted a kiss on the soldier's dirt encrusted neck. Disgusted, she allowed him to kiss her full on the lips. A rush of nausea overcame her.

Upon hearing the tap, Rassia lifted herself from the cot and peered out the window. The path to the forest was clear of soldiers. With little effort, she lifted herself out the open window and she ran.

Suddenly, the door flew open, and bright torchlight flooded the room. Tnasha covered her eyes. General Luig entered. "What is all the noise in here?"

Tnasha pulled away from the window and stood with her back against the wall, still shielding her eyes from the painful light.

With a quick scan of the room, he realized Rassia was missing. He rushed to the open window she had left by only moments earlier. "Corick, Demar, Rarick! One of them has escaped you morons! Go after her!"

Without question, the soldiers obediently ran into the forest in pursuit. The general faced Tnasha, his eyes wide with rage. Deep crimson crept up his neck and into his cheeks. "Where is she?"

"She's gone. You're too late." Tnasha gave him a condescending smile. She could not mask the defiance and hatred she felt. Her expression hardened. She only hoped Rassia had enough time to distance herself from the pursuing soldiers.

"You are coming with me." The general grabbed her firmly by the shoulder and pulled her from the room to High Priest Morvack's private quarters.

The Kersian sorcerer did not ask any questions. He seemed to know immediately what had happened. "I'll watch her. You find the other one."

"Yes, sire." With a final glare at Tnasha, the general left in haste.

CHAPTER 7

Rassia heard the yells from behind her, then the quickening footfalls of the soldiers trailing her. With her face flushed from running, and her breath caught in her chest, her heart skipped a beat, thumping wildly - so loud she could hear it. She drew in a deep breath, realizing she had nowhere to go. The forest was dense and black. In the pitch, she could make out the faint outlines of trees. She ran to the nearest tree and stopped. With fear as her catalyst, she began to climb, ignoring the stinging pain of the bark cutting and scraping her bare knees and shins. Adrenaline drove her into the oak's highest branches. Just in time, too. She paused long enough to look down. While she saw nothing, she could hear the two soldiers run beneath her. She held her breath, aware of everything by the sound it made. Leaves rustled in a light breeze, and the haunting echo of mysterious beast noises seemed to drift on the darkness. The sounds of the pursuing Kersians soon faded into the forest, and suddenly she was alone.

She took a deep breath and sighed gratefully. As carefully as she could manage, she felt around and found a sturdy place to sit in the fork of two branches where she would be hidden from below. She needed rest. It was doubtful she would be able to travel far in the darkness. She quickly decided the tree offered the best protection.

●

The sound of rustling leaves and whispers jolted her awake. Bright sunlight assaulted her eyes. She looked around. The sun poked its head above the cliffs and crags of the mountains, shedding copper light that blended into the clear blue sky like the colors on an artist's canvas. She shook herself to alertness and searched the sea of leaves for movement.

It took a few moments for her to spot them. Further off in the trees at the same height as herself, were a male and female, both dressed in the common leather armor of the lesser ranks of Danaria's Sirus Horde. Her heart began racing again. She lifted herself, standing amid the branches in a dance of balance. She wanted to cry out to let them know she was okay, and that Lynae was in grave danger. Her message became more urgent. She lifted her voice to the sky and made the high pitch sound of what she thought was a bird.

It was the closest she could come to a hawk. Her eldest brother had tried to teach her the calls before he left for Arkeereon. More likely, the sound that emerged from her throat sounded like a dying cat at best. It did, however, gather the attention of the Danarian soldiers. They turned toward her, their eyes searching the trees cautiously. She waved. In the distance, from the direction of the small village, the rhythmic beat of a slow, monotonous drum echoed through the still morning air.

It did not take long for the soldiers to reach her. The blonde man was the first to speak. "You are Rassia, daughter of Kyran?"

"Yes," she said anxiously. "We have to go back and save Lynae. They'll kill her, I know it. Where are the other soldiers?"

"What other soldiers?"

"You're it?" Rassia asked, exasperated.

"Our legion needed time to regroup. We figured we didn't have that kind of time so we came alone. I was right." The man looked over at the young woman with him.

"Rassia, let us worry about getting Tnasha back. You should stay up here. They can't see you from the ground," said the blonde woman. She turned to the man. "Lynae?"

"You don't think she would have told them her real name do you?" The man snickered.

"Of course not, but Lynae?" The woman shook her head.

"We should sneak into the city before full daybreak and find her." The man looked around.

"If you'll let me go with you I can show you where she is." Rassia did not want to go back to the city, but she felt she had to. She could not knowingly let someone die. Especially since that someone had tried to save her.

"Let her come with us," the female soldier told him. "We may not have time to come back and get her. The Kersians aren't going to take lightly that we're taking Tnasha as it is."

Rassia crinkled her forehead in confusion. "Who is Tnasha?"

The soldiers ignored her. The man rubbed his eyes and yawned. "We should hurry. Tnasha might be closer to death than we'd like to believe."

"Wait. Do you have names?"

The blonde man lifted an eyebrow. "I'm Kolgern, this is Alena. The woman you know as Lynae, auburn hair, short, that's our friend, Tnasha. So, now that we've been formally introduced, let's go."

Rassia nodded in understanding. Getting up the tree had seemed an easy task the night before. Getting down was proving itself more difficult. Rassia clung to the rough tree bark, setting her foot down in several spots before finding her footing. She did not care that her undergarments were exposed as the tree tugged and lifted her ripped dress.

"It's amazing how far you can climb up a tree when you're scared half to death," she said.

"Fear can show you abilities you never knew you had before." Kolgern lent a hand, helping her down the tree slowly, until after what seemed like hours, Rassia finally reached the ground.

Her knees were shaking. "Maybe I'm not ready for an adventure like this."

Kolgern and Alena both gave her *the look*. The same look her parents gave her when she had done something she was not supposed to do.

"You don't have much of a choice now, do you? Unless you want to climb back into the tree?" Alena's voice was laden with irritation.

Rassia swallowed her fear. "You're right. I have to be brave."

The threesome moved carefully through the forest, through the thickest underbrush, closer with each step to the Kersian city. It was when she could see the tops of the Kersian buildings in broad daylight that a lump rose in her throat. Rassia swallowed hard and followed the Danarian soldiers. Something she once heard her father say to her brother kept running through her mind. *Do not let fear hold you back from doing what you feel is right.*

CHAPTER 8

The sorcerer Morvack did not attempt to engage Tnasha in conversation. He stared at her for some time with a look of contempt. His eyes hinted the crimson of his mana, which swirled about his body in restless fluidity. She did not sleep that night. Instead, she sat next to the hearth with her eyes cast at the floor. Suddenly the Kersian sorcerer rose and began pacing the floor in contemplation. He held his hands against his lips in prayer. The white robes he now wore swirled around his boot-clad feet. Tnasha counted the steps. One, two, three, four, five, six. He would then turn on his heal and take six more steps back before turning and repeating the process. The scent of worn leather permeated the room.

Just before dawn, Morvack finally stopped pacing and spoke. "Where did you tell her to go?" The anger in his voice threatened he would lose his temper at any moment. A deep, irritated sigh followed.

"I don't see why it matters. I told her to go into the forest," Tnasha said in a calm voice.

Morvack scowled at her, and his lips pulled back into a sneer. "Regardless, if she makes it back to Danaria we will only go back and take her again." His face softened then, and he smiled condescendingly, leaning in toward her. "And for your crimes against our god, you will die in her place."

Tnasha rolled her eyes. "You would have killed me anyway. Remember our whole sacrifice conversation? Or did you forget?" Her heart pounded in her chest, filling her ears with her own fear. "You already told me you were going to kill me."

"Perhaps. But not with the *sacred* ritual. Our god is sure to be angry for not providing a fitting sacrifice."

Tnasha tried to think of an unlikely response to his statement, wanting desperately to instigate a fight with him. The mention of *the ritual* made her stomach growl even though she knew his ritual and hers were two different rituals indeed. Morvack's words offended her.

"What do you mean? I'm as fitting a sacrifice as she was."

He sat next to her and looked her straight in the eyes. "You are not afraid to die. You are not afraid of me? What type of sorcery is this?"

The panic swelled inside her, and she swallowed hard. "I have no sorcery to speak of. I'm a soldier. And you're right – I'm not afraid. Actually, I'm quite bored."

She could feel the anger well up inside him. His crimson mana became more vibrant and took on a deeper hue. She concentrated harder to hide her own, feeling even more exhausted. Doing anything with mana took from a sorcerer's physical and mental strength. The fatigue was one of several drawbacks to using one's mana, and fatigue was one thing she could not afford right now.

The flesh on his angular face contorted into a hard mold and he stood, his fists clenched. "All of that will change. I promise you." Abruptly, he turned and left the room.

Tnasha sat back against the coarse, mud wall in triumph. Her bandaged ankle and wrist did not ache like previously. But then she had not moved in hours either.

Before long, Morvack returned with several armed men. "The ritual is about to start. Take her to the altar."

"Sherokean Red?" she asked under her breath. A smile slid across her lips.

"What?"

"Nothing."

Morvack glared at her. The soldiers heeded his command and lifted her to her feet by the elbows. They led her from the room and out of the cottage. The temple, the pit, and its altar of death loomed before her like a tomb. And that is what it was. Kersian soldiers gathered kindling and wood for the fire. Upon throwing all of it into the pit, they lit it with torches and it burst into angry golden-orange flames. The dream had sealed her fate.

But who were the people who came up the stairs?

She figured she would know soon enough. To the beat of slow drums, they led her up the stairs and onto the platform high above. After chaining her to the altar, they retreated. The townspeople began gathering at the temple's base as other prisoners were led up the stairs to stand behind her. Morvack ascended behind them and took his place before a pulpit at the front of the altar.

She could see the Kersian High Priest, Morvack, preaching to a multitude of people kneeling at the temple's base, whose faces remained blurred. Morvack unlocked the chain that held her and pulled her to the front of the alter, holding her firmly next to the pit of fire while the scent of scorched flesh rose from the flames and permeated the air. There were others waiting to die as she did. But she was to die first...

CHAPTER 9

Upon reaching the edge of the Kersian village, they knelt behind a dense thicket of bushes. No soldiers patrolled the outskirts. Instead, they patrolled the inner city around the temple lest anyone should disturb the ongoing ritual.

Rassia led them to the cottage windows. "This is the room we were kept in last night."

Kolgern and Alena each looked into the open window. Alena pursed her lips. "Why is that cot broken apart?"

"Lynae, er, Tnasha broke her ankle and wrist. We had to use the wood from the cot to make splints."

Kolgern peered around the corner of the building and sat back. "Hmm."

Alena gave him an inquisitive look. "Hmm, what?"

"I wouldn't have thought to use a cot frame for splints."

Alena gave an exasperated sigh and motioned to the inner city. "What's happening over there?"

"It seems the Kersians are having a gathering. Most likely Tnasha is a guest?"

"Yeah - as the main attraction," Alena snorted.

"She's going to be used as a sacrifice." Rassia's gaze wandered over Kolgern's shoulder to the temple. High above, she saw a man grasping a small woman's arm. It had to be

Tnasha, she was sure of it. Hanging on a line nearby she saw two white gowns left out to dry in the warm spring air. "Wait here." She ran to them and brought them back to the side of the building handing one to Alena. "We'll go into the crowd and wait. You'll know when it's time. I'll call to you both with the same sound I made earlier."

Kolgern grinned. "The dying pig noise?"

Alena stifled a snicker.

"Yes, the dying pig." *So much for a hawk call*, Rassia thought.

"No. I think a hand signal would be more appropriate." Kolgern laughed softly, and held out a rough, thick hand. He extended his fingers with his palm vertical, then closed his fingers into a fist. "That's the signal, Alena. We need a cohesive plan. You'll both go into the crowd. I'll get some horses from the stable. While I'm doing that, Alena, move toward the stairs. Rassia, when I come up you get hold of the horses and keep the soldiers away from yourself. Alena and I will signal each other, and I'll make my way up the stairs to Tnasha. Alena will cover me. Hopefully Alena and I will be enough distraction to keep the soldiers away from you, Rassia." He paused and waited for Alena and Rassia to acknowledge that they understood.

Alena nodded reassuringly and handed Rassia a short sword.

"I don't know how to use this! I'm only fifteen-years-old," Rassia said in protest, holding the sword with the tips of her fingers. Even if she did, she would be afraid to use it and she knew it. If she stabbed someone, could she handle the sight of blood? She shuddered at the thought.

"Age has no bearing. When it comes to your life, you'll know what to do with it."

"This is rash, Alena," Kolgern said with some concern.

"We haven't time to waste planning. If we don't move now, she'll die and we'll have to live our lives knowing we did nothing to save her." Alena gave him an annoyed look.

Rassia noticed Alena's eyes showed the same concern as Kolgern, but not for her own life. She wanted to save her friend. Rassia wanted to save Tnasha, too. After all, Tnasha put her own life in danger to save her. With a surge of bravery, Rassia hid the sword beneath the white robe she wore and followed Alena to the temple.

Upon reaching the base of the temple, both young women slid easily to the back of the crowd and knelt unnoticed. Other late arrivals joined them, all of them with heads bowed and hands held in prayer. Looking up, Rassia saw Tnasha, who blankly stared into the treetops of the forest. She tapped Alena on the arm lightly and with a nod of her head, motioned for her to look up. Alena took a deep breath. From the look on her face Rassia could tell it was the first time Alena realized just how close they were to kissing the lips of death.

The silence was immediately shattered by a booming voice from far above the crowd. "Let us bow our heads and pray to the one true god, denied by all of those who are the embodiment of evil, who would kill our people in the name of their elements." Morvack held up a pale hand. "The one true god has chosen our people! We shall crush the infidels if they will not come willing to the waiting arms of the nameless one, the one true god. For in him, there is salvation, redemption, and purification."

Rassia looked around her, her head bent forward slightly. The patrol soldiers gathered next to the crowd also kneeled in prayer.

From above, the priest cried out. "Oh nameless one, we bring you offerings of flesh. Those condemned shall be purified in your fire!"

The shrill sound of the word *fire* resounded throughout the small village, reaching the highest treetops. The crowd of worshippers, adorned in white robes, stirred and looked up, their faces masked with adulation. Rassia convincingly mirrored the same reverent gaze, though her eyes searched for Kolgern. From the corner of her eye she saw Alena, and the hand signal. The worshippers finally settled back into their silent prayers with heads bowed. And just as they left themselves unguarded for that brief moment, Kolgern raced into the clearing with four horses, sword drawn. Rassia jumped up to grab the horses as she was told. Alena followed Kolgern.

Tnasha felt Morvack's strong grasp pull her closer to the pit of fire, ready to push her in. Then she heard the battle cries and saw clearer two familiar faces quickly ascending the stairs with blood lust evident in their wild eyes, wielding weapons of war. When she realized who they were, she shoved her weight backward, knocking Morvack against the altar and breaking free from his grasp. She fell forward slightly, but caught herself and limped toward her friends. Alena thrust a dagger into her hand. Grasping the dagger's handle firmly, Tnasha sought shelter behind Kolgern's towering, lithe form.

"Capture them!" Morvack shouted, regaining his balance. He ran at Tnasha.

In her own fear and desperation, Tnasha grabbed Morvack by the arm, placing the dagger firmly against his neck using the arm with the broken wrist. Her adrenaline seemed to mask the pain. The soldiers approaching from the stairs stopped. Tnasha said nothing, but the threatening, clouded look in her brown eyes told them she had no reservations about killing their high priest.

She pushed Morvack forward to make sure his soldiers could see. Her voice quivered in anger. "Lay down your weapons or he dies."

Alena placed her dagger in place of Tnasha's and pushed Kolgern forward. "Let's get out of here."

Kolgern steadied Tnasha, helping her down the stairs. At the bottom, Rassia waited with the horses. A satisfied look adorned her tear-stained face. She had successfully killed a kneeling crowd of soldiers, fearing they would overtake her friends. She had killed three of them with one sweeping motion of her sword, and a long drawn out scream. Their bodies lay in a heap next to the opposite stairway. They had not even had a chance to stand.

The Kersian general was among those who set down their weapons. He glared at Tnasha as she and Kolgern passed. "You won't get away with this. You'll go back to Danaria and we shall come for you. Administrator Gavgal will hear about this."

"See to it he does," Tnasha said through clenched teeth.

In truth, she was scared to death. She would have a price placed on her head. Regardless, they had no inkling as to who she was, which helped matters somewhat. But it still did nothing to ease her mind about the dream and all that had taken place. The general was right. Going back to Danaria was certain suicide. She had to see the Sorcerer Kalath. That was where they would go. The Kersians would not follow them so deep into the Selenia Forest. At least she hoped they wouldn't. Behind them, Morvack went willingly with Alena, without struggle or words.

Kolgern grabbed Morvack away from Alena. At that moment, Tnasha relaxed while Alena helped her, and the violet mana sheen emanating from her skin shown so brightly that Morvack covered his eyes. As she turned from him, Morvack's hand shot out and caught Tnasha's neck. She jerked away, and hurried to mount one of the horses with Alena's help. Once all three women were safely on horseback, Kolgern swept his blade over the priest's throat, spilling Morvack's blood to the ground. He hurriedly mounted the remaining horse, letting out a final battle cry as they turned their horses toward the Selenia Forest and bolted at full gallop from the village without looking back.

When she felt it was safe, Tnasha sat back in the saddle, slowing her horse to an amble, then a full stop. She waited for the others to catch up with her.

"That was a little too close," Kolgern said breathlessly, shaking his head. He swept a wisp of his moist blond hair from his unshaven, tired face. It was warm as though the forest captured the spring heat and held it beneath the shield of trees overhead. The space between trees left little room for them to ride side by side. Instead, they let their horses pick their way single file between thickets, trees, roots, and brush.

"Where are we going?" Rassia asked, looking back at the mountains and noticing they were moving away from them.

"We should go to see the sorcerer Kalath. It's the only place we'll be safe. They'll undoubtedly find us if we turn back to Danaria." The look in her dark brown eyes went distant, and by that, they knew she was serious.

"Tnasha's right," said Kolgern. "We couldn't hope to go back to Danaria thinking we'd be safe."

Alena crinkled her brow. "What about her?" she asked, pointing to Rassia.

Rassia rode in silence, glancing up at Alena's mention of her.

"She'll be fine as long as she's with us," Kolgern said.

Tnasha chuckled to herself. "We can hope she'll be safe. We almost died back there."

"No thanks to you falling out of that tree, Nasha," Kolgern said in a playful tone bordering sarcasm. He rarely called her by her shortened name unless out of affection.

Alena did not join in the laughter. "I don't happen to think it's funny at all! I *warned* you two that one of us could fall. Didn't I?"

Neither replied.

"It's no one's fault but my own," Tnasha admitted. "Had I been paying attention to what I was doing I wouldn't have fallen."

Kolgern cleared his throat. "Speaking of which, how are you feeling?"

"I'm fine. My ankle aches and my wrist just plain hurts. But I'm sure I'll live. Us sorcerers heal fast. When I broke my finger it healed in three days." She held out her pinky finger to them and wiggled it.

Rassia spoke up then. "How long will it be before we reach Kalath?"

Tnasha shrugged her shoulders. "If we ride through this evening only breaking to rest and water the horses, we should arrive there well into the night."

"Do you think they're following us?" Rassia looked back over her shoulder.

"Doubtful. But I think Morvack caught a glimpse of my mana as we were leaving." Tnasha silently scolded herself for being so careless and so weak.

Kolgern shrugged. "Maybe that was enough to scare them off."

Tnasha said nothing. As they rode on in silence, she allowed her thoughts to drift back to the Kersians. She felt nothing but anger. It writhed inside her, ripping at her like clawed appendages running from her navel up to the back of her throat. The flesh lumped there. The bitter taste of iron mingled in with her saliva and her stomach went sour, her face pale. She had not eaten in over a day. Reining her horse to a stop, she dismounted and hobbled to the base of a nearby tree. Then her stomach went into spasms and she heaved the remnants of the pit's acrid smoke. She heaved the dryness again and again.

Kolgern dismounted and hurried up beside her. "Are you all right?"

Tnasha coughed and spat the foul tasting fluid from her mouth, then wiped her chin. "I'll be fine. I'm not feeling well. I'm hungry, I hurt, and I'm tired."

"Obviously."

She pushed away the hand he offered her and hobbled further in between the trees. The pain from her broken bones throbbed with a renewed sharpness. She winced. "We have to hurry. But first, I need a little privacy."

Alena dismounted and followed, motioning for Kolgern to stay back. Tnasha found herself a private area behind a rock and some trees hiding her from view. There, she pulled down her pants and commenced relieving herself only to feel a sharp pain in her rear-end. She jumped. "Ye-ouch! Can this day get any worse?!"

Alena hurried around the tree with a look of panic adorning her face. "What happened?"

"By Natyis!" Tnasha jumped back, sending pain through her injured ankle, her hand cupping the wound. There, just beneath the large rock a dranar viper coiled, poised to strike again.

Alena jumped back. "Poisonous snake!"

Kolgern raced from the path toward them with his sword drawn. "What?"

"Snake!" Alena pointed it out to him.

He immediately found the snake and cut it in two. He turned to Tnasha and Alena who had since moved away. Tnasha turned around and bent over, exposing her left buttock.

A hearty chuckled escaped him. He put his hand up to his mouth in attempt to stop himself.

"It's not funny, Kolgern. How are we going to get the poison out?" Alena asked, angry.

Kolgern took a sudden step back. "I'm not putting my mouth…"

She threw him an angry glance and pulled her dagger from its sheath. "Tnasha, stay as you are. This might hurt a little." Without warning, she slit the bite wound open and commenced sucking the wound to remove the poison.

Kolgern wandered back to the path with his eyes cast to the ground, murmuring beneath his breath. "That's not good. Wrong."

Rassia perked up at his approach. "What's wrong?"

"Snake bite," he said offhandedly, and mounted.

Soon after, Alena returned, steadying Tnasha as she hobbled slowly to her horse and clumsily remounted. Alena returned to her own horse and mounted with one last warning glance in Kolgern's direction.

"What?"

Alena just shook her head.

The conversation quieted as morning turned into afternoon and then late day. They stopped to rest and water the horses several times. All the while, Tnasha's thoughts turned to Kalath, her second father since birth. Kalath was an understanding man, with dark expressive eyes. One would think he caught every word, every motion with those eyes. For most of the time, Kalath remained silent and did little more than listen without passing judgment.

She believed his silence to be the product of his immediate surroundings. He lived in a small cave in the midst of the Selenia Forest. He left it illuminated with torches, and a plethora of tapered candles of various lengths and colors. Yet, his home remained bleak and dark and the trees around the cave had long since died from the ever-growing salt marshes that extended into that part of the region.

During this visit, Tnasha reminded herself to ask him about the scenes and sounds that plagued her dreams. She vowed also to tell him of how the dream came to life before her very eyes as she stood before the pit of fire. Only an adept sorcerer could explain these things to her.

Even though Kalath's home meant safety, she hated the long ride. She also despised the thickness of the green and blue trees that shut the sun out from above them. One never knew what she might find lurking in the outskirts of the Onx Mountains and deep into the Selenia Forest. On previous journeys here with her father, the darkness of the forest would choke her with silence as she fought to inhale the thick, suffocating air into her lungs. The humidity left her entire body feeling soaked to the bone.

She broke from her thoughts and looked around her. Her friends rode without word, following her deeper into the forest. The sun slowly slipped behind the Onx Mountains, folding the crimson sky into black pitch. She peered into the oncoming darkness, barely able to distinguish the crudely cut path that led to the marshes. The path was rough and uneven, yet the horses were able to make their way through with agility and grace. The horse she rode moved cautiously, sidestepping once or twice to avoid getting caught in the tangling underbrush lining the narrow path.

The moon was already well into the sky when they reached the marsh. The waters of the marsh stagnated, unmoved by the night winds that whipped at the dead branches of the trees. It was not cold, but rather damp. Tnasha would have been grateful for a simple light wool cloak to keep the chill off. She patted her horse's withers, wondering whether the horse felt the chill at all.

An old slat bridge lay directly ahead of them, lined by now dead, stolid trees. Salt encrusted their dry, cracked trunks. The bridge appeared unsteady. It wavered over the water. Moist air soaked into the decaying fibers of porous, dry, wooden slats. The smell of rot lingered. The horses remained skittish about crossing the rickety bridge. One hoof at a time, each moved carefully, testing the first few slats by pawing at them gently. The boards creaked and bowed with their weight. Once each horse determined it safe, they bolted across it in fear it could crumble beneath them at any moment.

On the other side, in the distance, Tnasha saw the single

lit torch that marked the entrance of Kalath's reclusive home. For years, Kalath's had been a safe haven where she could think clearly and relish in the old man's tales of magic and mystery. She wished that could be the nature of her business here this time. Even so, thoughts of a warm fire and memories of fragrant herbs, music, and Kalath's deep, melodic voice relaxed her. She was glad they had come.

CHAPTER 10

Aragel awoke the next day in the damp hull of the ship amongst the crates of Captain Adarack Vogman's cargo. The room twisted around him and the loud crashing, splintering noises of the storm's fury pierced his ears. He put his hands to his throbbing head in attempt to steady himself. Upon standing, he immediately lost his balance, falling to the floor as the ship jerked violently. The sounds of the storm outside became muted for a moment as another large wave washed over the bow of the ship. Aragel came to full awareness then and realized what was happening. He could hear the cries and shouting of the men above as they fought to keep the ship on course despite the devouring ocean.

The ship rocked as another large wave slammed against the hull. Aragel's stomach turned. Damp salt water slowly seeped into the hull through the cracks and hatches. He heard the captain, his loud voice coming from somewhere else inside the hull. Aragel crawled to the nearest ladder, which led to an outside hatch. He noticed the outline of a door next to it. Pressing his ear against it, he could hear the captain's voice more clearly on the other side.

"If we can get ten leagues north of here, we should be out of it. This is a bad one," Adarack was saying.

Aragel recognized the voice of Shadon. "By Natyis! I swear this is my luck. We are going to die. Aithian despises me because I despise his serpents!"

Adarack laughed. "Great Lord Aithian, however, does favor me, my friend. He will not let me die, nor you, nor the prince."

"You think so? I'll believe that when we reach the shores of the Danarian mainland alive and in one piece. I need a drink to calm my nerves." Footsteps moved across the room.

"Try not to spill my good wine. I need to go above. You need to relax."

"Relax? Ha!"

Aragel heard the captain climb a ladder, open the hatch, and go above, shouting hurried orders at his crew. Another wave hit the ship. Aragel lost his footing again, this time falling to the floor, and hitting his head against the thin worn door.

As he struggled to regain his footing a second time, the door opened. Shadon stood there, looking down expectantly.

"So, look who's awake," he said, bracing himself in the decaying doorframe, grasping a bottle of wine in one hand.

"There's some water coming in, the floor is wet in here." Aragel pointed to the spot where he had woken up and rubbed his head where he hit it.

"Not enough to sink us." Shadon looked up as a large thud sounded from above. "Not yet anyway. Come in here. We're not experienced with these storms or with mariner's duties so we stay down here." He moved out of the doorway so Aragel could enter.

"What if the ship starts to take on water?"

Shadon shook his head. "Rule number two, never stay in the hull of a sinking ship. Rule number three, while I'm thinking about it, never run away wearing clothing of the aristocracy. Rule number four, never go anywhere with anyone you don't know. And lastly, for now, rule number five, use common sense and don't ask foolish questions."

Shadon pulled the cork from the wine and took another drink straight from the bottle. He sat down, corked the bottle, and put his head in his hands. Closing his eyes, he took several slow, measured breaths.

"About rule number four..." Aragel began.

Shadon answered before the boy-prince could complete the question. "No. You should never have come with me as willingly as you did. I could have killed you. You're lucky it was me and not an assassin out to murder you. You really need to be more careful and think before acting in the future."

"Well, you seemed harmless enough. You are my cousin, right?" Aragel sat down on a bench affixed to the wall. His eyes bore expectantly into Shadon. Whether or not Shadon was his cousin had not been established yet. Or had it? Paranoia washed over him. He did not know what was real anymore.

Shadon took another deep breath and looked Aragel straight in the eye. His face bore was grayish green hue from the dim light. "Do you know what I do for a living? Honestly?"

Aragel shrugged. "You're a spy of some sort..."

"Right. I steal documents and gather information. I've occasionally been paid to kill people. I'm good at what I do. I'm your cousin by blood, but I'm not who you think I am."

"You were paid to kill people? By who?" Aragel's eyes went wide with disbelief and fear. He grabbed at a wall for balance as another wave slapped at the ship.

"That's not important right now. What is important is that you're here and Hermond is delayed." He pulled the cork from the wine bottle again and took another drink.

"Who paid you to kill people?" Aragel asked again, firmer this time. He went for his short sword still firm in its scabbard affixed to his belt. Garik was right, he was not Aragel's cousin as he had once known him.

Shadon noticed this and jumped toward the boy, knocking him against the wall as another wall of water clawed violently at the ship. "Never pull a sword on me, cousin! I'm not going to hurt you, so put it away or so help me..."

Aragel could not move, pinned beneath Shadon and the wooden slats of the bench. "Let me up. I'm heir to the throne of Sherok!"

Shadon let the prince up with some reluctance. "You think that your aristocratic status will change the way I'm going to treat you? No, I don't think so. Don't forget, I was aristocracy once, too. Remember? Here and now, *you* are just a kid. You wouldn't have made it out of Sherok without my help."

Aragel's eyes clouded as he searched the floor for his pride. He thought of his status and then he became angry. "Why should I be grateful for your help? I knew I was going to Danaria before you had even figured out what Hermond was doing in Sherok." He smirked and rolled his eyes despondently.

Another wave hit the ship, yet this time, with less force. The men above still shouted.

"No. I knew Hermond was up to something long before you knew what he was up to. Don't deny that you didn't have any idea how you were going to get to Danaria until I provided the solution." Shadon held onto the wooden rail along the wall where he sat and rode each wave as it hit.

"You think you're so smart?" Aragel braced himself in the corner. "You're a nobody. A sniper, a thief. That's what you told me. So don't flatter yourself with your delusions of grandeur!"

Shadon raised an eyebrow, "My birth given name may be Garik Darak, and undoubtedly I endured the same education as you. I just chose to use it differently. The difference between you and I is I needed more than Sherok. You have a narrow world- view, cousin. *Sherok* is *your* world. The *world* is *my* world."

Aragel's mouth dropped open. He had no response to that. He was not sure he knew what Shadon meant.

Shadon pulled the family sigil pendant from where it hung around his thin neck and threw it to Aragel. "Unlike you, happy with the prospect of a throne, I wanted to travel. Difference was I used to sneak out of the castle and visit Sherok. Made a lot of friends that way. So, when I did decide to leave unnoticed, I had help. I was naive, yes. But I wasn't as foolish as you." He smiled at the memory. "I wasn't meant to be a king. I know now that I was right. I enjoy my life. I answer to no one unless I choose to. My responsibilities are far more… exciting."

Aragel stared at the sigil. "So, how many people know who you really are?"

"Very few. I won't tell anyone if you won't." He laughed and then fell silent. No more shouting came from above and the waves merely lapped at the sides of the Narassa. Aragel set his jaw, crossing his arms over his chest. He stared at the wall in front of him.

Shadon stood and walked cautiously to the ladder that led to the deck. "What the ...?" He slowly climbed the ladder. "Stay here and keep quiet," he told Aragel in little more than a whisper.

Aragel's eyes followed him until he vanished above. There he remained, unmoving and angry. Shadon was right. Aragel was naïve. Inside the Sherokean castle. The market of crops. The growing season. These were things Aragel knew. The only things. He felt betrayed. Like he had been sheltered on purpose. Why did his uncle not allow him to travel? It was probably Shadon's fault, he decided. Had Shadon, Garik, not run away, Aragel may not have been as sheltered.

"Well, if anyone should be angry, it should be me," he said aloud to no one in particular. He looked at the hatch, wondering what had happened above. A dragon maybe. Aragel's imagination ran rampant. The strange silence made him nervous. Then he heard footsteps and talking from above.

Shadon descended into the captain's quarters again. This time, the captain followed along with a gangly, unshaven fellow who Aragel recognized as one of the deck hands. A young man only slightly older than Aragel.

"What happened?" Aragel fidgeted with his tunic, wiping at the dirt stains.

"Well, we lost a few lads to the mighty sea, rest their souls," Adarack said mournfully. He held something small, wrapped in an old rag in his hand. After placing it on the table, he peered at it and touched it. The thing wrapped in cloth began squawking.

"It probably has er broken wing cap'n," the blonde, dirty deck hand said.

"Poor thing is wet and shaken." Adarack moved to the table bolted to the wall on the far side of the room. He waved his hand at Aragel to approach. "This is going to be your first job, lad." His eyes slid over Aragel's thin frame disapprovingly. "I don't want you to hurt yourself on deck."

Aragel ignored Adarak's gaze and went to the table to see what the dirty, wet cloth held. A raven, wild eyed, squawked at him. The poor bird was soaked and one wing looked awkward.

"What shall I do with it?" he asked.

Aragel never had time for animals aside from his horse. His uncle was allergic to everything with fur including horses and often took a carriage to keep some distance between himself and the beast that pulled it. Snakes and insects had been out of the question also. Serena's fearful tantrums regarding insects and serpents only sent the king into anger, and Aragel to his quarters.

"I was thinking you could nurse the bird back to health. Keep it as a pet until it is well." Captain Adarack held the bird out to him. "It will give you something to do and keep you out of trouble. Now, I need to arrange a funeral rite for those who were taken by the sea." The captain turned then, and without word, left them. Shadon remained silent. The air was still with grief.

Aragel turned to Shadon, trying to ignore what his imagination envisioned. Large waves crashing over the ship so forcefully that men were knocked overboard only to be lost in the raging sea below. He shook it off. "I know nothing about birds. What they eat, how to mend a wing..."

Shadon did not reply. Instead, he pulled a small flute from his bag and began playing. The song, filled with sorrow and loss, drifted to their ears, weighted with melancholy.

The normally chatty deck hand spoke then. "Eya, I know how to care fer a wee bird like 'iss. Ya need ta wrap the wing in a splint. Jus as you would a person. Ya have ta be careful though. Darn thing'll peck ya if yer not careful."

"So what does it eat?" Aragel asked, his tone more melancholy this time. The dark mood of everyone had shoved its way upon him. Above, the men sang a solemn song in a language he did not understand.

"Grains an' such, I s'pose," replied the young man. He shrugged his shoulders, not really knowing if that was indeed, what ravens ate.

Shadon stopped playing his flute and looked thoughtfully at the bird. Its shrill cries pierced the chamber.

"Don't you think you should name it?"

"How's we gonna do that if we's don't know if it be a male er a female?" the deck hand asked.

Shadon lifted the flute back to his lips.

Aragel sighed. "Nah, it needs a name having something to do with the storm."

"Well, you think 'bout it whiles I get er some bandages an' dry cloths so we's can fix er up."

Aragel looked at the bird, closer this time, but not so close that it could peck out his eye. The bird shivered, struggling to find a warm spot on the table. Names like Blackie and Hero went through Aragel's mind and he tossed them aside as being stupid. The bird deserved an honorable name that would do him justice.

Shadon ceased playing once more. "Beaky Buzzard," he suggested with a half-hearted laugh. The bird flopped around hopelessly in obvious discomfort and pain.

"No. How about Grarnek, after the chivalrous Arkeeronish warlord?" Aragel liked that name. He distantly heard Adarack saying a prayer to the god of water, Aithian, for those who had died.

Shadon laughed. But the laugh was not genuine. "That's a bit too bold, I think."

Jerred entered the cabin once more with the necessary dressings for the bird's injuries. He wore a startled look on his face. "It's the damnedest thin'. It's snowin'. I ain't seen nothin' like iss in 'ese waters. Is too warm, eh?"

Shadon chuckled and said offhandedly, "Maybe we should call the bird Snow." With that, he rose from where he sat and went above. He had to see this for himself. It never snowed on the southern ocean.

"Snow?" asked Aragel. It had been years since he saw snow. Not since he was a small boy. Having lived in a southern land for so long where snow did not exist, the memory had vanished.

"Go up an' see fer yerself." Jerred gave him an awkward smile, then set to work on the injured raven.

Aragel did as Jerred suggested. As he lifted the hatch, he

was greeted by cool air and chilly wind. He emerged fully from below and stood on the deck as white flakes of snow whirled around him. The snow melted as quickly as it fell from the air because even though it felt cold, it was much too warm for snow. And still, it managed to snow instead of rain. The evening sky was pale pink and cast a reflection so mesmerizing on the surface of the water that every man aboard the ship stared wistfully into the ocean.

"This is unnatural," whispered one of the men.

Another answered with, "These snowflakes be a work of sorcery."

Aragel sighed deeply, feeling alive and free. It was a feeling he had never experienced before. It was wonderful. Suddenly, he felt an urge to run across the deck and shout with joy. To laugh and take in this wonder called snow.

Instead, he went to Shadon and Adarack who were as deeply entranced as the others. "This is a sign, from the gods," whispered Shadon. "We're going to make it."

Adarack merely nodded in agreement and smiled broadly even though moments earlier he had been praying for the dead. He saw the snow as the answering of his prayer from the great lord Aithian. The wind picked up and with it, the speed of the small freight ship.

"It is a sign," said Aragel. Then he recalled the words he heard from one of the men only moments earlier. Snowflake. Frozen white rain, which did not describe the bird at all, but he liked it. "It's a sign that I'm going to name my raven Snowflake."

Adarack lifted a dark eyebrow.

"They say no two snowflakes are alike," Shadon said, still staring out over the water.

Aragel turned and hurried back to the quarters below deck. He wanted to share the bird's new name with Jerred. As he descended the ladder, Jerred was finishing up on Snowflake's broken wing. The bird was silent and standing upright, its left wing bandaged. Jerred put a small cup of grain and another of water next to the bird. "There ya are. I was wonderin' how long you'd stay an' gawk at tha' snow."

"I'm naming the raven Snowflake," said Aragel with a

big smile.

"What?" Jerred turned to him wide eyed. "Why, tha's a sissy name. No respect'd bird would allow 'isself to be called a snowflake! Iss stupid!"

"It's not stupid and I don't think it's a sissy name. Besides, the bird likes his new name. Don't you, Snowflake?" he asked the bird. He gently petted the bird's now dry head. The bird let him.

"Well, if it's not a sissy name it's a silly one. I don' thin' he likes it. He looks depress'd now. I'd be depress'd if I had a name the likes of Snowflake," Jerred finally concluded.

"You don't have to like it. I like it. After all, I'm the one who's going to be feeding and taking care of him. Why do you care?"

"If tha's what ya want. Fine. I can't argue with tha'. I'll show ya how to change er bandages later. An' by the way, I think er's a girl bird," said Jerred. He muttered one last comment about the bird's new name and went above to see if the snow had stopped.

Aragel picked the bird up carefully and carried it over to the small box Jerred had prepared for it. He placed it gently on the cloth lining.

"I don't think you have a silly name, Snowflake," he said.

Snowflake watched him with black, beady eyes and squawked as if to agree.

Then, as an after thought, Aragel added, "And I think you're a male."

The bird did not reply this time, not that Aragel expected it to. It moved around as much as it could manage flapping its good wing until it finally settled comfortably in the cloth lining of its new box home.

Shortly after, Shadon entered the cabin only to find that Aragel had fallen asleep on the floor with the bird in its box, on his stomach. He decided not to wake the young prince up. It was incredible how attached Aragel became to the bird in such a short matter of time. Then he remembered. King Darak was not fond of animals. They were not allowed in the castle. It was no wonder Aragel gladly accepted responsibility for the bird's care. Shadon shook his head, knowing his cousin probably led a boring life consisting of nothing more than schooling, swordsmanship, and appropriate courtly behavior. He remembered it all too well and shrank back at the thought. It was all a heap of horse manure and cow droppings. He had hated that life. With that in mind, he decided to get some sleep. It had been a long day at sea.

●

They both awoke the next morning to the cry "Land!" shouted by Adarack from above. The bird jumped around restlessly in the confines of his box, making soft chirping noises deep in his throat. He seemed to be feeling better.

"We couldn't have reached Danaria this quickly, it's only been two days." Shadon jumped up from the floor and wiped the sleep from his eyes.

A jug of clean water and two loaves of bread sat on the table. Aragel saw this and got up as well. He took Snowflake to the table and offered him his cups of grain and water, then set about getting his own morning meal out of the way. He noticed he had not felt sea-sick since he had woken up in the hull the previous day.

Shadon pulled his cloak on quickly and started toward the hatch. As he reached the ladder, Adarack was coming down. "We'll be at the ports of Orana Tulk before nightfall," he announced.

Aragel felt a brief moment of panic and patted his tunic, relieved to find Commander Corigerg's note still there.

"So fast?" asked Shadon, still amazed by their speed.

"The winds saved us a few leagues and the wind was heavy last night after that odd bout of snow. I told you I had the fastest freight ship on the ocean." He scratched his beard and peered into the box, examining the bird.

Aragel was already eating. "Jerred is going to teach me how to wrap Snowflake's wing today," he told them through mouthfuls of bread.

"You're taking the bird with you, I hope?" Adarack

asked.

"Oh yes."

"The bird seems to like you. It will also keep you company during the ride to Danaria. That trip is going to take much longer."

"Do we get to ride horses?" Aragel asked, excited as if he had never ridden a horse before. Of course he rode, but often had been confined to riding once a week. On that day, he would bathe directly afterward to save his uncle any distress from his allergy.

"Yes, of course we'll be riding horses." Even though he knew the circumstances, it still shocked Shadon to see Aragel so happy over a simple bird. Aragel had not even asked about Danaria yet. Shadon did not begrudge his cousin some time away from the terrible situation at hand. However, the subject of Hermond had to be addressed. In-depth. He was not quite sure how to bring it up.

"Adarack, I need to talk to, uh, Aaron," he said carefully, just in case one of Adarack's men was within earshot.

The captain did not seem surprised. He simply nodded and left, giving them the privacy Shadon asked for.

"Before we get to Orana Tulk, we have a lot to talk about. When we get into Orana Tulk, we cannot speak as openly about anything."

Aragel nodded in silence and listened.

"The political climate between Danaria and Exavia is strained. Exavia fears and envies Danaria. Danaria does not trust Exavia for several reasons. First, Prince Hermond runs illegal shipments of black market items into Danaria. It is against their trade agreement with Danaria. That trade agreement is the only reason they even have dealings with one another."

Aragel put his elbows on the table and continued to eat bread. "Why?"

"Let's just say the Exavian monarchy has lied to, and cheated the Danarian government and its people one too many times. The Danarians also suspect that Exavia has treaties and agreements with the Kersians." Shadon paused. That was no longer a suspicion, it was fact according to what Adarack had told him. "Danarian's hate Kersians."

"Because they have a different religion?" Aragel stuffed more bread into his mouth and poured himself a cup of water.

"And because the Kersians force conversion on people. And they sacrifice kidnapped Danarian women and children to their god. They seek out and try to capture Danarian sorcerers and sorceresses. Mainly because they believe they can take their mana by drinking their blood."

Aragel took a drink of the tepid water and set the cup on the table. "I don't think I'd like the Kersians either. Especially if I were a sorcerer."

"Well, they're constantly at war with one another. It's the whole reason Danaria boasts a military for its government. It's safer that way."

Aragel's tone turned serious. "So what does all of this mean for Sherok?"

"You said Hermond was talking to someone called 'Your Eminence'. That is how the Kersian administrator, self anointed high priest, is addressed by his subjects."

Aragel stood from the chair. "You mean that the Kersians are the ones who want uncle Darak and me dead?"

"That is what it sounds like."

"But why? We never did anything to them."

"It doesn't matter, but I suspect if they're controlling the Exavians and the Exavians control Sherok, it give the Kersians control. There is a political agenda at work here. On our way to Danaria we had better find out what that agenda is."

Aragel stared at the wall lost in thought.

"You need to know how to act in Danaria. The behavior and mannerisms that won't draw too much attention." Shadon waited for Aragel to acknowledge him. "First, don't be aggressive. You don't want your behavior to instigate a fight. Second, if you see sorcery, don't panic or make a big deal out of it."

"Sorcery? For real?" Aragel knew there were sorcerers in Danaria. Everyone did. But he never imagined he would be interacting with them.

Shadon chuckled. "It's real enough. It's also

commonplace. The Danarians breed sorcerers like one might breed horses. They also keep detailed pedigrees of family lines to make sure the lines don't cross."

Aragel sat back down. "What happens if they cross?"

"Mana degenerative disease, or worse. Basically, the sorcerer's mana will collapse in on itself killing the sorcerer slowly over time. But sometimes the progeny of inbreeding go insane. They rarely live past fifty if they have the mana degeneration. If they're insane, the other sorcerers will hunt them down and kill them. A healthy sorcerer, on the other hand, can live well past a century." Shadon sat back and yawned. "Any questions?"

Aragel shook his head while his mind remained on sorcerers. "No." He stood. "I need to find Jerred."

He hurried from the room. Worrying about the bird instead of worrying about himself, political issues and sorcerers, seemed practical. His mind needed a rest from more serious issues.

CHAPTER 11

Upon reaching the cave's entrance, she saw him. Kalath's frail frame knelt beside the containers of herbs he grew for his extensive collection of healing salves and potions. His mana was a pale blue. He did not turn at their approach.

"Settle your horses then go along inside and help yourselves to the broth I have prepared."

Tnasha smiled and dismounted. Undoubtedly Kalath also knew why they were there, even though he would not admit it. Foreseeing the future was a gift many adept sorcerers learned over time.

She handed her reins over to Kolgern and approached Kalath. "Is that any way to greet me?"

"Is there another way?" Kalath asked, standing. He turned to her with a soft expression in his brown eyes. "It's good to see you, child. You've gone and hurt yourself, I see." He looked her over, shook his head of receding gray hair, embraced her briefly, then urged her toward the entrance of the cave.

As she limped toward the cave, her stomach growled. It was no wonder she was in so much pain. Food is what her body needed so it could begin healing itself.

Rassia and Alena stayed behind with Kolgern to care for the horses.

"What kind of broth?" Tnasha asked playfully.

Kalath followed her inside. "The kind you eat. Or

perhaps drink."

She snickered, finding comfort in the familiar surroundings. The entrance of the cave proved narrow and dim, but opened to the main room, which stood aglow and welcome. Fragrant sandalwood filled the air, and in a crude hearth raged a warm fire. The scent of pork broth lifted from the steam of the large kettle there. Kalath searched the shelves along the walls for bowls for his guests. Upon finding five bowls, he settled next to the fire and began scooping generous amounts of broth into each one.

"It isn't much I'm afraid."

Tnasha limped over to the hearth and sat on the hard ground next to him with a wince. Her left buttock burned with searing pain. A day of riding had numbed it. But it was not numb now. She placed a thin hand on his shoulder. "That's all right. It's just nice to be warm. Presently, I think we'd all be grateful for anything in our stomachs, even hot water."

As if hearing this, Kolgern and the women entered the cave.

Alena and Rassia both mumbled in agreement and came over to take their bowls of broth, each thanking Kalath politely. Kolgern took up the rear. Tnasha could smell the pungent odor of horse sweat coming from them.

"How are those horses?" she asked.

Kolgern set down the bridles and packs. "I think the little bay mare Rassia was riding has a bruised frog. I'm going to need some cotton bandages and a good salve so I can pack the hoof. She should not be ridden hard, or over rough terrain for a few weeks."

Kalath looked at the jars of salve lining the wall. "I have an herbal tar salve that should help. We will have to watch for thrush with all this moisture. You do not want her lame."

Tnasha nodded and sipped at the steaming broth, feeling the warmth make its way down her throat and into her growling stomach. "Mmm. This is good. It's the first meal I've had in two days."

Kalath boasted a hearty chuckle. "It's hardly a proper meal. You should have breads and vegetables with it. It would help your body heal," he said with a smile.

Tnasha shrugged and continued to sip the broth.

"I can make some fresh bread tomorrow. Granted you haven't the proper stove for it, I could improvise," Rassia offered. As graceful as any aristocratic young lady, Rassia lightly sipped at her broth, wiping her mouth each time.

"I'll take you up on that. It's been awhile since I've had fresh bread. I have a barrel of flour somewhere here." Kalath's gaze traveled over Tnasha's injuries and he shook his head again. "After we've eaten we'll go into the other room and I'll set those bones proper."

"I think Rassia did a fine job for what we had to work with," she told him with a wry smile. "Alena, on the other hand, could only do so much."

He looked at Rassia and Alena approvingly. "Of course. They both did a fine job."

Tnasha fussed over the broth and gave herself a second helping before finally agreeing to step into the other room. She knew the re-setting of her broken bones would hurt and she wanted to avoid the pain. Then there was the small matter of the snake venom in her rear. Kalath would have to look, in the very least, to make sure the remaining venom was somehow neutralized. Knowing she could no longer prolong it, she stood and allowed Kalath to help her into the chamber that served as his ritual room. Once there, he helped her onto a long stone platform along the far wall.

"And how did this happen?" he finally asked.

"You know how it happened. Besides, it really is a long story." She winced as his cold hand moved across her ankle.

"Wait a moment." He strode over to one of the shelves and pulled down a bottle of salve. He placed it next to her and continued to work on her ankle. "The finer details of the story have eluded my sight. So please indulge me. I have plenty of time."

Tnasha smiled and leaned back against the wall of the cave, trying to ignore the pain that shot through her ankle and calve. "I can give you the short version," she offered. "Rassia was kidnapped by the Kersians. I tried to save her, along with

111

my legion, but I fell out of a tree and was also captured. How's that?"

A smile slid across the old man's lips and his eyes lit up. "I see. And how did you manage to escape the Kersians?"

"Rassia got away and...OW! That hurt!" With a pained look, she jumped. She heard the bone break as surely as she could feel the pain split through her leg. Tears came to her eyes.

"Of course it hurts. Did you expect less?" he asked. His face showed some concern while at the same time, helplessness. Tnasha knew he wished he could ease the pain. He held his hands over the spot, allowing his pale blue mana to mend the bones together.

She whimpered. "I didn't expect it to hurt as bad."

"Why not tell me about the escape and perhaps it will not hurt as bad. Take your mind off the pain."

She looked down at her ankle and noticed it was black and blue. In between were the various shades of crimson and purple. Her mana, in the injured areas, seemed a deep blue instead of its usual violet. He started to wrap her ankle.

Tnasha nodded, eyes closed, and continued. "Rassia got away and found Kolgern and Alena who'd followed the Kersians. Then they came back and got me."

Kalath took her wrist into his hand and unwrapped the crude splint. "Sounds like you have had quite a day."

"Try two days. Are you going to re-break this one, too?" she asked. Her wrist felt numb and throbbed a dull ache.

"That depends; do you ever want to use it again?" He gave her a reassuring look and a fatherly smile.

Tnasha hated it when he did that. She knew she had no choice but to let him break it. "Yes, I want to use it again."

"Good," he said.

With that, she heard and felt the snap. Like a piece of clay pot breaking even. She tried to pull away. The pain shot from her wrist up her shoulder, causing her to feel light headed. Once again, blue mana came from his hands, encircling her wrist to fuse the bones.

"Now, I suppose, you must turn over so I can assess the snake bite."

Reluctantly, Tnasha pulled down her leggings, exposing her left buttock. She turned over. A cool sensation covered the bite. It began to sting. A searing pain shot up her back, sending her muscles into spasms. Then, everything went black.

CHAPTER 12

Morvack choked back the taste of iron that surged forth from the back of his throat in thick bubbles. He sat on the ground, and held his hands to his neck. One hand clutched a turquoise amulet. He had pulled it from the prisoner's neck before he was wrestled from her. The amulet radiated the same violet mana the sorceress' body breathed forth. He coughed, spitting up thick streams of crimson mucus, and gasped for air. A strange sensation drifted over him. It was numbing. Suddenly, there was no pain and no fear, only warmth and a sense of safety. He could feel the violet mana closing the wound. Sealing it shut. Repairing the flesh. Staring into the sea of horrified faces, the faces of his people, he closed his eyes. With a final gasp for air, he realized he could breathe again. He inhaled deeply, feeling the air enter his lungs as if there had never been a hole in his throat at all. Upon opening his eyes, he held the amulet away from him. There was nothing extraordinary about the amulet itself. It was a plain turquoise disk on a silver chain. On its front, inlayed in silver, a sigil to a heathen god stared back at him. The sigil itself resembled an ocean wave pierced by an arrow. A *demon's* calling card.

Morvack coughed and let out a deep breath. "Send them away!"

Immediately, the soldiers pushed the crowd back, urging the people to return to their homes. General Luig helped

Morvack to his feet. A genuine look of awe and concern remained solid on the general's face. He gazed at the amulet Morvack held, watching it sway on the thin silver chain. He reached out, his fingers grazing Morvack's neck where the gaping wound had been only moments before.

"My Holy Liege, what sorcery is this?"

"I wondered why I could not read her mind. She was blocking it from me. We almost killed an anomalous fifth generation sorceress." It did not emerge from his lips as a statement, but rather a dull observation.

"Should we go after her?"

"No." Morvack tipped his head to one side and rubbed his neck with his free hand. "She will come to us when she realizes we have this amulet. She is weak and untrained. We will overcome her quite easily."

"It's a necklace. Fanciful heathen jewelry. Why would she return for it?" The general did not hide the disgust he felt for the heathens.

"That is where you are wrong. It is an amulet of magick, General Luig. It obviously holds great healing powers. Who knows what else could be accomplished with this." Morvack held it up to the general at eye level. "This amulet is more important than you know. Let the people know today's ritual has been postponed. I must have time to think."

Morvack left then, retreating to his cottage. Inside, he cleaned the blood from his skin with a damp cloth, changed his clothing, and sat down to further examine the amulet. The Kersian sorcerers' bloodlines were dying. Meanwhile, the heathen bloodlines flourished. The unfair situation angered him. The Danarians refused the Kersian's request for intermarriage centuries ago. Demon gods often caused such chaos. He wondered then how the girl, Lynae, was able to hide such strong mana. He sneered. Her name, Lynae, was much too common a name for a sorceress. Undoubtedly she was from an established bloodline. A bloodline carefully managed and bred within Danaria's strongholds. She was young, strong, and beautiful. Surly she would be a prize addition to Gavgal's breeding stock, and able to bear many children during her years. He narrowed his eyes and clamped his jaw shut.

A heavy knock on the entry door broke the Kersian Sorcerer's thoughts. "Is that you, General Luig?"

The general stepped into the room. "Yes, Your Holiness. I have news."

Morvack lifted an eyebrow in expectation. "What news?"

"The Danarians have replenished their forces and are less than a two days ride from here. What are your orders?"

The Sorcerer Morvack set the amulet on the table next to him. "I was going to have a messenger take this amulet to my brother. But since the situation has changed, gather the people. Tell them to travel to Kasana where they will be safe for now. You and twenty soldiers will come with me, back to Zul. Send two men ahead to summon one of our war ships from the Exavian port at Sergon. This amulet is the nameless one's gift to our people. It will bring us prosperity beyond our hopes and dreams. Hurry! We must not delay. Our business is urgent."

"Yes, My Liege." The general took his leave, closing the door firmly behind him.

When Morvack was alone, he once again picked up the amulet. His brother, Gavgal, would be pleased. Morvack would be rewarded. Undoubtedly the sorceress would want her amulet back. When she came for it, they would overpower her. Gavgal was quite adept, more so than Morvack, and could easily take down a young, inexperienced sorceress. He smiled at the amulet for all it would do for them. Magickal items were a rare attainment, and very few sorcerers could create them in such a way that others could wield them. Regardless of the amulet's nature, it would lure her onto their ground, whether by her own will or by Gavgal's. Perhaps it would even bring more sorceresses to Zul in search of such a powerful object. That thought alone set his heart racing. It meant one thing.

Yes, Morvack realized that this meant the Kersian's sorcerer bloodlines would survive, and Gavgal's dream of a Kersian world in service to the unnamed one would manifest itself before their very eyes. Paradise would be theirs, and the unnamed would once again walk the land. His brother had promised it to the people. More importantly, he had made that promise to Morvack and his brothers ever since they were small children.

Gavgal was much older and wiser and had raised Morvack and his two brothers by his own hand without complaint. He was the only parent they had ever really known, for their father was slain in battle and their mother died in childbirth. Her mana was not strong enough to survive the birth of a child with more mana than she possessed. Morvack would sometimes visit the burial grounds on Zul and talk to her. Sharing his dreams, hopes and fears with the ocean breeze. They had no sisters. There were no sorceresses left on Zul.

A feeling of joy swept over him. He looked up to the ceiling, bringing his hands in front of him in prayer. "Thank you unnamed one, the one true god. For even though I almost died, you have given me the greatest gift of all."

By his god's hand, he would finally have a consort and would not face his many remaining years alone. The Holy Scriptures denied him marriage to a human woman. But if she were a sorceress, he could be wed in the eyes of the unnamed and could start a family of his own. He put the amulet over his head and shoved it beneath his tunic. A tear came to his eye. He would finally know what it meant to be loved.

CHAPTER 13

A cool breeze and the smell of bread woke her from the blackness. Tnasha opened her eyes only to find herself sleeping upon a bed in a small cavern off the main room. She was stripped down to her underclothing. Her ankle and wrist felt much better, but not strong. The violet mana surrounding her body was still a deep blue hue in the injured areas. Now that her body was regenerating, her mana felt free and flowing. She knew now that hiding it had caused some imbalance. Slowly, she lifted herself from the bed and hobbled to the curtain-covered doorway. Pulling back the course fabric, she looked out. In the main room, Alena and Rassia tended to the preparation of the bread. They were also wearing nothing but their underclothing. Tnasha stepped from behind the curtain.

Alena was the first to notice her. "Good morning." She was almost too happy.

Tnasha rubbed granules of sleep from her eyes and nodded. Thoughts of doing another ritual to Liale filled her mind. But the soil here was tainted and she had not brought any with her. Squeezing her eyes closed, she said a quick prayer. *Liale, give me strength.* An impending sense of urgency swept through her. She felt cold.

Rassia took a cup from one of the nearby shelves. "How

about some spiced tea?"

Tnasha nodded again. "Where is Kalath? I have to talk to him." She stumbled from the room, still limping slightly.

"He's out with Kolgern, tending to the mare with the bad hoof," Alena said, holding the cup while Rassia strained the spiced tea through a small square of cheese cloth.

"How bad is the mare?" Tnasha asked, sleep disintegrating from her voice. She opened her eyes wide, lifted her arms skyward and stretched with a yawn.

Alena handed her the cup. "Just the stone bruises, I think. Probably from that hard gallop when we were trying to get away from those maniacs yesterday. She should be fine as long as she hasn't developed shin splints."

Tnasha shook her head. "We should have rested them more."

"She didn't seem to go lame until we reached the bridge. Then she seemed to stumble a little," Rassia said thoughtfully.

Just then, Kalath and a bare-chested Kolgern stepped inside the cave. Kalath carried one of his salve bottles with him. "The mare should be fine. However, next time you should check before taking a pregnant mare," Kalath said.

"She's pregnant?" Rassia's eyes lit up. She stood from where she knelt at the hearth.

Kalath smiled. "Indeed." He noticed Tnasha. "Good morning, child. Did you sleep well?"

"Yes."

"Good. I do hope you will be able to take yourself to bed for now on. I had some difficulty carrying you. I am not as young as I once was."

"I didn't mean to put you out of your own bed," Tnasha apologized. She felt foolish for having passed out from the pain. Reaching back, she rubbed her rear. It itched terribly.

Kalath waved a hand at her. "It was nothing. Sometimes it is good for an old man like me to sleep on the ground. It does wonders for the back."

Tnasha smiled. Then she remembered that she needed to talk to him. "Um, Kalath, can I talk to you?" As if suddenly remembering she was half naked she added, "Where are my clothes?"

"Alena and I washed them. They're hanging outside to dry." Rassia hurried toward the mouth of the cave and disappeared outside. She returned almost immediately with an armful of clothing.

Kalath turned from his shelve of herbs and handed another jar of salve to Kolgern. "Get dressed first, have something to eat and then we shall talk."

Tnasha took her clothes from the pile and began dressing. They were still damp. "All right."

They sat in silence sipping spiced tea until the bread was finished. It emerged from the hearth hard and deep brown. Almost burnt.

Rassia cringed as she cut it, handing each of them a thick slice. "Sorry." She shrugged.

They ate the morning meal in silence. Once they had finished eating, Kalath stood. With an outstretched arm, he pulled back the curtain that hid the entrance of the larger room. "Come then, Tnasha."

She followed him, entering the darkened room only to be met with the smell of healing herbs. Strong valerian mingled with wormwood. She wrinkled her nose in disgust, wondering if it had smelt this way last night and this morning. She did not recall the odor being so strong.

Kalath moved to one of the old wooden chairs and settled into it. He motioned for Tnasha to sit across from him. "Now, what is it?" he asked in a gentle, deep voice.

"I've been having dreams. Not like the ones I had when I was younger," she started. "You know, my nightmares?"

Kalath cocked his head as he listened. He said nothing.

She stared into the blackness. "They've changed. For a year now, I dreamt of the fiery pit, the Kersian's sacrificial temple, and him. High Priest Morvack. I never knew what the dreams were until yesterday, when the dream came true." The hair on the back of her neck lifted as she spoke those last words. Her gaze drifted to her lap and she waited for Kalath to say something.

Kalath nodded. "Alena and Kolgern were kind enough

to tell me what happened in great detail. You never told me they intended to sacrifice you. Do you know what would have happened had they succeeded? How did you manage to hide your mana?"

Tnasha lifted her brown eyes and looked at him. "Hiding my mana is the only sorcery I can manage successfully." She almost told him about the ritual, but paused and decided against it. "I learned how to hide my mana when I hid from my parents as a child."

"You are capable of so much more than simply hiding your mana. You can obviously *see* to some extend if you dreamt this would happen. That can only mean one thing. The prophecy has started. Had they succeeded in killing you, all hope for Danaria's sorcerers would be lost."

His gaze fell to her neck and he gasped so suddenly that Tnasha jumped in fear.

"What?" Her hands shot to her neck and whisked at it, just in case there was a large spider or something equally grotesque crawling on her. Then she realized what was wrong, or rather, missing. "My amulet!"

Kalath stood and strode to the altar on the far side of the room. "We *must* find it. The amulet, in the wrong hands, could split the world in bloodshed as happened in the beginning." Kalath's voice lingered, foreboding, on the still air. "Foolish girl. Your mana was on that amulet. With it they can track you, even kill you. It is *you* who stand between life and death in this world. Had you been practicing your sorcery from the beginning none of this would have ever happened!"

"Maybe, if I had been told that to begin with!" She stopped herself and held her tongue. Kalath had never been as strict. In shame, she moved to his side, and peered into the scrying bowl on the top of the altar. It was still and black.

"You were not told because the priestesses of the temple Dagon insisted it would put too much pressure on you. I did not agree with them, but I did not interfere. I should have." He waved his hands over the top of the water and closed his eyes. "Lord Aithian, show me where the amulet is."

The water turned gray for a moment then cleared again.

121

On the surface of the clear pool, Tnasha saw the amulet. She clutched at the sleeve of Kalath's long, black robe and took a deep breath. The amulet was around the neck of Morvack. He lived. All that remained of the wound Kolgern had given him was a thin scar, crusted with a scab of dried blood.

"But Kolgern killed him," she protested. "He slit his throat!"

"Your regenerative power is in that amulet. It must have healed him," Kalath whispered in disbelief. He turned to her. "Did he see your mana?"

Tnasha stood, paralyzed by fear as his gaze bore into her. "At the last minute he may have seen it. Yes. He shielded his eyes."

Kalath turned from her, practically running from the room. "We have little time to prepare. We must get started immediately."

CHAPTER 14

Hermond pushed the lone serving maid who came to his call toward the door. "Hurry, the king has suffered a heart attack! Fetch a doctor, woman!" She stumbled, regained her footing, and bolted from the room to do his bidding.

Prince Hermond smiled triumphantly. This was easier than he had expected. With the King dead, and Aragel missing, that left two items on his agenda. His smile faded sober as the royal physician ran into the room wild-eyed and frantic. He dropped next to Darak's still body, putting his ear to the King's chest. He felt for a pulse. Hermond looked on, trying to remain somber.

"Is he...dead?" Hermond asked, feigning fear and shock.

The physician sat back on his heals and took a deep breath. Soldiers and servants soon flooded the room to hear the news. "The King is dead," the physician announced.

Several women began crying. Commander Corigerg entered with two volunteer soldiers tailing him. "What is happening here?"

"The king is dead," a serving maid stifled a sob. Clearly, the king was loved among his people.

Corigerg crossed the room to view the body, then fixed his eyes on Hermond. "How did this happen?" Somewhere in the back of his mind, he could sense the prince had something to do with it. The King had been healthy and active only that morning.

"He stood, clutched his chest, and fell over. It was so, so sudden." Hermond took a deep breath and lifted a hand to shield his eyes. He had to make sure he looked upset. Focusing, he brought tears to his eyes by remembering the death of his childhood pet. A gray pony named Dappy. In truth, the death of a horse was the only thing that ever brought him to tears. He pulled his hand away and swallowed, letting a single tear fall down his cheek. He hoped Corigerg would notice. The success of this mission would determine his later standing in the new world. So far, the Kersians had kept their promises.

When Serena entered the room, the crowd went silent and parted, leaving a lone pathway to her father's fallen body. She began wailing uncontrollably. "Father," she cried. She ran to him and fell next to him, sobbing.

"Corigerg," Hermond started. He looked around the room making sure all ears were listening. Another tear fell and he wiped it away. "We have a problem. With Prince Aragel missing, it stands to reason that Serena and I shall make haste to keep order." He chose his words carefully, scanning the Commander's expression for signs of disagreement. Obviously, Serena was in no condition to put anything in order, and both men knew it. Which left Hermond free rein.

Commander Corigerg fought back several tears, set his jaw and glared at the Prince knowingly. His expression clearly implied he was not easily swayed by the prince's show of emotion. "There's little I can do to stop you."

Hermond wiped his eyes and forced a reassuring smile. The commander's face displayed resignation to the inevitable. Hermond sniffed and rubbed his eyes again - for good measure. "Good. I see we understand each other. This is a most unfortunate chain of events."

"Indeed," Corigerg said through clenched teeth. His gaze left Hermond's face and shifted over the crowd. In every Sherokean present there was pain. "The Sherokean people do not deserve this."

Hermond took a deep breath. "No, but there is nothing

that can be done. I am glad you are here to help me. I need you to send fifty soldiers to the docks to meet several ships. Have someone take Serena to her chambers. I will have the king prepared for burial." He looked at Corigerg, trying to gauge his response. "I would like to see you in the main hall."

Commander Corigerg glared at him. "We have less than fifty soldiers on duty."

"I realize this, but we need to be organized. We need to find Aragel, and we need to maintain order. The people of Sherok need us to be strong right now." Hermond turned and walked quickly away, leaving Corigerg no choice but to follow.

When they reached the adjacent room, Corigerg closed the door, and spoke immediately. "What do the ships carry?"

The prince sat down. "When the hurricane came, I sent message to several of our military vessels that were training near by. I figured the extra hands could help Sherok recover from the inevitable damage more quickly. Perhaps they can help us find Aragel. We must coronate him immediately. A nation without a king is an invitation to usurpers."

Corigerg narrowed his eyes. "It is," he agreed. "I was not aware you had war ships near Sherok for training."

"Oh, our war ships sail these waters often in training exercises. I just hope they were unaffected by the storm."

"I'm not sure I believe you." Corigerg stood firm with his arms crossed over his chest.

Hermond took another deep breath. "All right. I am not being completely truthful, but I did not want to cause panic. Perhaps my father is somewhat paranoid. He always fears my assassination when I travel and sends war ships to follow. But our soldiers do train while they are waiting to follow me back to Exavia."

The commander was confused. For a moment, he believed the story, but then doubt crept in. Maybe Hermond was not lying, he told himself. Nonsense. War ships? Who sends war ships with legions of soldiers aboard to keep a single person out of harms way? The chain of events were too perfect and playing out too quickly. Corigerg bit his inner cheek. "I suppose we're fortunate then. We could use help rebuilding and fortifying several piers. And it would be wise for us to find Aragel as soon as possible."

Hermond smiled, knowing that Corigerg did not trust him. "Good. I shall see to preparing the king's funeral, then I will check on Serena. She needs me." Hermond stood and left the room without looking back.

With reluctance, Corigerg set out to gather his soldiers. He was afraid, and clearly outnumbered.

●

A light knock sounded from the door. One of Serena's handmaids hurried to answer it. Hermond stepped inside the room, motioning the servants to leave. Once they were gone, he went to her, taking her small hands into his. "My poor Serena."

Serena dabbed her eyes with a handkerchief.

He sat next to her and pulled her to him. Enveloping her in his arms, he kissed her forehead gently. "I do love you, and nothing will ever change that."

She felt safe in his arms. Hermond, now, was her only solace with Aragel gone. She closed her eyes and buried her head in his chest. "What will we do now?" Several tears rolled down her cheek.

The Exavian prince smiled, lifted her head, and looked into her eyes. He did love her. "I won't let anything happen to you, or Aragel, or Sherok. I sent word to several of our nearby ships. Some are carrying soldiers who will come here to help with rebuilding the port. Others will search for Aragel. That cousin of yours," he laughed. "He has an imagination."

"I cannot believe my father is dead." Serena began sobbing again.

He drew her closer to him, holding her tightly. "Unfortunately we will all die, Serena. Nothing will bring your father back." He began thinking of his pony again, feeling the tears burn his eyes. "But we have to move on. He will always live in our memories."

Serena pulled away and wiped her eyes. "You're right. I will be strong."

After wiping his own blue eyes, he reached over and cupped her chin in his hand. "We'll make it through this together. Get some rest."

●

Serena awoke that evening to the sound of voices and commotion. She stood and went to the window. Far below in the courtyard, twenty Exavian soldiers casually chatted, while lounging comfortably on the grass. She went to the door and opened it only to find two blonde Exavian soldiers standing guard.

That seemed odd. "Have you seen my ladies in waiting?"

The soldiers glanced at one another. "Prince Hermond sent them away so you could rest, M'Lady," the tallest said.

The second soldier stepped forward. "I will go see if I can find them for you. M'Lady."

"Oh no. That's all right. I'll find them myself." She stepped forward, as one of the men stepped in front of her, blocking her way.

"We were told to keep you in your chambers, M'Lady. Prince Hermond does not want anyone to upset you right now."

"That's nonsense." She ran a hand through her long dark hair. "I'll be perfectly fine."

"If we do not obey our orders…" the tall soldier started.

"You have my permission to disobey them. I will tell Hermond that myself. Now stand aside."

The shorter soldier, whose hair was thinning, shook his head. "No. M'Lady. We do not take orders from you. Please step back into the room. I will find your maids and bring them to you." He stepped forward, gently took her by the arm and pushed her back into the room, closing the door behind her.

Serena felt anger swell inside her. What insolence! She paced her quarters frantically. With her father dead and Aragel missing, she felt terribly alone and afraid. Why would Hermond lock her away? It seemed impractical. He seemed sincere enough in trying to help, but this was too much. When she saw him next, she told herself, she would explain to him that he would not have her confined to her quarters. They were not married yet.

Her shoulders slumped. Perhaps she was being too hard on him. Maybe he was afraid, too. After all, three disasters in the course of several days seemed enough to put anyone into a panic. The Exavian soldiers made her uneasy, but Hermond assured her it was okay. He insisted she stay in her room to rest. That he would take care of everything. She sighed. She loved him.

●

With the funeral arrangements made, Prince Hermond had unfinished business. His top general entered the room with a salute. "Your Highness."

Hermond did not waste time. "Where is Prince Aragel?"

"He is in Orana Tulk. We are making arrangements, My Lord. He will be taken care of immediately."

Hermond ground his teeth. "It *must* look like an accident."

The general nodded. "I understand, Highness. What shall we do with Corigerg?"

"After the King's burial tomorrow, take him aside and give him a chance to swear his allegiance to us. It would be much easier if we had his full cooperation. With his help, more Sherokeans will be likely to accept our presence. He should be given a chance."

"And if he refuses, My Lord?"

"If he refuses, kill him. The same applies for any Sherokean who resists. Now leave me. I must resume my marriage plans. If all goes well, I will be King of Sherok very soon."

The general saluted again, turned and left the room obediently.

CHAPTER 15

Tnasha sat at the edge of the clearing outside the cave staring into the sea of dead trees around her. The clear patch of sky above once again promised little relief from the warm summer sun. She looked to the west. Deep, gray, storm clouds loomed menacingly. She stood corrected. Leaning back onto the rock she sat on, she stared pensively into the sky. Even then, her thoughts chose to fall back on Morvack. For all that was great in the world, Tnasha could not understand her luck. Or more properly, her lack thereof. *Why does this always happen to me?* she wondered. She closed her eyes in hopes of waking to find that all of this had been a terrible nightmare. But the warmth flooding down on her skin told her otherwise.

Kalath sat down next to her. She could feel his presence. "You're wondering why this is happening to you," he said.

Tnasha opened her eyes and looked at him curiously. "How do you know?"

He folded his arms across his chest. "Being a seer aside, I suppose in your situation I would wonder the same. It is not as terrible as you think."

"Which part?" Tnasha asked, her voice heavy with worry.

"Being a sorceress, unable to utilize the powers within, must be frustrating for you," he said, forcing a smile. "All of this *is* fairly bad, I'm afraid."

She groaned and put her head in her hands. "You certainly know how to cheer me up."

Kalath chuckled and put an arm across her shoulders. "All things happen for a reason, my dear Tnasha. Whether it be good or bad, these things make us stronger."

"Well, I wish it would happen to someone else." It did not seem fair. For everything she had, it seemed she always had to work harder than anyone else. Even for the simple things.

Kalath sighed deeply and met her gaze. "You can feel sorry for yourself all you want. But it will not go away. You can be sure of that. The gods have other plans for you, and willing or not, you shall end up taking your destined path all the same."

"And what if I don't believe in destiny?" she asked, her voice laden with insolence.

"I thought we had this discussion when you were about sixteen years of age. Did we not?" Kalath looked at her in question, waiting for her to remember.

Tnasha did remember. It was her choice. She *chose* what she did and did not believe. She chose not to use her mana to impress the priests and priestesses. In defiance of authority and expectations, she chose to refuse all the help and training she had been offered.

She nodded in defeat. "So what am I going to do about it?"

Kalath stood and motioned her to do the same. "Learn sorcery, of course. I am afraid there is little I can teach you in such a short time. However, I can give you the basics. A text. Time is of the essence. You will have to leave soon. You must go to Zul and get the amulet back."

"Me? Zul?"

"Yes. You are much stronger than you know, Tnasha. Don't worry. You will have help and you will not have to go to Zul alone."

"You will go with me?" A spark of hope flickered in her eyes.

"No. But you have friends who care about you. They would never abandon you."

She lifted an eyebrow. "Well, I guess they did come to

rescue me while the rest of my legion left me to die. But I've already put them through too much. They didn't have to come back for me."

"No, but they did. You should be grateful. Not everyone has friends who care about them so deeply. Now come along. I must give you that book."

Tnasha smiled even though her heart pounded in her chest from the anxiety she felt. Kalath was forever giving her texts on one thing or another. The fact that he would give her texts to teach her sorcery made her laugh. "I should have expected as much," she said with a forced grin. She stood and followed him back into the cool air of the cave, all the while trying to swallow the lump in her throat.

The remainder of the day Tnasha spent her time away from her friends, practicing sorcery. For her first task, she decided to spend her time working with the elements. She was quick to pick up the art of tree magic, bringing to life an oak, long dead from the tainted ground. Equally, she practiced water magic. Finding the water magic emanating from her hands like natural waves, she discovered her counterpart of whom Kalath had spoke years ago. Deep in her heart she felt the tides ebbing and swaying, lifting her soul in cool, slicing waves. The lightning flowed from her fingers like fine threads of gold and the rain fell in crystalline shards from the skies, giving life to the tree she had spent the morning nurturing.

The fire magick was more difficult. Each time she worked with fire the energy conflicted with the water, giving her gentle tingles of shock. Small sparks emanated from the tips of her fingers, but never quite flourished as she had hoped. At the same time she was thankful. She could only imagine what would happen if the fire energy came forth freely, burning the forest to the ground before she could stop it. The air magick was also difficult for her to manipulate. The air slipped through her fingers so easily it was as if the wind found her penetrable through bone and flesh. She could only control small wisps and currents. She practiced until she was able to move a leaf around.

Hours later, exhausted from overusing her mana, she asked Kalath why two elements seemed so easy, the water so natural. Kalath took her to the tree, and beneath the shade of its full branches, explained it to her.

"I'm impressed with your progress in such little time. It only confirms my suspicions." He looked up at the now living tree and smiled. "Water energy is cunning. When fire touches water, it nullifies or scatters causing something akin to being hit by a lightening bolt. When earth touches water, it becomes thick and slow moving. Sometimes the earth energy, if allowed, causes an elemental imbalance in the sorcerer because it becomes firm and unmoving." He paused and looked into her eyes as if waiting to see if she understood what he said.

Tnasha nodded for him to continue. It all seemed so complex.

"Air has a difficult time moving through water. It can graze the top of the water, but it will never truly pierce it. And you, because you are the earthy part of water, have difficulty because your energy is slow building and somewhat incompatible with the other elements." He looked to the deadened forest around them. "All of the answers you shall ever need to help you in your sorcery you will find surrounding you."

"So essentially, what you are saying is that I'm going to have to deal with being ineffective as a sorceress. But this is supposed to save me?" Tnasha was puzzled.

"I think you have missed the point, my girl." The old sorcerer laughed and smiled. "Water is one of the strongest elements. Like the hurricane - a magick cast from a water sorcerer is a silent assassin. It comes on without warning and hits fiercely, leaving destruction in its wake."

"Great. So I could unintentionally kill people? I could get killed and so could the people around me? If sorcery is so dangerous it should be labeled lethal!" Tnasha rolled her eyes. She doubted she would ever understand it.

Kalath laughed again. This time more deeply with some reserve. "Not if you learn to manipulate all of the elements in conjunction with what already comes naturally."

Tnasha took a deep breath and sighed. "I'll work on it." She was disappointed. This was not something she could learn by reading. She would simply have to do it, and she would have to figure it out quickly. Zul was home to several Kersian sorcerers much older and adept than she. If it came to magickal warfare, she was clearly defeated before she had even begun. Now, she was not sure what she would do.

Kalath stood and departed, leaving her once again to practice. Tnasha began flipping through the pages of the grimoire. She needed a plan. Preferably, something that included a magickal attack by water or earth.

CHAPTER 16

Adarack chose a table in the far back corner of the small tavern. Orana Tulk was smaller than Aragel expected it to be. Excitement filled his every nerve. He was anxious to smell new things and taste foods he had never tested against his palate. He held back his excitement, remembering why they were here. Sherok was in grave danger. Sadness overwhelmed him. He turned his attention back to the bird, fighting back a sudden onrush of fear. Snowflake fluttered about in the small cage Aragel and Jerred had made for him from small flats of wood. The bird only occasionally squawked. The intermittent cries of the raven were followed by stares from the commoners native to the village. But the people did not stare long. They were too busy with their daily lives to worry about travelers.

"I will be leaving you in the morning after the last of my cargo is unloaded, and the new cargo loaded," Adarack said in a monotone whisper. He eased back in the rickety pine chair, which creaked under his stout weight.

"We'll be heading west. I have some horses and a few Sirus soldiers waiting for us at the next outpost." Shadon scratched his ear, then leaned his elbows on the table. He hoped the message he sent upon his arrival would reach the outpost in time.

Aragel said nothing, just listened and glanced down at Snowflake now and again. He placed the bird's light cage beneath the wooden table, at his feet, and the bird quieted. With him, he carried his satchel, now fuller than before with bandages and food for the raven.

"We'll be staying at the inn across the way for tonight," Shadon said to Aragel, bringing the boy's attention from his new pet.

"Will we have beds?" Aragel asked. He hoped they would. He longed for a real bed after two nights of sleeping on the floor of the ship's cabin. His aching arms and legs were a reminder of how uncomfortable it had been.

"I would think so. With as much as I'm paying for a room, there had better be."

Aragel was grateful when a young woman approached the table and asked them what they wanted to eat. He was tired of meager meals of hard bread and fish. He selected the spiced divanish, wanting to fully explore the food of this strange, new land. He had never had foreign food before and suspected nothing when both Shadon and Adarack cringed and shook their heads. They both decided on salmon, not being as adventurous as the young prince. When the food finally arrived, Aragel stared in disgust at his plate. Upon it lay a small, sliced octopus, which was indeed, covered with numerous spices.

"This is an octopus!" he said loud enough for everyone in the inn to hear. Sherokeans rarely ate anything other than fish and shellfish. Other sea creatures were not fit for eating, according to popular Sherokean opinion.

Shadon and Adarack burst into laughter.

"That's an octopus all right. Divanish is the Danarian word for octopus. Think of it this way- Sherokean's eat insects as delicacies." Adarack let out another hearty chuckle. Others at the surrounding tables also joined in the laughter discreetly.

"You both knew I ordered an octopus and you didn't say anything?" Aragel found the joke less amusing, then decided to show them that he would eat it regardless. He would choke down every last bite if he had to. With his knife, he cut a small piece from a tentacle and placed it into his mouth. He chewed the rubbery substance trying to forget what it was he was eating then took a deep drink of weak ale to wash it down. *It's not half bad*, he thought. With that thought in mind, he put his full concentration into devouring the octopus.

As they finished their meal, a young man approached the table and handed Shadon a folded piece of parchment. Shadon opened it slowly, looked over his shoulder for prying eyes, then read it. Afterward, he folded the note and shoved it deep into a pocket on the inside of his tunic. He frowned. "We may be here for several more days."

Adarack took a swig of ale, then wiped his mouth on his sleeve. "Problem?"

"It seems there is a Kersian legion northwest of the outpost. The Danarian's cannot send soldiers to drive them off right away."

"Interceptors?" Adarack asked.

Shadon frowned more deeply. "We're not going to rush over there to find out."

Aragel said nothing. He felt helpless. Would Shadon be able to get him to central Danaria? The fear of failure reared its ugly head. Aragel began wheezing. *Concentrate on your breathing*, he told himself. He focused on his breath, trying to calm himself. Adarack put a hand on the prince's shoulder.

"Shadon, perhaps you should take Aaron to the room at the inn. He looks like he could use a good night's sleep."

Shadon nodded and stood, helping Aragel up. "Come on, cousin. It's been a rough week."

Aragel rested the remainder of the day. That evening Shadon returned and began readying himself for sleep in the small, cramped room of the inn. Aragel was awake. He sat up. Two beds with feather mattresses took up the whole of the floor space, barely leaving enough room for movement, let alone the small night table between them.

That is when Aragel asked the question. "Why does Uncle Darak tell people you were killed by assassins?" He lay back down, staring at the heavy wooden beams of the ceiling.

Shadon put his satchel down and eased onto his bed. It took him awhile to answer, but finally he said, "I didn't know he was telling people that. I don't know. He could have been embarrassed that his only son would abandon his right to the throne. My father was always so...demanding." He turned his head to look at Aragel whose attention had not left the ceiling.

"He always acts sad, then tells them you were killed by assassins. Commander Corigerg told me you ran away, but that I should never let Uncle Darak know that I knew the truth." The prince paused for a moment. "It's your fault, you know."

"My fault for what?"

"For the way he treats me. He's overprotective. Afraid to let me sit in on trade agreements. He won't let me travel. Always watched and never allowed to do anything," he said with some malice. "But I do want to be king. I just want to be able to learn how to be king before I get there. You understand, right?"

Shadon nodded. "Some of that is your imagination. If he were that careful, would you have gotten out of the castle? Would I have gotten in?"

"They know I'm gone by now."

"Of course they do. It's been a few days. They'll be frantically searching for you. Maybe thinking you've been lost at sea with the hurricane. Maybe that's best. If Hermond thinks you're dead, maybe he'll let it go. I'm just worried about what he's going to do next. When you told me Hermond mentioned 'Your Eminence' my heart almost stopped. Are you sure that is what you heard?"

"I would swear my life on it. I only wish I knew why the Kersians were involved."

"You and I both. Obviously, if Hermond got rid of you and the king, he could marry Serena and Exavia would inherit Sherok. Maybe the Exavians want to expand their territory?" Shadon followed Aragel's lead and stared at the ceiling thoughtfully.

Aragel sighed. "That would make sense if the Kersians weren't involved. What would the Exavians want with the Kersians?"

Shadon shook his head. "More appropriately, what do the Kersians want from the Exavians? Why do the Kersian's want Sherok? Food, supplies? I don't know."

"Maybe the Exavians converted their religion to worship the no-name god. Now they want Sherok to convert? That would make sense." Aragel looked over at Shadon with wide eyes.

Shadon sat up on his elbows. "Maybe so. But it sure seems like an awful lot to go through just to convert people. Then again, maybe not." He sighed. "We should get some sleep." With that, Shadon blew out the oil lamp on the small night table between them, and both he and Aragel settled into their beds for a night of restless sleep.

●

Orana Tulk was Danarian territory. However, the people living there spoke several languages for the sake of the trade market. Being as small as it was, many cargo shipments made their way through Orana Tulk, en route to Carinth and deeper into Danaria, sometimes all the way to the capital city, Central Danaria. Shadon knew Orana Tulk well. Here, he captured a large majority of black market goods shipped into the country. His primary concern, or what had been the past few years, consisted of trade agreements, shipping embargos, and those people who violated the laws surrounding them. It was here that every aristocratic criminal attempted to sneak something by the Danarian government, though further up the coast was a city called Mengala. Mengala was usually the second port the offenders tried. It was just north of Mengala where Hermond's war ships had been harbored. Undoubtedly they were not there now. Shadon had no idea where they were. That is what he planned to find out.

Security was lapse here. Or so it seemed. In truth, however, Danarian intelligence was everywhere. At some point in time, every bit of political information in the West Ocean Mainlands came through the port. The spies and agents gathered it and sent it to the council and high military officials for dissemination.

Shadon woke early that morning and went to the open market. He had to find out what was going on. Moving through the crowded streets and searching for a familiar face, he spotted a man behind a tomato stand. Ambling to the stand, he picked up a tomato, squeezed it gently and began examining it. "Morning."

"Morning." The short bald man behind the stand wore a tattered tunic and patched pair of leggings. He looked idly over the stand at Shadon.

"Are these from Mengala?" Shadon asked cautiously.

"They left Mengala the day before yesterday. They only arrived by here yesterday." The man said, examining the tomato with Shadon.

Shadon picked up a second tomato. "Two?"

"Yes. Two hundred each I believe," he said.

"Do you have any Sherokean tomatoes?" Shadon asked.

"The Sherokean tomatoes died before harvest," the little man replied with a somber look.

A cold chill slipped up Shadon's back. "When did this happen?"

"News travels fast. Faster than you."

Shadon pulled five shinder from his purse. "Thank you for the tomatoes."

"Eya," the man said, turning his attention to a woman approaching from the other side of the stand.

When Shadon returned to the inn, Aragel was already awake and dressed. "Let's get our things and meet Adarack for breakfast. We have to stay here until I can confirm we have free passage to the capital holding. While we're here I'll try to find out what's going on."

Aragel shrugged his shoulders. "All right."

At the tavern, they found Adarack sitting at a far table in the back of the room. Shadon and Aragel joined him without formal greetings.

"I'm hearing things," Adarack finally said after a waiting girl served them with juice and tea. "I have to stay two more days. I have another three wagons of cargo coming in, and the other shipment only just arrived. It will take as long for them to transfer the goods."

"Where are you going next?" Aragel asked with great interest. It entranced him to imagine the captain's adventurous life. All the exotic places he had been.

"Arkeereon," Adarack said with a yawn. "Well, Cabalia. Same thing."

It was here the discussion became political. In a hotbed of spies, Shadon found himself determined to keep their conversation amongst themselves. For surely if Danaria had agents working the city, so did every other government including the Exavians and the Kersians. In Orana Tulk, nothing was sacred.

Shadon waited until the serving woman had taken their meal requests and left them. He leaned in to the center of the table. "Word is those two shipments I mentioned are heading to Sherok. Four hundred items in cargo." He sat back up and looked around to see who was listening at the surrounding tables.

"Something has happened," Aragel whispered back. "Otherwise they would have waited." He had not thought of the Exavian warships Shadon mentioned back in Sherok until now. He scolded himself for not being more attentive and serious. War was not a matter to be ignored no matter how inexperienced he felt. He knew that now.

Shadon shook his head and put a finger to his lips, telling Aragel to be quiet. At the next table, a man sat reading a ledger. Shadon knew better. No one read a true ledger in the open. There were too many thieves about to be so careless.

"Well, hopefully the shipments missed that hurricane and arrived safely," Shadon said in a loud voice. The man closed the ledger and stood to leave, only pausing to drain the contents of his cup. He turned and glanced at the three of them with a brief acknowledging smile.

"Spy?" Adarack asked after the man left.

"Likely." Shadon closed his eyes and rubbed them. He was tired. The serving girl came back to fill their drinks.

"It looks like things are going to slow down a bit," she said with a bright smile.

Shadon lifted an eyebrow. "Storm?"

"From the north," the young woman said, picking up the empty cup from the table behind them.

"Hmm." Adarack scratched his beard. "I suppose I

should get that cargo loaded as soon as possible. Maybe I should take you and Aaron with me. Cancel our order, there isn't time to eat right now."

Aragel crinkled his forehead in confusion.

Shadon handed the woman several shinder. "Our tour has been delayed."

"I could use the company anyway," Adarack concluded. The men stood. Aragel got up with reluctance and picked up Snowflake's cage. The bird had been quiet all morning.

Aragel tapped the side of the cage and followed Shadon outside.

As they stepped outside the tavern, Shadon noticed the man with the ledger. The simulated ledger, that is. He was speaking to another man whose appearance suggested another shady character. Shadon yawned, rubbed his eyes, and then narrowed them. He recognized the taller, gaunt man the ledger man spoke to. A known Exavian spy who went under the name of Ramath. Still, seeing them together did not lend further information toward the plot afoot.

Aragel tugged at Shadon's sleeve. "Are you going to stand there all day?"

Shadon looked down at his young cousin. "You're becoming mouthier by the day."

"I'm tired of being quiet. I feel like I need to take a more active role in what is happening." There was a hint of scorn in the prince's voice.

"You don't trust me?"

Aragel gave him a bored look. "I trust you well enough, but we're not getting anywhere."

"Patience, cousin. Patience. If we hurry off without finding out what's going on, we may never make it to Central Danaria."

"I had a bad feeling about that."

"Yeah, me too."

"What are we going to do about it?"

"Lay low."

"What will that accomplish?"

"It will ensure your safety."

Aragel was not convinced. "Will it?"

"What do you mean? Of course it will." Shadon gave a quick nod toward the two men. "That man was reading a ledger behind us while we were eating. He's now talking to an Exavian spy."

"Which means?"

"Prince Hermond most likely knows you're here." Shadon gave him a tight smile.

"That's impossible."

Shadon leaned against the building and motioned Aragel to come closer. "You don't know how quickly these people can move and disperse information. They will run a horse to death if it means traveling one hundred miles in a day. They're paid quite well, I assure you."

"What does this mean?"

"They probably have every city from here to Central Danaria crawling with assassins, just waiting for us so they can kill you."

Aragel's eyes widened. "So now what?"

"Maybe Adarack will take us further up the coast. The problem with that is the other ports are less secure than this." Shadon really had no idea what they were going to do. But he did not want to tell Aragel this. It had been hard enough to convince his cousin to trust him to begin with.

"He wouldn't leave us to the wolves like that."

"No, he wouldn't. Not in good conscious, anyway." He paused. "We'll figure it out. There is a way out of every bad situation. Come on."

Aragel followed. "Is that another rule?"

Shadon chuckled. "Yes. I suppose it is."

CHAPTER 17

Kolgern smiled as he told his favorite story."Before the world split, all horses were black. The sorcerer god, Lord Natyis, gave the horses instincts to detect and avoid danger so that his soldiers could avoid ambush by Kersians while traveling the land. Well, one day, Lord Natyis' firstborn son, Behmot, who was also the best soldier in Natyis' military, was delivering a message from Natyis to a legion in the northern part of the land. As Behmot and his war horse descended into a rock quarry, a Kersian leapt from behind the rocks on his right, sword drawn. The Kersian went straight for Behmot's neck, wanting to cut off his head. But the horse, the horse had instinct. So, he sidestepped to the left and the Kersian missed his mark, fell to the ground and broke his ankle. Thus, Behmot was able to draw his sword and slay the man without incident. If I remember it correctly, that's how the story goes."

"It's been years since I've heard that tale." Kalath's deep brown eyes showed a hint of appreciation. "Traveling on the left horse black. The moral of the story being sometimes it is best to follow your instincts. There are times we must use our instinct to avoid danger, or to get ourselves out of a dangerous situation. Oftentimes, people ignore their instinct, when in fact we must learn to trust it."

Tnasha sat in a dimly lit corner of the room pouring over the ancient text Kalath had assigned her to read. She lifted her nose from the book and closed it gently. "What I want to know is how the world split the first time."

Kalath smiled and looked at the waiting faces of his guests. "You have never heard how that happened? Well now, let me see." He paused, taking a sip of his homemade ale and relaxed deeper into his chair. "In the Book of Fire it is writ the Dark Lord Natyis alone created everything. Lord Natyis created all the earth and the sun, moon, and stars through his sorcery. When he had finished his creation, he lit the sun and out of eternal black night, there came to be light. The world was a mass of rock and soil and so was birthed water that fell from the deep red folds of the sky. It fell for many a moon until the earth's deepest chasms filled and only the highest land masses lay uncovered. Then Lord Natyis created creatures not unlike himself, who also bore powers of sorcery. They became gods, the Imperial Hierarchy of the land of Arkeereon."

Kalath took another sip of ale before continuing. "Plants and trees were set upon the ground and made to grow in various climates with many colors. The land transformed into hues of green and blue. Lord Natyis created creatures then, from the smallest insect to largest of mammals. With them, he created more mammals like himself, yet these creatures bore no powers of sorcery. That would entail the majority of the common folk." He motioned to Alena, Rassia, and Kolgern.

"It is said that weak faith turned some of these latter creatures against Lord Natyis." Kalath shook his head and stared off into the distance. "During those years, Natyis married. The young queen, Unsere, gave the Dark Lord Natyis many sons and finally, a daughter. This daughter bore great powers of sorcery. Yet, as the queen lived happily with her infant daughter within the great fortress of Arkeereon City, a rebellion swept the land. During the upheaval, the fortress was attacked and the daughter of the Dark Lord was taken and lost forever to the Kersians who took her."

"Did they sacrifice her?" Rassia asked, twirling a long strand of blonde hair around one finger.

Kalath shrugged his shoulders. "No one knows. But that is the general belief. For years, the Kersians and armies of Arkeereon waged war upon one another until one day, the land split from the massive earthquakes conjured by Natyis himself. He unleashed his anger in hopes the Kersians would retreat and return his daughter to him, if only out of fear. The ocean swallowed much of the land into its dismal depths and spat up new lands. Regardless, the Kersians did not falter. Instead, a new generation of those faithful to Natyis and others indifferent traveled to the new lands and birthed cities and kingdoms. That is how Danaria, Sherok, and Exavia came to be."

"And Zul," Kolgern interjected.

"And Zul," agreed the old sorcerer.

"So what happened then?" Kolgern asked.

"Well, the Kersian forces grew, and again, tried to take Arkeereon and the new lands from their rulers. The world was at war and there was much bloodshed and death. Out of this battle, there came to be an alliance amongst the lands."

"The Kersians against everyone else," Tnasha said. Her gaze fell on the hearth and she stared, entranced by the golden-orange flames.

Kalath nodded as if remembering. "Prophecy was born after that. Seers, hundreds of them, came and told of prophecies that would bring the daughter of the Dark Lord Natyis back to him."

"Is this prophecy, the one that I'm in, one of those?" Tnasha asked hopefully. She hoped it was. If so, it would certainly make her feel better about risking her life for an amulet. Maybe she would be the one to save Natyis' daughter? A born hero? She laughed at herself.

"Indeed, it is a large part of that prophecy as a whole. This is the first prophecy of three," Kalath said matter-of-fact. He poured himself another pint of ale from the barrel next to him.

The room stood silent for several minutes before Rassia spoke. "So do you think she's still alive?"

"Who?" Kalath asked.

"Natyis' daughter, of course."

"Not her original incarnation. No. According to the

prophecies, she was reborn. Or rather her mana was," Kalath explained. "Although no one knows for sure."

Rassia stared dreamily into the fire in front of her. "I wonder where she is right now. She could be anyone... even Tnasha."

Kalath smiled. "She could be in the land of the dead. Perhaps the prophecies mean to resurrect her."

"Now that would be a tale worth telling." Kolgern yawned. "Nothing like a good ghost story to fall asleep to."

Tnasha let out a nervous laugh. "I don't know. Prophecies seem so...silly."

"There are only three for this generation. Every generation breeds new prophecy," Kalath said. "So how is the book coming along?" He stood and walked over to her.

"Elemental balancing?" she asked. "What happens when your elements are imbalanced?"

"Simply put, your energy implodes on itself and kills you."

Kolgern yawned again and lay down. "Yikes. Better you than any of us."

"Thank you, Kolgern. I was all set to learn sorcery and now you're telling me not only could I accidentally kill myself, but I could also implode from an imbalance?" She could feel the disbelief make its way across her face.

Kalath placed a hand on her shoulder. "I never said sorcery was without its limitations and dangers. It is a skill like any. Nothing is ever easy regardless of how easy some people make it look."

"So I'm destined to a life of elemental balancing rituals?" she asked, somewhat disturbed by the idea.

"If you want to use your innate abilities of sorcery, yes. It is not as hindering as you seem to think it is, girl."

"Fine, I'll do one right now." She stood, clutching the book to her chest. "Can I use your ritual room?"

Kalath nodded. "Of course."

Alena shook her head. "If she's a sorceress, why all the practice? Shouldn't she be able to do those things naturally?"

Kolgern lifted his head. He was interested in the answer,

too. "I've never seen Tnasha do amazing stuff or nothing like that. No one ever taught her."

Kalath nodded in agreement. "It must be taught. Think of it as a skill. Rassia can cook. She had the ability to learn to cook, but she did not know instinctively how to cook."

Alena looked somewhat disappointed. "That makes sense I guess."

Tnasha went to the ritual room, closing the drape behind her. She could hear the muffled voices of her friends telling more tales in the other room.

She had already read through the book. Whispering aloud to herself, she scanned the walls around her. "Okay, I need one red candle, one white, one brown and one blue." She shuffled through the shelves until she found the needed items. "I need a black candle and another white candle." She shook her head, laughing. Then said aloud, "I can see me running all over the place carrying all these candles."

With all the candles assembled in front of her, she placed each in a separate candle holder. She looked at the book again. "White goes to the east for air. Red to the south for fire. Blue to the west for water. Brown to the north for earth. It seems simple enough."

She placed each candle in its perspective place, the black candle on her right and the second white on her left, then sat back on her heels to survey her work. "Now I suppose I light them."

The dim light from the torches on the walls cast dancing shadows over the pages of the book. She read the next part aloud in a boisterous voice. "Thou shalt ignite these tapers from thine own fire element. So what does that mean?" She read further. "To conjure fire whence lighting torches or tapers, place palms together."

With a broad smile, Tnasha put her palms together and read on. "Imagine the fire, hot and burning between thine palms whilst imagining the fire element's red glow. Fine." Tnasha executed the next bit of instructions. She envisioned herself holding hot fire that seethed angry red. She moved her hands to the candles and touched the wick of the black candle lightly. The wick burst into a golden-orange flame. Tnasha jumped back, startled.

She jumped from where she sat. "Kalath!" she called. "I've lit a candle!" She lept up in her excitement only to land on her partially healed ankle. A dull pain reminded her to be careful.

Kolgern's voice rang out from the other room. "We're very proud of you, Tnasha. Lighting a candle is by no means an easy task." She could hear Alena and Kolgern snicker.

She was disappointed that her friends did not understand sorcery or sorcerers, even though Kalath had tried to explain the process of learning sorcery to them. They seemed to ignore the explanation and continue with their own tales and stories. She did not expect them to listen. After all, the prophecy was of no concern to them. A pang of guilt emerged in her chest. Her friends were not to blame for her situation. It was fate. Her fate—*hers*—not theirs. She sat back down with a deep sigh and followed her ritual, ignoring her thoughts.

Only after the hazy lights from the elements had dissipated in rainbows streaking through the dark, did Tnasha rise and extinguish the candles. She came from the room feeling wonderful and refreshed. Kalath looked at her expectantly. "Well?"

"I must've done it right. I feel amazingly... light. I can't think of any other way to describe it." She smiled and looked around. Her friends and Rassia had fallen asleep close to the hearth. She yawned. Sorcery still made her tired.

"Now you understand how magick works. It's all in how you focus your existing energy." He lit his pipe and took another sip of ale. "Perhaps tomorrow you can focus on healing your bones even further until they are strong again. Self-healing is a valuable skill to have. You may need it."

Tnasha smiled. She had other plans for her sorcery practice in the morning. Healing could come later. She pulled a blanket from a nearby shelf. "I should rest."

Kalath nodded wordlessly with a look of contentment and retreated to the other room.

Tnasha wrapped herself into the blanket and fell

quickly to sleep.

That night she dreamt something odd. The dream was set on a small ship. A freighter perhaps.

Above, on the deck, the men sang a solemn song to Eurynomous, the god of death, in ancient Danarian.

"Grains an' such, I s'pose..." said a young, blonde man. He shrugged his narrow shoulders.

A large man with a black beard and a full head of black hair held a small raven. The bird looked injured. "Don't you think we should name it?" came a voice from afar.

"How's we gonna do that if we's don't know if it be a male er a female?" the young blonde man asked. Their faces were blurred.

"Perhaps I should give it a name with regards to the storm," another voice suggested.

"Well, you think 'bout it whiles I get er some bandages an' dry cloths so we's can fix er up."

A dark-haired young man looked at the bird, closer this time, but not so close that it could peck out his eye. The bird shivered, struggling to find a warm spot on the table. "Beaky Buzzard," said someone within the haze. The bird flopped around hopelessly, in obvious discomfort and pain. "Or perhaps Grarneck, after the chivalrous Arkeeronish war lord?" he suggested to someone in the haze. In the distance, someone prayed to the god of water, Aithian, for those who had died. Tnasha was not sure who had died, but she knew someone had.

The blonde lad entered the chamber once more with dressings for the bird's injuries. He wore a startled look on his face. "It's the damnedest thin'. It's snowin'. I ain't seen nothin' like iss in 'ese waters. Is too warm, eh? Go up an' see fer yerself, Cap'n," the young man said as he set to work on the injured raven.

"Maybe we should call the bird Snow," said the voice beyond the haze.

As he lifted the hatch, Tnasha felt the chill of the wind as the snow swirled around the dark haired man-child. The snow appeared like stars, and the details were fuzzy. A crowd of men stood on deck of the ship staring out at the water. What were they staring at? As if coming from a cave a voice echoed, "This is unnatural, these snowflakes be a work of sorcery."

"I think we'll name the raven Snowflake," came another voice. "These snowflakes be a work of sorcery. Sorcery!"

The dream stopped there. Tnasha bolted upright. Sweat poured from her forehead. She was confused. It had a different feel than the prophetic dream. This one was more distant, as if it had happened. It was a dream of the past? The present? She wasn't sure. She was not there so it could not have been prophetic. She put her head in her hands. It was just a dream, she reassured herself. Just a normal, strange dream. After all, not all of her dreams had to be prophetic.

Kolgern gave her a puzzled look. "You look as though you have been contemplating the creation of the world all night." His voice startled her. He sat close to the mouth of the cave reading one of Kalath's many books.

Rassia and Alena were busy eating the gruel Rassia prepared for the morning meal, while Kalath was busy labeling jars of herbs.

"I just had a strange dream," she said, her voice absent of emotion.

"Was it like the last?" Kalath asked with a genuine look of interest.

"No. As silly as it was," she paused. "It was about a shipload of people who found a raven and named it Snowflake."

"Sounds normal enough to me. Too much of Kalath's spiced tea before bed," Kolgern assured her. "So why would anyone name a raven Snowflake?"

"Because it was snowing when the bird came aboard their ship with a broken wing," Tnasha answered matter-of-fact.

"That's as a good a reason as any." Alena tipped her head with a shrug, stood, and took a bowl of gruel to Kolgern.

"I'll eat later, I have something I want to do." No one questioned her as she stood, took a jar of calamus from the shelf, and went outside. Before the morning meal, she decided to try the something she had thought of the day before. If water sorcery came so naturally, she would try more weather working. This would be her defense against the Kersian sorcerers. It stood to reason her natural abilities were bound to protect her. Her intention was to bring on a light drizzle of rain. For practice.

Outside, it was a bright and beautiful day. The sun felt warm on her face. She looked around and the sullen landscape, then at the tree she had brought to life the day before. It was perfect. She pulled the wide cork from the clay jar and pulled out a handful of calamus root. Drawing a deep breath, she focused. Once she had found the balance of her center, she threw the handful of calamus root skyward, then poised her hands, palms upward, at several clouds. She focused her mana, willing it gray and blue, and imagined it flowing in a stream of light, filling the clouds with rain. A light drizzle would ensure a cooler day. But just as her thoughts insisted on a light drizzle, the sky opened into a sudden downpour. Immediately, the rain poured mercilessly onto the already sodden swampland, and within moments, Tnasha was soaked through and the waters of the marsh began to rise.

Kalath hurried from the cave to see what had happened. When he saw the rain he shook his head, and pulled Tnasha back into the cave's entrance, leaving the clay jar of calamus on the ground outside. "I did not realize *it* would happen this way. We have no choice but to abandon our morning meal, take whatever we can carry and leave. We shall be flooded out in a few hours."

Tnasha stared at the muddy ground and the splashes of rain pelting it. "I really didn't mean to...."

Kalath shook his head. "Well, there isn't time to cast blame. Too much Calamus Root I think. Perhaps you could save weather working for a drought?"

They hurried to gather what few things they had. "I will take Rassia back to Danaria. Undoubtedly we will run into a scouting party." The old sorcerer pulled the hood of his robe over his head to shield himself from the rain.

Kolgern began packing his things. "Alena and I will go with Tnasha like we discussed last night."

"We will? I thought you were the only one going..."

Kolgern smacked her arm. "Yes, *both* of us will go. We're not letting her go to Zul by herself. She's our friend. She's like a sister."

Tnasha felt a warm feeling overtake her. They must have discussed Zul while she was doing the elemental balancing rite. She suddenly felt guilty for thinking they did not understand. "Really? You would go with me?" She wanted to cry.

"Of course we will." Alena smiled with tenderness.

"Of course we will." Kolgern mimicked. "You were ready to run the opposite direction."

"Shut up, Kolgern. I didn't know *I* was going. I was surprised, that's all."

Kolgern hurried outside to saddle the horses.

Finally outside, in the pouring rain, Tnasha put her arms around Kalath and hugged him. "Thank you. Take good care of yourself and Rassia."

"You, too, my child. Remember the left horse black. Always follow your instincts." He handed her a purse. Inside were several shinder. "You may need this. Be careful."

Kalath smiled back at her as he and Rassia, with the pregnant mare, disappeared west into the Selenia Forest. Tnasha, with Kolgern and Alena, grabbed their hastily filled packs, and finished saddling their horses. Mounting without delay, they rode east toward the coast. If they hurried, they could be in Orana Tulk by the end of the day.

Left Horse Black

CHAPTER 18

Morvack and his men left early that morning. Now, the Kersian village, nestled deep in the Selenia Forest where it had gone undisturbed for years, stood empty, since the villagers had left the night before. The sounds of the horses echoed off the empty buildings. When the Danarian heathens came, they would find nothing. He felt content. It would be welcoming to see Zul and his fellow countrymen after so many years' service on the foreign mainland. Without doubt, Gavgal would be surprised to see him, and would wonder what had brought his youngest brother from his post. It was certain he would not be upset once he learned what Morvack brought him.

General Luig seemed uncertain. His gaze fidgeted from the path before him to Morvack. After a long stretch of uneasy silence the general spoke. "Your Holiness, I have often wondered how it is sorcerers know one another and why our blessed god would cause so much upheaval among his creatures."

Morvack squinted at the rays of sunlight that shined at them through the trees. "The unnamed gave sorcerers the gift to see one another's mana. Though why we fight amongst ourselves has nothing to do with him. It is the heathens and their gods who create strife. They have not been purified and cannot see the path the unnamed has paved for us. All of us."

"If he wanted us to survive, would he not provide us with all we need?" The general furrowed his brow in question.

"He places us in difficult situations to test our resolve and worthiness. Only those who die serving him, or who survive in his service are worthy of paradise," Morvack said, matter-of-fact. He remembered when he had asked his brother, Gavgal, the same questions. He had memorized the answers just as his brother taught him. His brother was a wise man.

Morvack's answer did not seem to comfort General Luig. He fidgeted with the mane of the horse beneath him. "I do not understand the nature of sorcery, though it must be difficult."

"It is why my brothers and I lead our holy cause. It is a sorcerer's work to lead the people."

"If I may ask, Your Holiness, how does it work?"

Morvack lifted an eyebrow. "What?"

"Mana. How is it from mana comes power to do so many wondrous things?" The general knew he was treading on uncertain territory in asking. Were he serving with Morvack's brother, Seth, he would not have asked such questions.

But Morvack answered, undaunted. "Each mana has its own gifts. I have faith the unnamed gave us the mana in hopes we would use it wisely to make our world better."

Luig's forehead wrinkled with more uncertainty. "It comes naturally then?"

"Indeed."

"Then would it not be prudent for us to assume the sorceress who bore that amulet is not the harmless creature we assume her to be?"

"Luig, as with any natural ability, it must be trained. The more it is used, the stronger it becomes. But exertion of mana can also make one weak. The sorceress *is* weak. Hiding her mana exhausted her."

"How could you tell, Your Holiness?"

"She could barely lift herself to her horse."

"But she was also injured."

"Those injuries did not heal as they should have. What

does that tell us?" Morvack's eyes beckoned an answer.

Luig shrugged. "That she is untrained?"

Morvack smiled. "Precisely. She cannot heal herself."

General Luig said nothing more as the morning wore on; probably contemplating his worthiness, Morvack mused. As well he should, for a general serving the one true god must be loyal and worthy.

The morning sunlight soon slipped behind deep black, rolling clouds, bringing with them a sudden pelting of rain that slid to the ground in crystalline sheets. Before long, each of them was soaked through. Soon, instead of solid ground or thick mud, the horses carefully made way through water that rose well above their fetlocks.

Morvack anticipated meeting no one along the path, for the path was not heavily traveled. Though clearly ahead of them, he saw a lone horse, led by two people trudging knee high through the water. One of them bore a pale blue mana. He was old. Morvack tapped General Luig's elbow with his riding crop to get his attention and reined his horse to a stop, leaning back in his saddle. "We must not leave witnesses to our departure lest we want the Danarian's following us."

General Luig spurred his gray gelding forward, followed by his men to apprehend the travelers.

At their approach, the old sorcerer stopped and held his walking stick firmly in front of him. "We have no quarrel with you. Please let us go in peace," he said.

Morvack approached at a steady pace, recognizing the daughter of the Warlord Kyran, and the infamous sorcerer immediately. A sly grin slid over his lips. "I must be blessed this day."

The old sorcerer scowled at him. "We have nothing to offer you."

"On the contrary, old man. You must be Kalath the Seer. I know of you. Your scrying abilities are renowned." He dismounted along with several soldiers, choosing his words carefully. Rassia had been with the two Danarian soldiers who took Lynae from him. "I remember Rassia quite well. If I recall, one of your progeny took her from me. Which leaves me to wonder where the sorceress wench has gone. Is she here?" Morvack looked around for any trace of the violet mana.

"One of my progeny? I have no progeny. You must be mistaken. I found this girl alone, wandering the forest. I am taking her home, to Danaria." Kalath put a protective arm up in front of the girl, who cowered behind him.

Morvack shook his head. He did not believe Sorcerer Kalath was so foolish. Certainly, he would have foreseen this. "You know better, old man. You both will come with me. Rassia shall surrender herself to the call of the unnamed one. It is her destiny to be purified. We may have use for you. Your scrying ability will be utilized. My brother and my god will be pleased to know that my men and I did not fail them after all."

"Is your brother your god? Are they one in the same?" Kalath narrowed his eyes, and held his staff up in the air. He noted Morvack's deficient reaction, then closed his eyes and began reciting the incantation.

"Stop this nonsense this instant. You know as well as I do that my brother is merely the vessel through which *the one with no name* speaks."

Kalath sopped his recitation of the incantation. "I see how you reason it. But is your reasoning truth, or faith?"

"Does it matter?"

"I suppose not." Kalath closed his eyes, continuing the incantation from where he left off.

Morvack motioned one of his soldiers to Rassia and drew his sword. "Cast a working of sorcery and I shall kill the girl here, leaving her corpse for the heathens to find."

Kalath opened his eyes again. "You would kill her regardless."

Rassia shot Kalath a hurt look.

A treacherous grin adorned the Kersian Sorcerer's face. "Here she would die slowly. Sacrifice is a more fitting death for a creature so enchanting."

"Have you Kersians no hearts? Take me, and leave the girl alone. She cannot harm you as I can."

"A compromise?" Morvack laughed. "I do not negotiate with heathens. I doubt you could hurt me, old man. Your mana has seen many years. It is degenerating before our very eyes. Take them."

With every ounce of strength he could muster, Kalath built the blate slowly. A yellow-orange light emanated from the palm of his hand, growing slowly into a ball of energy. He hurled it full force at Morvack. Morvack stood solid, not even attempting to step out of the blate's path. It seethed deep yellow and orange, moving through the air like a bolt of fire. On impact, Morvack's own mana absorbed it without effort or disturbance.

"Your blate and I are of a similar element, Sorcerer Kalath. Were you wise, you would have used your natural mana, but even then your blates cannot hurt me. But mine, mine could increase your willingness to come along. Healing and scrying, old man, are no match for a more permanent fire."

Without warning, Morvack allowed a single shard of mana to slip through his fingers. It struck Kalath in the chest, throwing him backward and knocking him unconscious on contact. Rassia let out a scream. For the second time that week, Rassia found herself gagged and bound, and lifted to horseback under guard of a Kersian soldier. Kalath's limp, unconscious body followed with another soldier behind them.

Morvack remounted and rode ahead.

"Should we take this horse, Your Holiness?"

"No. Leave the lame animal. It is useless to us," he said. He did not look back.

CHAPTER 19

King Darak's funeral had been brief. When it was over, Serena was escorted with her maids back into the castle. Commander Corigerg did not have a chance to speak with her. Had he had the chance he would have not had enough time to gather the information he needed to plan a counter defense. He watched helplessly as she was led away, then turned to find the Exavian general and two guards behind him. "Ah, General. I did not expect you to be standing there."

The general was as tall as Corigerg, but younger, with a sturdier build. His stark blonde hair, blue eyes, and pale skin stood out in contrast to his dark brown uniform. He tipped his head respectfully. "Commander Corigerg, may I speak with you privately?"

Corigerg nodded, leading the way to his command quarters.

Once inside, the general ordered his soldiers to stand guard outside the door. With the door closed, he turned to Corigerg. "We have a situation with which we need to procure your full cooperation, Commander."

Corigerg sat down. "And what situation would that be? Have I not given my full cooperation so far?"

The general smiled wryly. "We intend to coronate

Hermond to the Sherokean throne. You can do one of two things…"

"Nonsense!" Corigerg jumped up. "Prince Aragel is heir to the Sherokean throne and I intend to secure it for him until his return."

The general laughed. "Do you actually think the boy made it that far?"

Corigerg's eyes widened. He could feel the rage pumping through his body. It crept into his cheeks a crimson red, hidden somewhat by his deep brown skin.

"He did make it as far as Orana Tulk. I gave the orders to have the city, and everyone in it, destroyed." The general wore a smug look of satisfaction. "You can join us in cooperation or die. It's quite simple, really."

"When Danaria finds out about this…" Corigerg felt his stomach tighten. He wanted to unsheathe his sword and plunge it deep into the general's heart. The only thing stopping him was his oath to protect Sherok. To protect Serena. The only remaining member of the Sherokean monarchy. He would see her queen long before he allowed Hermond to reign as king. For that, he had no choice but to go along.

"Danaria will not find out. The attack has been cleverly disguised as a mercenary raid." The general was obviously quite proud of himself. "So what will it be?"

"Why do you give me a choice?"

"Were it my decision, I wouldn't have. I would have killed you immediately. But Prince Hermond believes he has use for you. *I* do *not* trust you."

Corigerg paused before speaking, concentrating on his breath. "Nor do I trust you, General. I will cooperate. But not because I have allegiance to Exavia. I will cooperate for the sake of Serena and all of Sherok. No other reason."

The general smiled. "I expected as much. I shall share your decision with Prince Hermond immediately."

"You do that." Corigerg's gaze followed the general as he left the room. After he was gone, Corigerg decided to go into the city for a drink and a mid-morning meal. *Tomatoes*, he thought.

•

Prince Hermond and Serena sat in the private dining hall. Serena toyed with the vegetables and meat on her plate with a blank stare. She merely glanced up when the general entered the room. The general saluted.

"And what was the answer, General?" Hermond did not look up from the plate of food in front of him.

"The commander has given his full cooperation in the matter. Though not out of allegiance, My Lord."

Hermond nodded, swallowed, and took a drink from the cup of ale in front of him. "He may very well change his mind."

"I doubt it, My Lord."

Hermond glanced up at the general, noting his sober expression.

Serena threw Hermond a hurtful look. "What matter?"

"You are obviously upset, my dear. Do not give it another thought. I am taking care of everything."

The anger that she had tried so hard to suppress surged forth. "Do *not* tell me I am upset. I *know* when I'm upset. I have *every* right to know what is going on. I have *every* right to come and go within this castle as *I* please. You will *not* lord over me. If you expect me to marry you, I suggest you start by treating me with some measure of respect and giving me credit for being more than a, a brood mare!" Serena stood and threw her napkin to the table. "Well?" she challenged. Her dark eyes seemed almost black and seethed with anger.

The general looked on without a change in his expression, but Hermond was obviously shocked by her sudden outburst. If he wanted to keep Serena under control he would have no choice but to say anything that might calm her. He stammered for words. "I, I never meant to make you feel as though your opinions... I did not want to upset you. With your father dying and Aragel's abrupt departure... I guess I wanted to protect you."

"This is ridiculous. I am taking charge here," she announced in a bold voice. The fierce determination in her eyes burned with intense passion. "General, find my cousin and bring him back here. Go!"

The general, taken aback to a woman giving him orders, looked to Hermond for approval.

"Don't look at him. Do as I say. I am just as well your princess now as I will be later."

Hermond smiled. "It's okay, General."

The general, obviously disgruntled, turned and stomped from the room with his jaw set.

"Serena, please calm down. We are looking for Aragel already. The last time he was seen he was on a ship heading toward the Danarian coastline. We know the port; we shall find him and bring him back. He should be home by the end of the week."

"Fine. Now, what is Commander Corigerg cooperating on?" She held her ground, crossing her arms over her chest.

This would be more difficult than Hermond expected. He had never seen Serena like this. He talked as fast as he could. "I suggested additional soldiers should patrol the cities. After all, a city without a king begs for marauders. We do not want to risk an attack. Commander Corigerg did not agree. The general was finally able to get him to agree, even though he did not like it." He gave her a quick reassuring smile.

"Uh huh. I'll be in my quarters." She turned from him and walked away. As much as she loved him, something did not seem right. Did he think she was naive? Serena knew Corigerg well enough to know that Corigerg was paranoid. He would have agreed with such a plan without question. He would not have to be coerced.

She went to her quarters and summoned her most trusted maid, Carolyn. A petite woman with deep brown skin and long tresses of black hair hurried into the room.

"You called, My Lady?"

"Carolyn, I want you to summon a supplier to me. I must go about my business of running the castle. We need tomatoes." Serena gave Carolyn a quick glance as if to ask if she understood. She once overheard the commander tell her cousin, several years ago, that *tomato* was a word used by spies to gather information. She remembered thinking how silly that was.

Carolyn nodded at once as if she understood the code. "I know a man who sells wonderful tomatoes that you will be quite pleased with. I shall summon him immediately." She turned to leave. "Can I get you anything else, Lady?"

"Tomatoes will be all for now."

•

It was late evening when the tomato merchant arrived and met with Serena in the kitchen. He was an older, graying man dressed in common merchants garb. His eyesight was poor. She could tell by the way he squinted at her.

"My Lady." He bowed. "I am Davin Vore. I own the Thirsty Sailor."

"You sell tomatoes as well, I suspect?"

"Indeed. I own several acres of farmland. One acre of it is tomatoes. The early tomatoes are fairing well this year despite *the locusts*. I have a full crop not yet reserved for anyone."

She lifted an eyebrow, wondering if she and the merchant were discussing the same thing.

He winked at her in return as if sensing her confusion.

She decided to continue. "How many?" The persistent feeling of something not quite right ate away at her.

"The best in all of Sherok. Over *five hundred* bushels. Commander Corigerg has inspected my tomatoes recently. He can assure you they are good. He will be thrilled to know you are buying them. He is one of my best customers. He comes into the city more often these days."

"Has he been by within the last few days?"

"I believe he stopped by this afternoon for a drink. He mentioned the *diseased tomatoes* you received only recently, *disguised* beneath a few good ones."

"Yes."

"My Lady, sometimes the *bad* tomatoes are *hidden* at the bottom of the barrel. You do not notice them. Perhaps blinded by their *outward appearance*. But, if one is diseased, it can *covertly destroy* the whole barrel. The disease *takes over*."

Serena took a deep breath and frowned. In her mind, she

tried to figure out exactly what he was trying to say. A look of confusion masked her face. "What about the younger tomatoes?"

"A mature, diseased tomato will disease the young and upcoming crop quite easily just as it may destroy the older, perfectly ripe ones." The man wore a somber look and shook his head. As if realizing she did not understand, he put his hand across hers. "Your father was old, but healthy. It was a disease. A *foreign* disease."

Her stomach twisted.

"They become *poisoned*," he said quietly, shifting the topic back to tomatoes. His eyes kept shifting from her to the door.

Tears came to Serena's eyes when she realized what he was saying. "I hadn't known that."

"Be careful of the bad ones, My Lady. Their only purpose is to destroy and take over the good crop. I assure you will have our healthiest at your disposal. They are strong and good and will destroy the plague upon us."

She held back her tears and forced herself to become strong again. "Very well. If Commander Corigerg approves of this, then I'm sure I will, too. He's very picky about his... vegetables."

"With good reason."

"Are you sure you'll be able to coordinate the delivery of all those bushels?"

"Oh, easily. But you should not concern yourself with that detail. Let me deal with that."

"When can I expect delivery?"

"Before your wedding, My Lady. You'll need them just before the ceremony's conclusion."

Serena stood in contemplation for a moment. If she was translating the conversation correctly, a covert Sherokean uprising would happen the day of her wedding. "Is there anything I should do in preparation for delivery? Clear some space?"

"My Lady, please allow the delivery men to worry about that. All you need to worry about is attending your wedding."

"Wonderful. Thank you."

Just as the conversation ended, Hermond entered the kitchen. "I've been looking for you. The ladies are decorating the hall. I thought you would want to oversee it." He looked over the tavern keeper. "Who is this?"

Serena forced a smile and looked up at him. "Vegetable merchant. I've just ordered some vegetables for the after wedding meal. I absolutely love tomatoes."

"Good ones, I hope?" Hermond asked.

"Yes, My Lord. They will be picked the evening before delivery to ensure freshness. They are so wonderful you could eat them like apples."

Hermond nodded approvingly. "Well, off with you then."

The man hurried from the kitchen. Serena forced another smile. She stood and hugged Hermond lovingly, holding back the urge to punch his face and rip out his eyes. Hermond would soon learn that she could pretend love, too. She decided then that she would kill Hermond herself. Did he think he could poison her father without the threat of retribution? In her heart, she felt a small part of herself die. Inside her head, she wept, and hoped the gods could forgive her for what she planned to do.

CHAPTER 20

They arrived in the small port village of Orana Tulk late that evening. After traveling all day with only a few stops to rest and feed the horses, they were tired.

"We should take the horses to a stable and board them for a few weeks," Kolgern said.

Tnasha nodded and searched her belongings for the few Shinder Kalath had given her. She handed the small purse to Kolgern. "That's everything I have."

Kolgern snorted and pulled his purse from his belt. "With this and what you gave me that should set them up nicely, and we could probably get a room at an inn for the night. But what are we going to do if we want to eat?"

Alena was quick to answer. "I have some Shinder."

Tnasha decided to point out another obvious problem. "What about securing travel to Zul?"

Kolgern shrugged his shoulders. "We can probably do various work on a ship in trade for passage."

"No. I'm not scrubbing a ship deck," Alena told him without hiding her disgust. "I'm an archer, not a cleaning maid."

"We really don't have any choice, do we?" Tnasha asked her. "If I have to scrub a deck I will. But we shouldn't worry about that now. I'm tired and the horses need some rest."

Alena gave in, following them toward the city. "Well, if Tnasha will do it then so will I. But I won't like it."

Upon entering the small city, they found a suitable stable almost immediately. Kolgern and Alena stayed to take care of the horses while Tnasha set out to find them a room for the night. Newer wooden buildings framed wide cobblestone streets busy with merchants and horse-drawn carts. Tnasha spotted an inn almost immediately. The initial attraction was a tall sign that announced "Rooms Available" headed with the simple statement: "INN."

Tnasha opened the wooden door and stepped inside. The main floor, as was typical with Danarian inns, housed a rough, rustic tavern. Along the back wall stood a staircase leading to the rooms above. She approached the bar counter and summoned the innkeeper. "How much for a room to sleep three?"

The tall man with a thin face scratched the side of his nose, then wiped his hands on the apron he wore. "I have a two bed suite available." He looked her up and down as if trying to gauge how much money she had. "Four shinder for the night."

Tnasha nodded, noticing Alena and Kolgern coming up from behind her. She turned to Alena. "Four shinder for the night."

Alena reached into her purse and pulled out the crystalline shinder, handing them to the man. He took the shinder with a smile and handed them a key. "Up the stairs, third door on the right."

They retreated to a table near the staircase and ordered a meal.

Kolgern lifted an eyebrow. "Should we have secured a ship tonight?"

Tnasha leaned back in the pine chair and closed her eyes. "Let's do it in the morning. I'm too tired."

"Me, too," Alena agreed.

Kolgern folded his arms on the table and rested his head in his arms. "Good. After we eat we can get some sleep."

After they had finished their first real meal in days, the three ascended the stairs weary and content. The small, dusty room was barely large enough for all three of them. The straw filled beds took up the entire room. Beyond caring, all three fell quickly to sleep.

●

The fog cleared. Wood splintered. The pounding of hooves roared through the streets. Through the thick shadows, she could vaguely make out the outlines of mounted horsemen carrying torches, and cutting down whoever stood in their way. Dust took to the air with smoke and orange-golden flames. The smoke burnt her eyes and her throat. She choked. People screamed and ran. The chaos faded in the fog. Distantly, someone was still choking back the thick, black smoke.

Tnasha opened her eyes, bolted upright, and realized she was choking on her own saliva. She coughed, took a deep breath, and surveyed her surroundings. A thin beam of daylight filtered beneath the dusty, curtained window. She jumped out of bed and pulled the drape back, looking down onto the busy streets of Orana Tulk. The sun was almost midway in the sky. They had slept in too late. "Get up! It's almost noontide."

Kolgern rolled over wearily and pushed his arm out, knocking Alena off the bed. "Almost noontide?"

"By Natyis, Kolgern Starkweather!" Alena lifted herself from the narrow space between the beds.

Kolgern sat up, rubbing his eyes. "What?"

Alena brushed herself off. "You shoved me off the bed. Remind me never to sleep next to you again. You're a bed hog."

Tnasha stifled a giggle, and ran her hand through her dirty, brown hair, pulling her fingers through the tangles.

Alena put her hands on her hips. "It's not funny." She followed Tnasha's lead and began pulling her thin fingers through her own blonde hair. "Ewww. I must look and smell as if I've slept in a sty."

Kolgern swung his legs over the side of the bed and scratched at his scalp. "Don't we all?" He yawned, scratching at his shoulder. "We probably have fleas."

Tnasha laughed.

Alena's eyes widened in horror. "Great! Do you know

what kind of diseases you can get from fleas?"

Kolgern shrugged his shoulders. This was how he had lived the majority of his life.

"Don't forget lice." Tnasha smiled, enjoying the game of feeding Alena's paranoia.

Alena bent over and roughed her dark blond hair up, running her fingers from her scalp to the ends of her hair. "Great. Maybe you two don't mind being covered in dirt, but I'm used to bathing once every few days. It has been a good four days!"

"We'll dunk you in the ocean before boarding ship." Kolgern fought to keep his amusement hidden.

Tnasha's expression turned sober. "Maybe it's time we quit fooling around and got moving. We need to find a ship leaving for Carinth or Arkeereon sometime today."

"Why Carinth or Arkeereon?"

"A ship heading in that direction is more likely to pass close to Zul," Kolgern said.

Without so much as another word, they left the small inn behind them and ventured on to acquisition a ship to take them to Zul.

It was upon their approach at the piers that Tnasha saw him. He stood next to the long lines of fishing nets on one of the piers leading to the docks. He seemed to examine each net with a cautious eye. Many of them were in need of repair.

"That's him," she said aloud. She looked back to make sure Kolgern and Alena were still with her. They had stopped several paces behind her to gaze out over the water.

A dark haired man stepped up next to her. He seemed more interested in chewing on a fingernail rather than the bustle around him. "Who?" he asked nonchalantly.

She smiled wryly. "Nothing." She stepped away from the stranger, who seemed familiar to her as well. A young boy joined him.

"Adarack," he called. The man examining the nets turned and smiled. The dark-haired man and the boy hurried to his side.

Tnasha looked on. Something was not right. Her silly

dream about a bird named snowflake did not seem so silly after all. She began to wonder about her most recent dream. She shook her head, shoving it to the back of her mind. She did not have time to deal with that dream now. Not when finding passage took precedence, especially with the more current dream from last night, which had given her that same feeling of dread as the dream of Morvack's sacrificial pit of fire.

Kolgern and Alena joined her. "What's going on?" Kolgern asked.

Tnasha pointed to the man dressed in dirty, wrinkled clothing. She took Kolgern by the hand and led him and Alena toward the unsuspecting sea captain and his mates.

As they approached him, Tnasha snapped her fingers and stepped up to the captain with confidence. "You."

Adarack turned to her with a defensive posture. "What is it you want?"

"Passage on your ship."

"My ship? That's out of the question. I don't take passengers. Cargo and crew. That's it."

"You could do it this once, couldn't you? Please?"

Adarack turned to her and shook his head. "No, I'm sorry."

Tnasha took a deep breath. Convincing the captain to give them passage was going to require more effort than she thought. "Look, you have a young man aboard your ship. With a raven named Snowflake. I know that because I have prophetic dreams. In my dream, you took us where we needed to go."

Aragel warily lifted the bird's cage. The raven squawked inside.

"Snowflake?" Tnasha asked with a smile.

Aragel nodded wordlessly, with a quick glance at Shadon.

"Hmph. Prophetic dreams my foot." Adarack turned to Shadon. "Have you ever heard such a thing?"

Shadon was busy studying the woman. "Tnasha…"

Tnasha extended her hand. "You are?"

"I know your father. I've seen you several times. I'm Shadon Longbowe."

Tnasha's eyes lit up. "Of course. I know of you, but we've never been formally introduced." Shadon Longbowe was a name she recognized well. It was the name the council used when referring to information acquisition. It was the name she heard when whispers of spying were heard behind closed doors. She narrowed her eyes, then shrugged off the uneasiness. It was not so strange for intelligence agents to be in Orana Tulk. It was one of the few information centers in the West Ocean Mainlands.

"Ahem," Adarack cleared his throat. "Indeed. We must be on our way. It was nice meeting you." He nodded to Shadon and turned to leave.

Tnasha grabbed onto his sleeve. He turned around. "I'm afraid I didn't catch your name."

He turned around. "Captain Adarack Vogman."

She took his hand and shook it. "Now that we've been formally introduced, please may we have passage on your ship? We will not be a bother. I promise."

Shadon lifted an eyebrow and smiled. The daughter of Termark O'Schoitt had the reputation of being a bit odd. Most fifth generation sorceresses did. But this was beyond anything he would have expected.

Adarack answered without hesitation. "I already told you that I do not take passengers."

"But you never explained why."

"Because of the liability."

"But you will. I saw it in my dream," she lied, "which means you will." Tnasha glanced back and forth between Adarack, Shadon, and Aragel. She stepped up to Adarack, only inches from his face. "We need passage to Zul. We don't have much in the way of money, but we could easily exchange free labor for passage."

Shadon pulled her back. "Sorry, Adarack, she's a little excited. High strung."

Why a sorceress would want to go to Zul was beyond his comprehension. Surely there was something amiss for a young woman to be willing to place herself in the hands of the enemy. A foreboding feeling rose in Shadon's gut.

Tnasha pushed Shadon away with a gentle shove and introduced her friends. "This is Alena fen Rishen and this is Kolgern Starkweather."

Adarack held out his hand curiously. "Indeed? Does your friend always greet strangers so oddly?" he asked with a smile. The deep brown creases of his face were covered in a layer of thick black hair, and beneath his eyes dark circles from many sleepless nights.

"Captain Vogman, I know you're going to Arkeereon. You are going right by where we need to be." She refused to give up.

Adarack gave Shadon a more than puzzled look. "Is she military intelligence? It seems to me when she gets an idea in her head she won't let it go."

Shadon stifled a nervous chuckle. "She's the daughter of a Danarian warlord," he paused, then looked at her strangely. "Why do you need to find a ship going past Zul?"

"Why else? We have to go there," she said with a tight smile.

It was clear she would not share more information. Shadon could tell by the look in her eyes.

The captain still wore a puzzled look. "Zul, eh? That's an odd request. What would the three of you want with Zul? You're not Kersians, are you?"

Alena snickered, while Tnasha gave him a wordless look of contempt.

"No. We just need someone to take us close to there," Kolgern finally said.

"Zul is no place for the curious." Adarack gave Shadon a knowing glance and Shadon shrugged his shoulders in response.

Kolgern tried to further explain. "We have business there."

"We also need a paddleboat to hold three people, too," Tnasha added with a big smile.

"A paddleboat?" The captain stared at her in obvious shock. "By Natyis! I've never heard anything so daft in my life! To Zul in a paddleboat?" He began mumbling to himself.

Aragel and Shadon looked at each other. Each wondering if the other was thinking the same thing. They were. Was it possible the three strangers were somehow involved in something? A grand scheme was surfacing and it did not look good.

That is when it happened. The *storm* hit. It was Tnasha's dream from the previous night unfolding before their very eyes. A chill ran its way up her neck. Battle cries echoed throughout the city like a diabolic wind, leaving a moment of deaf silence in its wake.

"Barbarians!" came a shout from someone near them. The city's bells sounded and everyone, it seemed, made haste to the nearest ship hoping it would pull from the harbor in time.

Kolgern paused and started back to the stables. "The horses!" he yelled frantically.

Shadon grabbed hold of Kolgern's tunic and pulled him back. "Leave them! There isn't time, you idiot!"

With reluctance, Kolgern followed Tnasha and Alena with Shadon pushing him forward. Aragel ran ahead with Snowflake to board the *Narassa*.

CHAPTER 21

As morning turned to noon, Rassia found herself staring straight ahead seeing everything and nothing. She was afraid and emotionally numb. Nothing in her life had prepared her for this, and now, she had lost her will to fight. If she was going to die, it was the will of the gods. She only hoped that her death would be remembered, and that others would learn from it.

The forest around them began to thin, leading to open, hilly grassland. She could see the coastline far below. The soldier with whom she rode kept a tight arm around her. His hand sat firm and unmoving on her abdomen. Anger replaced her fear. His touch was annoying, even violating in its own way. She bit down on the dirty cloth rag in her mouth.

"The horses are slowing," said a voice from behind her.

"Nonsense. The horses are not slowing. We are tiring. We will ride straight through to the port north of Morasta. We must be on the ship by night's fall," said another.

Rassia did not avert her gaze.

"The girl is not struggling."

"Perhaps she has come to peace with the destiny our god has ordained for her," said her captor.

"Silence, all of you," Morvack said. "We do not want to attract attention. Wrap the girl and the old man in blankets. We will peaceably move along the outskirts of Morasta to the port."

The soldiers quieted in obedience. Midday turned to afternoon and afternoon into evening. The steady pace of the horses lulled Rassia to sleep. When the horses finally stopped her eyes flew open in surprise. She listened carefully. She could hear the wind, the steady fall of rain, and the sound of surf crashing onto the shore. The smell of brine assaulted her nose. The black blanket covering her made it impossible to see anything, not even a sliver of light.

We are by the ocean, her mind screamed. But who did her mind scream to? *Tnasha*, she decided. *Kalath and I have been taken prisoner*, her mind called into the wind. For some reason, she hoped Tnasha could hear her.

She felt her body leaving one set of arms to another, until finally one man carried her. His footfalls echoed off planked wood. The sound of water got closer, louder, almost deafening.

"There is no sense in you calling to your sorceress friend," the man who carried her said.

For a moment she did not know who was speaking, then realized the blanket muffled Morvack's voice.

"I can read your thoughts. A glorious gift bestowed upon me by the unnamed."

Rassia felt her heart skip a beat as the incline changed. The terrain was steeper here. Her body was nestled next to his. He held her firmly. No matter how hard she tried to move away, she could not. They boarded the ship.

"You have good senses, girl."

Quit talking to me, you ass, she thought.

"The things heathen children think. You are not worthy to live. Perhaps the unnamed will show you mercy in the afterlife."

Is he as cruel to his own children? she wondered.

She felt her body drop, unsuspected. When her side hit the ship deck, it knocked the wind out of her. She fought to inhale through her nostrils. The humidity made the air thick, almost too thick to breathe.

"Put the sorcerer here, too," Morvack said with a hint of anger in his voice.

Was it something I said? she wondered with a silent laugh. Had Morvack heard her?

She was pulled from her thoughts as Kalath's body fell beside her with a dull thud. He did not move, though she thought she could hear him breathing. Clearly, she heard the steady clack of Morvack's heavy boots move away. From where she lay, she could feel the ship move, as if she were one with it. The ship shifted with the waves. The wood of the deck smelt of fish and damp wood. She bit down on the cloth, noting some of the threads had snapped under the pressure of her bite. She began biting the cloth bit by bit. After some time, the cloth began to loosen and she spit it from her mouth. It fell around her neck. She took in a deep breath. The blanket smelled moldy.

It was then she began to fidget, slowly moving her wrists and fingers in hopes she could pry loose the thin, course rope binding her hands. She was careful not to make any rash movements in hopes the Kersians would not notice. Only when her hands were free would she be able peek from the blanket at her surroundings, and wake Kalath. Trembling, she emptied her mind, afraid to surrender any thoughts in case Morvack was somewhere nearby. The thought came anyway. *What if Kalath is dead?*

Just as she felt she had made some progress in loosening the ropes, the approach of soldiers caused her to stop. She felt a tug on the blanket, and immediately was hoisted to her feet.

The soldier with thick lips and a square head pulled her along and looked over at his companion. "She got the gag off."

The other soldier sighed and put it back in place, tightening the knot.

They dragged her to the hatch, down the steps and into a dark, cavernous room below deck. There Morvack sat in waiting. "Bring her in here, remove the gag and leave us."

The soldiers did as instructed and left the room. Between her and Morvack sat a small table with an oil lantern bolted to it. The light from the lantern cast a soft light across the small room, softening Morvack's square, angular jaw and the sharp jag in his nose. Rassia shifted her jaw and swallowed. The taste of the dirty rag lingered on her tongue.

"Perhaps if you were more quiet. Cooperative. We could leave your mouth unbound."

Rassia shivered. It was cold and the torn dress she wore offered little warmth. "I'm not accustomed to being a prisoner."

"Nor am I accustomed to taking prisoners."

She could feel tears welling up in the corners of her eyes, but she managed to hold them back. Her voice emerged small, childlike. "Why couldn't you just let me go? I don't want to die."

"None of us wants to die. But death is the natural conclusion to life. You have nothing to fear. I promise it will be quick and painless."

"Why?" A lone tear traveled down her cheek.

"You must be purified. It is the only way to save you from yourself and the heathens who have brought you into their world."

Rassia thought about her father, her mother and brothers. *Were they worried about her?* Those thoughts alone brought on soft sobs.

"Please don't cry." Morvack's voice toned a note of irritation.

"I can't help it." She wiped the tears from her cheek with her shoulder. "I'm never going to see my father or my mother again. Or my brothers. Or my grandmother." She began crying harder.

Morvack turned his head and wiped at his face. "I have no choice."

She continued to choke back the tears, trying to stop them altogether. "You do have a choice! You could spare Kalath and me. You could turn this ship around right now, let us go and you could hide somewhere where they would not find you. The Danarian legions will stop looking for you if they find me."

"It is my duty." Morvack wrung his hands.

"Duty? To whom? To your brother? Like Kalath asked, who do you serve? Your god or your brother?"

"Who I serve is none of your business."

Rassia took a deep breath. She knew she had touched on something. "If you are going to take my life of fifteen years, I think it *is* my business. You became angry when I wondered if you would treat your own children this way. Why? It is because you would *not* treat them this way. I know it is."

"I have no children," he said in a solemn whisper laden with anger.

Suddenly it dawned on her. Perhaps Morvack wanted children. "If you had children and your god commanded their sacrifice through your brother, would you obey? Can't you see what you are doing is wrong?"

He did not reply.

"If you could have children would you? Would you leave your life as a tyrant and become a more humble, quiet man? What would you do?" She paused, waiting for his reply. He offered none. She felt a surge of anger emerge. "Answer me!"

"Enough." He stood, taking a blanket from the ground. "I don't even know why I had them bring you down here."

"You wanted to have this exact conversation." Rassia hung her head in defeat. Clearly, she was not as strong as Tnasha. The sorceress would not hear her. She and Kalath would not be saved.

"If you knew what it was like…"

"I would not want to know."

"I cannot marry and have children," he said.

"I suppose that is because most women would not marry such a cruel person."

He sat back down. "I am a sorcerer. We have no sorceresses left. I could not have a family even if I wanted one."

She looked up at him, noting the sadness in his eyes. His answer surprised her. "So you do not take sorceresses for their blood?"

"Humph. That is a lie perpetuated by your heathen elders. They use it to turn their offspring against us." He met her gaze.

"If you wanted a wife there are plenty of ways to get one other than killing people and destroying their villages," she uttered with dirision.

Confidence resurged in his eyes. He tossed the folded

blanket to her. It fell on her lap. "My god will reward in the afterlife for my service."

"I hope so. It sounds like a lonely life. I would rather live fifteen years as I have, than your life far into old age." She looked down at the blanket. "Could you please help me with this? My hands are tied."

Morvack stood and walked around the table. He draped the blanket over her, extinguished the lantern, and left the room angry and in haste.

CHAPTER 22

The brief silence ended with shouts and screams and the pounding of hooves. Clanking metal and the roar of consuming fire seemed to linger in their ears. Adarack led the way, shoving past anyone in his path, making way for Aragel, Tnasha, Alena, Kolgern, and finally Shadon. The noise of running footfalls rang heavy on the wooden planks leading to the ship. The ensuing minutes seemed a blur as the planks were withdrawn. The sounds of chain being wound by cranks as anchors lifted, and the sharp snap of unfurled sails whipping crisply in the wind. As the uproar of calamity died down, Tnasha and her companions found themselves on a small freight ship headed out to sea.

Arrows with flaming tips sailed toward them, falling short in range and dipping into the ocean with brief sizzles as each flaming arrow died. Shadon and Aragel stood near the threesome, waiting for some confirmation of their suspicions. They watched as, in the distance, mounted horsemen with torches marauded and burnt the city to the ground. Many stood on the beaches and piers still attempting to catch the *Narassa* with more arrows despite her speed. Adarack handed Shadon a spyglass. He looked through it and noticed something strange. The marauders, despite their attempt at subterfuge, had neglected to camouflage their swords. The combination of Exavian steel and Kersian markings wasn't easy to disguise.

Tnasha fell onto the deck of the ship and took a deep, cleansing breath. "Can my fortnight get any worse?"

Kolgern lifted an eyebrow. "You should know better, Nasha. Just when you think it has gotten bad - it really hasn't. Even though we've lost four horses and most of our money..."

"And what's that supposed to mean?" she asked wearily. "We stole those horses. Granted they were probably stolen from Danaria to begin with."

Kolgern started in on her, exasperated. "It means that you think you have it bad. Ever since Kalath's you have been going on and on with self-pity. I've had enough. This is only a week out of your posh life in your big castle. Some people live like this exclusively. Take for example - me," he said, glaring at her.

She turned to him in seriousness. It was not like Kolgern to get snippy with her or anyone for that matter. "What has put you against me? You're the one who said you would come with me. So we lost a few horses and some money. We could have lost our lives!"

"That has nothing to do with it!" He turned on his heal and strode off toward the bow of the ship.

Tnasha stared after him in disbelief. Alena and Shadon looked on wordlessly. "What's wrong with him?"

Alena shook her head. "With him, who knows? I certainly don't."

"He looks tired. The horses were an excuse. Having to run like this and not knowing what's going to happen next... You have to admit, Tnasha, this isn't a situation suited to everyone. We all cope in our own way. I think he'll be all right once he adjusts," Shadon assured her.

Alena turned back to them. "He feels helpless," she said without meeting Tnasha's curious gaze.

"Helpless?" Tnasha asked. That was not a word Tnasha had ever considered using to describe Kolgern. She pulled her hand through her hair. It was matted and stringy and beginning to annoy her.

Alena nodded. "Yesterday, when we were stabling the horses, he told me he feels angry that you're in this situation and he feels helpless to help you. He's torn between going home because there is nothing he can do and staying just in case you need him."

Tnasha suddenly felt humbled and embarrassed. She should have never pulled her friends into this. Sure, they agreed to come with her. She should have refused their company. But then she had not really asked them to come. All for an amulet. It did not make sense. "I didn't know he felt that way."

"It's not your fault," Shadon told her even though he had no idea what they were talking about. He sat beside her and put an arm over her narrow shoulders. "Some men tend to suppress their emotions because they want their friends to think they're strong. Then, when his emotions get the better of him, and he does show them, his feelings seem excessive and unwarranted. He'll get over it."

"Well aren't you sympathetic?" Alena remarked sourly.

"I'm trying to help," Shadon answered, unruffled.

Tnasha held a hand up. "Let's stop fighting amongst ourselves. Please?" She stood. "I need to find Captain Vogman and find out if he's willing to take us to Zul..."

A familiar voice cut her off. "The gods are not looking upon me kindly this day."

She turned to find Captain Adarack Vogman facing her. "Captain Vogman."

"Now that you and your friends are aboard, what, pray tell, will I do with you?" His dark eyes stared through her. She was on his territory now.

"Shadon herded us onto your ship. It was the one docked closest to us," she said carefully, hoping Shadon would not mind her placing the blame on him. From the corner of her eye she saw him nod.

"Well, I can't very well throw you overboard. So I suppose I'm stuck with you." His eyes traveled over her and Alena. He shook his head at Shadon, then turned back to her. "Your other friend didn't make it?"

"He's around here somewhere," Shadon said.

"I see. Well find him and keep him put with the rest of ya. I don't need land-dwellers underfoot my crew," he said sharply.

Tnasha smiled as she watched the captain leave them. "Is he always like that?"

Shadon laughed. "He's only joking. He has a dry sense of humor. He's really a kind hearted person, a dear friend, once you get to know him."

●

The hours passed in silence since Kolgern rejoined them. They sat in a small circle staring at the great expanse of water around them. Aragel went below deck, but Shadon stayed behind and sat with them.

"Kinda makes you feel insignificant," Kolgern whispered.

Tnasha turned to him. His eyes were transfixed on the deep, gray, waves. "Yes."

"Do you think we'll have to clean the decks so we can get something to eat?" Alena asked in a small voice.

"Why?" Tnasha asked.

"'Cause I'm really hungry." She held her stomach, her eyes pleading.

Shadon let out a chuckle and shook his head. "Come with me. I'll get you some food. Adarack is not as strict as he pretends to be."

Alena and Shadon stood, leaving Tnasha and Kolgern behind.

Tnasha could not stand the silence any longer. "What's wrong? I didn't mean to upset you if I did."

Kolgern kept his eyes affixed on the gray water. "When things get bad I can usually fix them." His voice trailed off.

Tnasha put her arm around him. "You can't very well fix everything. That's the nature of things. You just have to make do and hope everything turns out all right."

He shrugged his shoulders and met her gaze. "Yeah. I suppose so. But I feel like I'm losing control. I can't help. I can't do anything except wait and see what happens."

Tnasha was briefly taken aback. For the few years she had known Kolgern, she had never seen him cry. Seeing a grown man cry, young though he was, made her uncomfortable.

She pulled him close to her. "Just by being here you are doing more than you'll ever know. You've shown me that you are the greatest of friends. Nothing else can equal. I love you for it," she whispered, coming to tears herself.

Kolgern took a deep breath, straightened and wiped his eyes. "I wonder what your father is doing."

Tnasha wiped her own eyes and leaned back. "He's probably panicked and assembling a legion to find us. By now, he's terribly worried. Unless he happened upon Kalath. In which case he may be on a ship trying to arrive at Zul before we do."

Kolgern chuckled half-heartedly. "Well at least you know he loves you. Would do anything for you."

Tnasha nodded. "My father is a hard man. But I'm beginning to see why. The world is not a friendly place. You need to be tough." She stood and leaned on the railing, staring out over the water. "All this time that's what he's been trying to teach me."

Kolgern sighed. "You're lucky. The only thing my father ever tried to teach me was how to continue with the family business."

"The family business?" Tnasha asked. "What was that?" She slid back down to the deck and pulled her knees to her chest. Kolgern rarely shared personal stories, especially when it came to his childhood. He kept that side of himself hidden, like something best left clandestine, locked away in the deep recesses of his past.

"Ever since I can remember, I knew how to steal. I could take anything I wanted and slide away before anyone noticed. Then, one day, my father promised to teach me the art of killing another person for more golden Keldins and crystalline Shinders than I had seen my whole fifteen years. It was the way our family had always lived." His expression remained somber and his voice took on a more solemn tone than before.

"Assassinations?" Tnasha asked, horrified.

Kolgern nodded, continuing. "It was the reason my father took me to the death ground in Laran to show me the results of sloppiness." He paused as his face contorted with distress. "I remember how the gallows loomed before us like a gray skeleton, like the shadow of death itself. And I remember feeling the cold, spring, wind race down the back of my neck. I don't know why I remember it. I just do. I remember feeling cold, tingly. Like I could feel death, you know?"

Tnasha nodded wordlessly. She had never heard Kolgern speak so.

"And I remember three bodies swinging slowly on top of the platform by the ropes around their necks. Among them was one of my uncles. Uncle Damon was the unlucky one; caught in the castle of the Carinthian Warlord Coriman with a dagger up his sleeve." Kolgern took another deep breath. "When it was all over, I was numb, unable to move my eyes from the bodies just swinging there." Kolgern stopped and stared. "Then, when the crowd dispersed, my father said, 'You understand why you cannot be caught now, boy? Even a petty thief can find 'imself up there.' I remember it like it happened yesterday. I was really afraid."

Tnasha squeezed his shoulder. "Did you tell your father it frightened you?"

Kolgern laughed a snide laugh. "By Natyis, no! I was too afraid to say anything. So I quit stealing because every time I tried to steal something, those bodies—hanging there limp and dead—leapt into my mind. I told my parents that the merchants were being more careful."

"So what did they say?"

"They didn't believe me, of course." He sniffed. The air was becoming thicker and humid. "I spent a lot of time sitting behind the Temple Dagon. Thinking. And finally, one day a priestess approached me and we talked. She told me about how her father wanted her to marry a farmer and raise children. And she said she defied him and became a priestess instead."

"So you decided to take charge of your own life then?"

"Kind of. Well, yeah. But I didn't do it soon enough. I was still too afraid to say anything to my father. I didn't want to be a disappointment. I know you understand that," he said matter-of-fact.

"Unfortunately. I've always felt my father was disappointed because his only child was a female. So proving yourself seems the only way to gain acceptance and love." She sighed heavily. It was beginning to make sense now. It was the reason she had labored so hard to become a soldier. The reason she had to get the amulet back. But it was something deeper. Something about needing to prove she was worthy of respect, and had a purpose. She had placed those expectations on herself. Her father had not. Her father's expectations were simply what she envisioned them to be. The revelation left her awe struck.

"Perhaps we all face this challenge at some point. Having to live up to the expectation of someone else," Kolgern said, as if knowing what she was thinking. "One night, my father took me on an assassination excursion." Kolgern crinkled his nose in disgust. Then, in an exaggerated voice with a Carinthian accent he said, " 'Assassination is an art. It is an art that must be practiced with refinement. It must be planned carefully and the life you take must be extracted quickly and flawlessly. There is no room for mistake lest you be caught and find yourself in the gallows.' He made me remember that. Recite it, in fact."

Tnasha nodded, now realizing that Kolgern's father was far worse than hers had ever been or could ever be. Kolgern was right. She was living a privileged life.

"He was the one who killed King Abergorn of Carinth. I was there. I watched him. With poison - Raegnas. It was all too easy. Distract the guards. Not much of a problem since security was light. One small incision in the wrist. The king woke up, his breath caught in his throat and in one gurgle he died, falling back into the pillows of his bed. His eyes were still open." Kolgern stopped and swallowed hard.

Tnasha sat quietly and said nothing. What could she say?

"It still makes me sick to think about it." His eyes met hers. "We got away easily. I heaved at the side of the road on the way home and my father chastised me for it. So that night I ran away and never looked back. That was the end of it. I haven't seen my family since."

Tnasha knew Kolgern had brothers. He had mentioned it once briefly. "What about your brothers?"

Kolgern snorted. "Jace was the first to greet us when we got back. He said, 'Good job! Father, Kolgern!' and then he asks me, 'So, how was it?' as if he were asking about my first time with a woman rather than murder. I don't know. Let's talk about something else."

Tnasha agreed. "That sounds like a good idea. I'm sorry if I was prying."

"No. It's okay. I wonder what's keeping Shadon and Alena." He stood and wiped his hands on his tunic.

Metal buckets clanked against the ship's deck, and Tnasha and Kolgern looked toward the source of the noise only to find Alena and Shadon carrying buckets and scrub brushes.

"You can't be serious. Shadon?" Tnasha was not in the mood.

Alena gave her a wicked grin. "If we clean deck we can have food."

Shadon let out a laugh. "She's kidding. We volunteered to bring these things up for the deck hands to get them out of the galley so we can eat."

Kolgern laughed and Tnasha smiled. They left the mops and brooms above deck and went below. Aragel sat quietly in the corner, eating the bowl of stew in front of him. Tnasha sat next to him.

"What are you doing in this part of the world, Shadon?"

Shadon handed her a bowl of the rich fish stew and a spoon. "Funny. I was going to ask you the same thing. Luckily Alena gave me a brief rundown of your recent skirmish with the Kersians."

"Why do you look so... curious then?" Tnasha dipped the spoon in the soup and took a sip. It was salty enough to choke her. She coughed. "Sorry."

Aragel snickered.

She gave the young man an awkward smile.

Shadon settled in his chair. "Do you know who those people were who attacked Orana Tulk?"

"Should we?" She took another spoonful of stew.

"They were a subterfuge, a combined Kersian-Exavian attack force."

Kolgern looked up from his bowl. "If that's the case and Danaria finds out, which they will, the Kersians and Exavians had better pray for their lives."

Alena rolled her eyes. "What is their motivation in attacking Orana Tulk?"

"What?" Tnasha looked at her, puzzled.

"What is their motivation? Why would they do that unless something was in the bargain for them?"

"They wanted me," came Aragel's voice.

"Why?" Alena cocked her head toward Aragel. "See, this is what I mean by motivation. All evildoers have a motivation. They want to kidnap him? That seems like a lot of trouble to go through just to kidnap someone."

Aragel sat back and pushed the bowl away from him. "They want to *kill* me."

Tnasha crinkled her forehead. "Hmm. A raid. It would look like a horrible coincidence. They didn't want anyone to know they wanted to *intentionally* kill him."

Shadon nodded.

Tnasha turned back to Aragel and patted him on the shoulder. "Welcome to my world. The Kersians have wanted to kill me since before I was born. I'm a sorceress. Evidently you must be important if they want to kill you."

Aragel did not answer, but his eyes went wide when she said she was a sorceress. There was something unsettling about that fact. He had never been around a real sorceress before. She made him nervous. With that in mind, he inched away from her.

Shadon narrowed his eyes suspiciously. "If I tell you why they want to kill him, do you swear in blood to keep it quiet?"

Alena, Kolgern, and Tnasha exchanged glances. Tnasha tipped her head. "All right. Alena, dagger."

Aragel watched wide-eyed and in silence as Alena pulled a dagger from her boot, cut open her hand and handed the dagger to Kolgern. He cut his hand. Tnasha followed suit. She handed the dagger to Shadon. With a quick slice, he cut open his own hand. They all placed their hands on his.

Shadon nodded at Aragel. "Meet prince Aragel of Sherok. It seems Exavia has taken over Sherok for the time being. King Darak is dead. Murdered by Prince Hermond of Exavia, or one of his agents. Aragel and I were on our way to Central Danaria to gather reinforcements. We were forewarned about the attack and were getting ready to leave when we ran into you. So far, all we know is the Kersians and Exavians have a united plan to usurp Sherok's throne, placing Hermond at the helm."

"My uncle is dead?" Aragel shot up from his chair.

Shadon sighed. "I'm sorry I didn't tell you."

"How long have you known?"

"This morning. Before the morning meal." His gaze traveled to the floor.

Aragel sat back down and stared at his feet.

Tnasha patted Aragel's leg and gave Shadon a dumbfounded look. "You could have told him sooner, Shadon, and more gently. He's a king now."

Shadon shrugged. "I had honestly *forgotten* I didn't already tell him."

Tnasha took her hand from Aragel and leaned closer to Shadon. "We're going to Zul to get my amulet back. It fell from my neck when we were escaping the Kersians. The Kersian sorcerer Morvack has it."

"No." Kolgern lifted a finger. "*I killed him.* I think Kalath's vision was mistaken. It's probably just one of the Kersian..."

"Sorry Kolgern, you didn't. My amulet healed him. He's very much alive."

"How can we know for sure?"

"I looked into the scrying bowl, too. Kalath was not the only one who saw. Didn't Kalath tell you that? After all, he did explain to you why we were going to Zul, didn't he?" Tnasha shrugged and lifted her hands. She turned back to Shadon. "Within the amulet is not only the power of my mana, but also the power to control me. The sorcerer Kalath said the Kersians having control of me would place the world in a dangerous situation." She pulled back and pressed her bleeding palm on her knee.

Aragel broke the silence. "It doesn't make sense."

Tnasha nodded. "But, as is everything in the universe, it is all connected somehow. Let me tell you how I see it. If they have already taken Exavia, and now Sherok, and now they have my amulet, they could be planning to take over another kingdom next. World domination, perhaps?"

Aragel nodded wordlessly. "But that's awfully bold, isn't it? They could be planning to make money off the exportation of crops for all we know. Maybe they're not planning to take over the world at all. Right?"

"When you're insane, nothing is too bold. Whatever it is they're planning, my amulet could only help them. I'd rather not have something of mine helping them to reach their goals."

Shadon looked on, knowing that Tnasha was probably right. Somehow, it was all connected. How, he did not know. None of them did. But he was certain it was only a matter of time before they found out.

As everyone else continued eating, Aragel stood and went above. For him, a sorcerer was alien. What could he expect? *Quit being an idiot,* he finally told himself. *She is no different than anyone else. Except she can do unnatural things.* He had heard stories of sorcerers who could work the weather and control objects with their minds. They could heal the sick, and just as easily, kill. "What has Sherok gotten into?" he asked aloud to no one.

"Sherok has gotten into nothing. It is a mere casualty of war," came a voice from behind him. He turned. Shadon stepped from the shadows.

"I hate it when you do that. You need to wear a bell around your neck."

Shadon laughed. "Sorry. I didn't mean to startle you." He sighed deeply, adopting a more serious expression. "I'm also sorry I did not tell you about my father's death sooner. I suppose I wanted to spare you any grief."

Aragel didn't respond right away. His thoughts were

still on Shadon's previous statement. Sherok was a casualty of war. Aragel shook his head when the realization hit him. "Shadon, do you realize we're caught in the middle of a sorcerer's war. It makes more sense now."

Shadon did not understand. "What do you mean?"

Aragel forced a smile even though all hope seemed bleak and dim. For the first time he knew what was going on before his cousin did. "How Hermond got out of the room and downstairs so quickly. 'Your Eminence' is a Kersian sorcerer. You told me that, remember? The sorcerer must have gotten him out of the room, extinguished the fire…"

"That makes sense. But to what end? Or as Alena would say, what was his motivation? Why would the Kersians want Sherok, and an amulet of one sorceress among many? It seems to me the amulet was simply a lucky mistake on their part."

"Perhaps. What would sorcerers want with mortals though? Their end has to be driven by others of their kind. Enemies. Wouldn't you think so? What if they are building an army by taking over each kingdom one at a time? To fight a war?"

Shadon shook his head. "Conversion seems like an easier tactic. For all we know, all of this is mere coincidence."

"That's what we're going to find out. I knew there was a reason we ran into you." Tnasha had come up behind them.

Shadon jumped. "Don't do that! Sneaking up on people…" He shook his head.

Tnasha smiled. "Did I scare you?"

"Now you know how it feels." Aragel put on a big grin and poked Shadon in the side. "He's always startling me like that. It serves him right."

Tnasha smiled and laughed half-heartedly. She took a deep breath and looked Aragel over. She noticed a slight discoloration in the air around his neck. That was odd. She had never seen anything like it before. She said it before thinking, leaning forward to touch his neck. "Do you experience shortness of breath?"

He backed away slightly, then forced himself to stand still. She was not going to hurt him, after all. Both he and

Shadon looked at her, puzzled. A

Aragel finally answered. "Sometimes. When I get nervous."

"It's just anxiety of a new or frightening situation," Shadon said matter-of-fact. "Why do you ask?"

Tnasha decided to lie, a bit afraid to reveal her newly emerging abilities to anyone. "In my dream he was fighting to catch his breath. I just wondered."

"If I pay attention to my breathing I can calm myself down," said Aragel.

"You better watch that if you're going to be king."

"What does that have to do with being king?" Tnasha rolled her eyes.

"A king cannot show weakness in front of his subjects."

Aragel sighed. "It's not a weakness, is it?"

Tnasha waved her hand. "He'll grow out of it. He just needs to get out more."

Shadon put his tongue in his cheek. "He needs to get *out* more?"

"Sure. The more he gets out and interacts with a variety of people, the less likely he'll feel anxiety in a new situation."

"It sounds too easy."

"I can manage," Aragel said. "I have done all right so far."

Tnasha smiled in agreement. "I think so, too." She quickly changed the subject. "So there was a sorcerer in on Hermond's plan to kill King Darak, you were saying?"

"Can sorcerers do that? Disappear and materialize someplace else?" Aragel asked.

Tnasha shrugged. The idea of a sorcerer with such power gave her chills. "I don't know for sure, but I suppose it's possible."

Aragel squeezed his eyes shut and yawned. "I can't think about this any more tonight. I need to sleep to get my thoughts in order."

Tnasha nodded. At the same time, she was disappointed that she was not going to hear more about the sorcerer. Not tonight anyway.

Shadon did not want to discuss it anymore either. There were so many possibilities to the situation it was hard to keep them all straight. "I'm tired, too. I'm going to bed."

Tnasha did not push them. Instead, she joined them. Feeling tired, she too resigned herself to sleep.

●

Alena found herself standing alone in a quiet spot near the stern of the ship. From her pocket, she pulled a pipe and a small blue sachet half full of slightly damp tobacco. How it had survived the journey so far was beyond her. She had almost forgotten about it. After shoving a small amount into the pipe, she used a small stick of wood lit by the lantern she carried to light the tobacco. She inhaled deeply, letting the rich, fragrant smoke fill her lungs. She exhaled, watching the smoke trail off into the darkness.

"Do you mind if I smoke with you?" Captain Adarack Vogman had approached her in silence.

Alena offered her pipe.

"I've brought my own." He pulled out his own pipe, lighting it. "If you do not mind me asking, how is it you came to travel with a wayward sorceress?"

Alena smiled. "Who told you?"

"Shadon gave me some details. Things he's heard."

"I wouldn't call her wayward. Tnasha has never really used her sorcery until recently. I met her in military training. We were the only two women in training for the front line."

"Hmm. Why doesn't she use it? Her sorcery?"

Alena inhaled from the pipe again. "I don't know. She's always been kind of strange about it. The whole sorcery thing. I don't think she has a lot of faith in it."

"Any reason?" Adarack leaned on the railing and gazed out over the water.

"Not that I know of. It could be her father. He's quite…" she paused, searching for the right word, "…demanding?"

Adarack's gaze turned contemplative. "She seems quite grounded. She knows what she wants and she doesn't give up."

"She's smart, but stubborn."

"I take it you did not want to come along?"

She shrugged. "I couldn't let her go to Zul alone if that's what you mean. Like I said, she is too stubborn. If you ask me, it gets her into more trouble than not."

Adarack chuckled.

"I only came to help. And I really had nothing better to do."

He laughed heartily then. "It sounds to me like you have a stubborn streak as well."

She shot him a look of disagreement and rolled her eyes. "No, I'm more practical than the rest of them. I see this for what it is."

"And what, exactly, is it?" He raised an eyebrow, and began to fill his pipe a second time.

"It's the gods testing us."

"The gods?" He laughed again. "Nonsense."

"It has to be. There is no other explanation."

"What are they testing? Your strategic ability? I doubt very much there is a need for tactical superiority in the afterlife."

Alena tipped her head to one side. "No. They are testing our resolve and ability."

"If they are gods, they already know such things without having to administer tests."

"Are you sure?"

"Are you sure you are being tested?"

"The gods do not shout. They merely whisper."

Adarack shrugged. "Or perhaps they're always talking, but we're too busy living our own lives to stop and listen."

Alena looked up at him and smiled. "Maybe."

"I wonder what the gods would say about getting some sleep."

"They would probably say it was a good idea." She held her pipe over the ship railing and dumped the residue from the used tobacco into the water below, then rinsed the pipe out with a splash of water from her canteen. "It was nice talking to you."

Adarack continued to take puffs from his pipe. "Likewise."

She turned from him and walked steadily toward where her friends had set up sleeping arrangements above deck, wondering if the gods were always talking. For a moment, she stopped and listened to the silence, half expecting to hear the voices of the gods drifting on the warm wind.

●

Tnasha could not sleep. She thought about Kolgern. She thought about the necklace and of Morvack. She never noticed that the necklace carried any power. She did, however, notice Morvack's. His energy was crimson fire slipping through his body with fluidity. Eventually, the fire image drew her into her nightmare.

The horses were charging again. She stood on a cliff overlooking a deep blue ocean. The water below crashed onto jagged rocks; a cacophony of death. The sky was a dome of blood, heated by a single fiery orb. Then they came, hordes of them, dressed in their gold colored armor. Spikes protruding leather and chain mail with great broadswords affixed at their sides. They stopped before her, removing their helms of death. A man she did not recognize dismounted; his earth radiance jagged and chaotic around him. Around his neck was her amulet that now breathed its own violet fire.

The man's eyes were cold and unforgiving. Then she heard a voice. "You are nothing but an insignificant force. You will fail," it said. The voice was deep, dripping with anger. The man's lips did not move.

A vision of the serpent god Dagon flashed before her. Then the dream receded.

Tnasha woke with her breath caught in her throat and sat straight up. Morning's first light assaulted her eyes. But something was wrong. It was too quiet or too warm or too something. She could not quite place it. Then she noticed that the ship's crew, along with her friends, stood silent, staring into the gray water around them. Tnasha looked around, confused.

Shadon helped her to her feet and motioned for silence. She looked at him bewildered. "There's a large shark circling the ship just beneath the water," he whispered.

Tnasha raised an eyebrow. "A shark?"

Shadon nodded wordlessly.

Her eyes traveled to the bow of the ship where a lone man stood aiming a harpoon. The harpoon moved slowly, following the shark through the water below. Then suddenly, in one loud snap the harpoon let sail through the air as others followed. Tnasha noticed then that there were other harpoons following lead.

"We've got it!" cried one of the men. The crew cheered.

"Why are they using a harpoon on a shark?" Alena asked in a loud, disapproving voice. "Why are they killing sharks?"

Kolgern shrugged. "Why not? Sharks are just carnivorous fish."

Captain Vogman stood only a few yards away. "You like eating, don't you?" he asked her.

Alena nodded with an exaggerated smile. "Eating sharks... yummy." She mumbled something inaudible as she moved behind Kolgern.

Kolgern turned around to look at her. "What? I've heard shark is delicious."

Shadon nodded in agreement. "It is. The first time I ate shark I was a boy. I've had it quite a few times since then. I think it tastes just like any other fish. Perhaps better."

Tnasha shrugged her shoulders and sat back down against the deck railing. She closed her eyes. They were on their way to Zul and they did not even have so much as a plan to get the amulet back. It was clear that she intended to use her sorcery. She was still not sure how. A simple weather working was not going to save her or her friends. In her mind, a list began forming. She would use elemental magick—yes. But how?

Shadon and Kolgern joined her while Alena watched in awe as the crewmen of the *Narassa* hoisted the shark up with pulleys, chain, and rope, preparing to set it on the main deck of the ship.

"So what do we do for the next day?" Shadon asked.

Kolgern snickered. "We could help cut up the shark. But

we'll probably end up helping to clean the deck this time after they've finished with the carcass."

"I need to practice my sorcery," Tnasha told them.

Both men looked at her with narrowed eyes and crinkled brows. Shadon was the first to question her statement. "What are you going to do?"

"I'm going to turn the boat into a carriage." She realized her own sarcasm too late. "I'm sorry. I didn't mean to be rude."

Shadon was not offended. He had no reason to be. He could understand her frustration. He had been there a few times himself. Not with sorcery, but with his experience in gathering information in hostile territory. This situation was no different. "If all of this is connected like you suspect, I was thinking that maybe I should go with you to Zul. Perhaps I can find some answers and help to get the amulet back. After all, we don't need them having any more advantage over us, right?"

Tnasha felt her stomach jump. "I can't put you in danger."

"I'd be putting myself in danger."

"Who would protect King Aragel?"

Shadon did not have a quick answer for that question. It seemed strange to him to hear Aragel referred to as king. But it was true. Aragel *was* a king now. Who would take care of Aragel? "He could stay with Adarack."

"You don't sound convinced. Neither am I. The only protection he can get is from you, and us."

The idea was almost too inane for him to imagine it. "You mean I should bring him with us? They've already killed one king."

"Why not? He seems smart enough. Enough common sense is all you need for survival. I won't let them hurt him. I'm a sorceress, remember?"

"Hmm. On an island filled with Kersian enemies? And from what I've heard your sorcery is, at best, questionable. I don't know. It seems too risky."

Tnasha thought it over for a moment. "Do any of us really have a choice? Sherok is already under Exavian rule, and you're in hiding because between you and Danaria lyes a greater danger. The best way is to hit them at the source."

"What do you mean?"

"If we take down the Kersian sorcerers at the source, then we have a better chance of getting Sherok back. You know, Sorcerer Kalath told me what was about to happen was a fated prophecy. If this is true, then none of us has a choice. We all have to go."

"How do we know if we have a choice?"

The answer came from her lips quickly, as if it was not a conscious answer at all. "You'll have to follow your instincts." In a strange way, Shadon's support eased Tnasha's worried mind. "We need a plan and part of that plan lies in knowing how to fight sorcery with sorcery. Which is why I need to practice my *questionable* sorcery."

Kolgern, who had sat quietly without interrupting, nodded. "She's right. Shadon and I will worry about how we're going get into the city, and into Gavgal's palace. You worry about the sorcery."

"There's a slight problem. We don't know the terrain of Zul. How are we going to find what we need to find?" Shadon asked.

"You may not know Zul. But I do. Do you remember the Crystal Oracle?" Kolgern stretched his arms in front of him and yawned. A proud, boasting smile adorned his face.

"Oh. That's right," Shadon said. "I remember hearing about that."

Alena still watched as the shark was lowered to the deck, covering the mass of it. "What about the oracle?" she asked distantly.

"Who do you think stole it back from the Kersians?" Shadon asked her.

She turned her attention on them. "You mean Kolgern did that? I don't believe it."

Kolgern nodded proudly with a raised eyebrow. "All by myself."

Tnasha laughed lightly and gave Kolgern a playful swat. "Some things never change, but all for the better."

He grinned back. "Hey—I'm a good thief. Always have

been. It's all in who you're stealing from and why."

The four quieted and watched as Adarack's men worked, cutting the meat from the shark. Finally, Tnasha stood and walked away, looking for a quiet place where she could practice her sorcery.

CHAPTER 23

Termark O'Schoitt took a deep breath. Sweat dripped from his dark, brown hair, trickled down his forehead and cheeks, and finally soaked into his beard. His head throbbed a dull ache, and he was tired. Even his maroon mana seemed to move more slowly in fatigue. The only traces of Tnasha they had been able to find were bits of violet mana residue left behind. With each step, he feared he would find the unthinkable. Her broken body huddled somewhere along the path. He shuddered at the thought, feeling nauseated. The mere thought of his only daughter dying by the hands of his enemy was something he tossed to the back of his mind. His hopes of finding her spurred him on. Around him, hundreds of men spread themselves amongst the trees, and as one long line they searched for anything they could find that would provide a clue to what happened.

For the first time in years, the Sirus had failed. It seemed doubtful they would find Warlord Kyran's daughter either. Now, his daughter and her friends, Alena and Kolgern, were missing as well. A knot sat in the base of his throat, unmoved by hard swallows and deep sighs. Earlier that day they came upon a recently abandoned Kersian city hiding in the depths of the forest.

The Sirus legions destroyed the city immediately upon finding infant bones near an altar to the no-name god. While the coals were still warm, there was no evidence of a recent sacrifice. Though they had found traces of Tnasha's mana near the base of the temple, and a plethora of hoof prints leading from the city into the Selenia Forest. Whatever happened had interrupted an ongoing ritual, and caused everyone within the small city to flee. *Were they summoned back to Zul by their high priest?* Termark wondered.

It was his hope that Tnasha was still alive, even though she was a prisoner of the Kersians who had inhabited the clandestine encampment.

"We are approaching the salt marshes, Lord Termark. Should we stop?" a young scout asked the tired warlord, pulling him from his thoughts.

Termark did not want to stop searching. He hoped, no, he *knew* Tnasha was not dead. It was an instinctive feeling. His only solace was in Kalath. If Tnasha was injured, dead, or captured, Kalath would know. His scrying abilities were adept and proven. Very few sorcerers had the ability to see things as he did.

"We'll go into the salt marshes," he said to the soldiers. A young soldier relayed the order among the men.

It seemed they rode for hours. The narrow paths leading through the forest were well marked, torn asunder by the hooves of many horses. Much of the brush was broken. Tnasha had undoubtedly come this way, on horseback. The closer they got to Kalath's reclusive cave, the muddier the ground became. A storm must have come through as well. The paths became thick puddles of slurping mud left from the rain.

As they approached the clearing, the bridge leading to the cave came into full view. There, between several trees, they found a lone, pregnant mare grazing on some weeds. Termark could tell she was pregnant. He had kept many brood mares in his years. Her saddle hung half off and her bridle was broken. One of her hooves was packed with a stone bruise dressing. Near her lay a pack. One of the soldiers dismounted and picked up the pack. He opened it, peered inside, and brought it to Termark.

The warlord opened it immediately, scanning the contents. Inside were herbs, books, bread, dried meat, and several blankets. He handed the pack back to the soldier and looked around wordlessly. The ground was marred with hoof marks as if a legion had passed through this way.

Termark's mind began racing. "We will take the mare back to the city along with the items. Wait until we secure the area, first." He had a frightening thought and brushed it aside. There was a chance someone merely lost a horse, but he knew he was wrong.

Immediately, he found himself facing the rickety bridge. The horses and men moved clamorously through the thick, barren mud. Puddles of deep standing water stagnated in the heat. The rain had been heavy and flooded the already wet marshland. It was the season for such weather. He crossed the bridge into the clearing near the opening of the cave. Dismounting, he looked around. Potted herbs had been set on boulders, having survived the storm. Termark scanned the dead trees, until finally his eyes settled on one in particular. A violet mana emanated from the tree's trunk. As strange as it seemed, the tree boasted a full canopy of living, healthy leaves. He walked to it, around it, and finally tipped his head back looking up at it. He set his thick square hand upon the rough bark.

"Shall we go inside the cave, sir?" a lieutenant asked.

"Yes, secure the cave. I will be there in a moment." He took a deep breath and touched the violet mana. Clearly, Tnasha had been here. She had escaped the Kersians, it seemed. She would not have led the Kersians here. No. They must have come after her and recaptured her. It seemed the logical conclusion. Undoubtedly her friends and Kyran's daughter would have been with her.

With a moment of hesitation, he turned and went inside the cave only to find that most items had been hastily moved to high shelves, and Kalath was nowhere. Several bowls of dried gruel were left hastily behind. On a shelf on the far wall, Termark saw it. A bloody piece of torn black cloth from a Sirus soldier's tunic. If Tnasha was injured, she may have come here, though Termark could not be sure. Why did she not simply come home? Perhaps it was too dangerous. He trusted his daughter's judgment. If she came to Kalath, she must have had good reason.

He picked up a blanket similar to one they had found with the mare earlier. Then it occurred to him. It started making sense. They were interrupted. Something bad happened and they abandoned the cave quickly. Kalath had been trying to get back to Danaria, possibly with an injured Tnasha and friends, but they ran into the Kersians, who had abandoned their small city for some unknown reason. He shook his head.

Warlord Kyran stepped into the cave cautiously behind him. "Lord Termark."

Termark turned to him. "They were here when the flood came. They escaped the Kersians, The Kersians pursued them. Beyond that I'm not sure."

Kyran scratched his hand. His expression remained placid. "Where would the Kersians have taken them?"

"Zul." Termark looked at Kyran expectantly. Kyran was exhausted. He had been fighting a battle on the southern front of Danaria when his daughter was taken. It was doubtful he had slept much since. "Are you coming with me?"

Warlord Kyran nodded. "How many men will we bring?"

Without so much as a pause, Termark answered. "Three warships and six hundred men."

Kyran smirked. "Will that be enough?"

"They'll wish they had kept to themselves when we're finished with them." He put his hand on Kyran's shoulder. "We're going to find all four of them, and Sorcerer Kalath, too."

Kyran nodded with a half-hearted smile. They retreated from the cave to the soldiers waiting for them.

Termark wasted no time. "You." He pointed to one of the commanders. "Take thirty men back to Danaria with the mare. Inform the high council and General Daxin that we will be taking war ships to Zul."

The obvious surprise on the commander's face begged for some clarification of the order. Upon seeing this, Warlord Kyran lifted an eyebrow. "Don't question the orders. Follow them. If you run into any trouble on your way back, kill it."

Several of the other commanding officers snickered. When in doubt, save yourself by killing the threat. Perhaps the most violent of Danarian tenants of war, reserved only for dire situations. The commander in charge of the thirty saluted and picked his men. Upon finishing, they turned toward Danaria with the pregnant mare in tow.

Kyran and Termark exchanged glances. "You." Termark picked another commander from the soldiers. Take twenty men to Morasta. Assemble our legions and war ships. Meet the rest of us in Orana Tulk."

The soldier nodded, saluted, and did as he was told. The first rule of Danarian warfare. Do what your commanding officer tells you immediately and without question.

"The rest of you, follow us. We should be in Orana Tulk by nightfall."

They headed out at an even trot with one hundred fifty soldiers at their command. Late morning turned to afternoon, to evening and dusk. They arrived in Orana Tulk, or what was left of it, just as the suns last rays descended behind the Onyx Mountains in the west. Looking over the remains of their small port city, they realized the Kersians had been busy. Several survivors rummaged through the burnt out husks of buildings searching for the dead and any salvageable belongings.

Kyran turned to Termark. "How many times has it been now?"

"Fourteen in the last twenty-five years." Termark shook his head. "I guess we'll need to rebuild again. I've told the council numerous times that we need a permanent outpost here."

"I think they're worried we'll deplete our forces by placing so many soldiers on the front like this."

Termark laughed. "Perhaps it would discourage them, or in the very least, keep the damage minimal."

"It's all politics, my friend. It's less expensive and more convenient to keep rebuilding the city, rather than continually replenish troops."

A young woman carrying a bundle of rags approached them. "They were Kersians, I tell you. But they was with Exavians." She pulled a sword from the mound of cloth, and handed it to Kyran. "We killed one of 'em. My husband says he ain't never seen a sword like 'iss." She turned and walked back toward the charred remains of the buildings leaving the sword for Kyran's inspection.

Termark turned his horse and rode into what had once been the center of the city. "Hear me." When he was sure he had the attention of the remaining residents of Orana Tulk, spies and merchants alike, he continued, "We are at war with the Kersians. This time, however, we are not taking a passive defense. Make sure this message is passed on. All Kersians will be considered hostile." He paused, then added for effect: "We do not take prisoners."

It was a sure way to make certain the whole world knew that the Kersians had overstepped their boundaries for the last time. Termark was tired of the council's apathy. They did not seem to mind the continuing war games. But the soldiers and people of Danaria were tired. Many of them exhausted, broken men who wanted nothing more than a better life for their children. Deep down, Termark could feel the war coming on. Something like he had never seen in his entire fifty-eight years. It was just beginning.

The soldiers pitched camp and went about gathering information from Orana Tulk's determined residents. Termark and Kyran set to work laying out their battle plan. It took several hours before any of the soldiers returned with news.

A young soldier, no more than twenty, approached Termark and Kyran with uncertainty. "Lord Termark." He saluted.

"Speak."

"Tnasha, Alena, and Kolgern were all seen by the inn-keeper. They stayed at his inn and left right before the attack."

Termark was afraid to ask. He steadied his voice. "Were they among the dead?"

"No, sir."

Termark breathed a sigh of relief. He felt guilty because there was no mention of Kyran's daughter, Rassia.

Just then, one of the commanders approached. "Tnasha was seen talking to a ship captain right before the attack. It's likely they are on a ship and escaped the raid."

Kyran spoke then, not hiding the excitement in his

voice. "It sounds like they were not prisoners after all. But perhaps they were following the Kersians because *they* have Rassia."

Termark nodded wordlessly. "You are both dismissed."

When the soldiers had left them Kyran spoke again. "You have a brave daughter."

"When she gets an idea in her head she rarely lets it go." Termark smiled. She was, indeed, a brave woman. And very stubborn, which got Tnasha into trouble more often than not.

"You have to admire her perseverance. If my daughter survives it will be because of her."

Termark set his jaw and looked out to the ocean noticing the outlines of three Danarian war ships approaching the harbor in the distance. "Let us pray they all survive."

CHAPTER 24

Kalath awoke with a dull throbbing in his skull. He found himself covered loosely with a gray blanket, lying on the cold wood floor of a ship's cargo hold. The room was dark except for a small portal window high on the wall. A thin beam of light hit the floor. He could see an outline of someone else against the far wall.

He lifted himself from the floor. "Where are we?"

Rassia's voice, strangly calm, greeted him. "We've been captured by the Kersians."

Kalath jumped up only to discover his hands were bound in front of him. "Have they hurt you?"

Her voice came at him from the blackness, void of enthusiasm, and filled with resignation. "No. They put me in here with you this morning. Did you know Morvack's religion doesn't allow him to have a family?"

He began walking around the room, stumbling over crates. "Nonsense. Morvack's brother, Gavgal, killed all the Kersian sorceresses before Morvack was old enough to remember."

She gasped. "Why would he do such a thing?"

He finally made his way to her and sat down beside her with some effort. "Gavgal is impotent. He could not beget children. As punishment, each woman was killed when she did not become impregnated. He killed his own mother."

"No. Truly?" The horror was clear in her voice.

Kalath took a deep breath and looked around again, leaning his head against the wood wall. "Of course it's true. I am a seer. What Gavgal did not anticipate in his own selfish rage, was that he would kill off his own family line by doing what he did. Thus forcing his brothers to endure the same sorrow and loneliness as himself."

"That's horrible. Poor Morvack."

Kalath could scarcely believe his ears. "Poor Morvack? Young lady, he means to kill you."

"I know, but it's still sad." She fidgeted with the blankets in front of her.

Kalath noticed this. Her hands were unbound. He held his bound hands up to her. "Since you are free, would you mind?"

"Oh. Sorry." She pulled at the knots, undoing them carefully one at a time until she finally pulled the rope from his hands.

He rubbed his wrists. They were raw and sore, much like the rest of him. His body had endured many years of discomfort. As he got older, he tolerated it less. "Do not worry, Rassia. Things will happen, as they should, as the prophecies have been foretold. We are but a small part of a larger war."

"I know," she said, again with defeat.

Kalath put his arm around her, pulling her to him. "I mean that things will be all right. You are not going to die."

"Are you sure?" she asked in a small voice.

Kalath bit his tongue. He knew Tnasha would arrive at Zul. But the vision stopped there. The fate of Rassia and himself was as much a mystery to him, though he did not tell her that.

Without warning the door cracked open, and three soldiers entered, swords drawn, a lantern lighting their way. The blackness of the room hid their faces.

"Get up, heathen sorcerer."

Kalath stood, looking down at Rassia. She hung her head, refusing to look up at her captors. He drew in a deep breath. "I assume I have been summoned by Morvack."

"He must be a seer after all," quipped another of the soldiers. They chuckled, grabbing Kalath by the arms and dragging him from the room.

They were much taller than Kalath. He saw no reason to struggle. It was a short distance between the cargo hold in which they were held and Morvack's quarters. When they entered the room, Kalath was tossed to the floor at Morvack's feet. The soldiers remained in the room.

"Stand and come to the table."

Kalath looked up at the Kersian sorcerer, noting the dark circles beneath his eyes. It gave him some satisfaction knowing the Kersian gotten no sleep. He took his time getting to his feet.

"You are going to prove your scrying abilities," Morvack said.

"Forcibly?"

"If I must." Morvack nodded at one of the soldiers.

Kalath felt the blade of a sword on his back, and for the first time noticed a bowl of water on the table next to the Kersian sorcerer. "I see."

"I certainly hope you do. For your benefit." Morvack motioned to the table and narrowed his eyes. "Now, I want to know where the sorceress is."

"And if I see nothing?"

Morvack's upper lip curled into a sneer. "You had better see something or you are worth nothing to me. I would just as soon throw your corpse overboard."

Sorcerer Kalath stepped past Morvack to the table. He took another deep breath, attempting to cleanse the negative energy from his mana. "I will need silence."

Morvack lifted an eyebrow with a quick sideward glance at the soldiers. "Fine."

He began then. Holding his hands above the bowl of water he crossed them, closed his eyes and slowly opened them. The water clouded, then cleared. With clarity he could see the images. Tnasha was on a ship on her way to Zul. "She is on a ship."

Morvack moved to his side, peering over his shoulder.

"Where is she?"

By the way Morvack squinted into the water with searching eyes, Kalath could tell the Kersian sorcerer saw nothing. He did not have the ability for sight. Kalath bit his lower lip and let out a sigh of exasperation. "On her way to Zul. Obviously."

Morvack's dark eyes bore into Kalath's only inches away. "Obvious to you, perhaps. Tell me more."

"What else is there to tell?"

"Her attack plan."

"I see images. I do not see thoughts nor do I hear words. I do not know what other information I can give you. I can tell you I see her clearly on a ship bound for Zul."

"Hmm. Then how is it you know for certain she is going to Zul?"

Kalath met Morvack's glare steadfast. "Because that is where I told her she should go."

"Look into the future then, old man. What happens when she arrives at Zul."

Kalath looked back into the bowl. "I can tell you we arrive well before she does."

The Kersian sorcerer smiled and said proudly, "Just as I planned. From which direction does she arrive?"

"I see nothing more than a small paddle boat in the midst of night."

"Which night?"

Kalath shrugged his shoulders. "I do not know that."

After pulling a chair to the table, Morvack sat down, leaning in to the scrying bowl as if searching for the pictures he could not see. "There must be something."

"I can give you nothing else. I see a ruined temple. A gathering of soldiers. Chaos. I see nothing else." Kalath was not lying. The pictures faded into the blackness of the water. The water cleared until finally, all he could see was the bottom of the bowl.

"Very well." Morvack stood. "Take the heathen back to the cargo hold. We will try again when we reach Zul. We should be there by morning."

"So quickly?"

Morvack grinned. "Let us just say that I have a way with wind working."

"That's good to know," Kalath whispered beneath his breath.

The soldiers led him back to the cargo hold where Rassia paced frantically. Once the door closed and they were alone in the darkness, she spoke. "What did he want?"

"He wanted me to scry for information." He crept to the far wall adjacent the door and slid to the ground, putting his head in his hands.

"Are you going to be all right?" She sat beside him and pulled her knees to her chest.

Kalath nodded. "I'll be fine. I tire more easily when I exert my mana. Nothing more than old age." His voice drifted off into silence.

Rassia let out a heavy sigh. "How long before we get to Zul?"

"By morning."

She gasped. "So quickly?

"It seems Morvack has the ability to manipulate the wind. This is a smaller ship. Tnasha will not arrive until late tomorrow night."

"Did you tell him that?"

Kalath gave her a shocked look. "By Natyis, no! I will feed him small amounts of weak information. Not anything sufficiently revealing to aid him."

"Good."

"May I get some rest now? You should rest, too."

Rassia sighed another heavy sigh, pulling the thin blanket Morvack's minions had provided tightly around her. "It's too cold to sleep."

"Come here." Kalath held his arms open. She leaned against him. He wrapped his arms around her and closed his eyes. That night Sorcerer Kalath drifted in and out of sleep, plagued by nightmares of serpents and a coming sorcerer's war.

CHAPTER 25

Tnasha found herself a quiet spot near the rear of the ship's deck. There she sat, staring into the water and gathering her concentration. For her part of the plan, she had decided upon an elemental spell to raise a tempest. A strong gale wind perhaps. But she would only let it blow for a few minutes. After all, she did not want to arrive at Zul any faster than intended. A violent storm, with lightening, rain, and heavy wind would surly work to her advantage on Zul. Provided the Kersian sorcerers could not counteract her. But no two sorcerers had the same gifts to the same degree. Not usually.

She gathered her will and focused, speaking the incantation from memory. "Icar. Yana. Hoet. Tempeste. Come forth and reveal thyself to me. Dagon, keeper of the skies, I pray thee. Come forth."

The incantation did not work. The wind remained as soft and gentle as it was before. Strangely, it even seemed to die down a bit. "Well that didn't work," she said aloud. She put her hand to her chin and began dissecting the incantation word by word.

Suddenly, the water broke and a serpent rose from the ocean's depth. Its eyes were the color of emeralds, its scales and horns a snake-like blend of yellow and darkest gray. One clawed appendage reached out, grabbing the ship by the railing and pulling it to a complete stop. Silence overcame the crew and captain. Tnasha winced.

She had just realized she said the incantation wrong. Dagon was the serpent God of water. "Oops," she said in a small voice. It should have been *Dagona*, and had she said it that way the sorcery would have worked. But it was so simple to mix the words up. And her concentration was focused on the water, which had not helped matters any.

She quickly decided to amend the magic. This time she focused on the sky above while avoiding the serpent's stare. "Icar. Yana. Hoet. Tempeste. Come forth and reveal thyself to me. Dagona, keeper of the skies, I pray thee. Come forth with gale and drive this serpent from here!"

She stopped, waiting to see what amending the incantation might do. She was not sure she should have done it. But it was done. There was nothing she could do now. The serpent moved to the side of the ship, keeping one glassed eye on Tnasha, and took the shark from the deck, carefully avoiding the people around it. In one swallow, the shark vanished into the beast. The serpent then turned to Tnasha and lowered its head to her. She did what any intelligent sorcerer would have done. She backed away.

"I appreciate the sacrifice. It was a kind gesture," the thing said, water seeping from its mouth. Hot, fish breath emanated from the serpent, hitting her square in the face.

Tnasha gulped at the knot in her throat. She closed her eyes tight. "This is a dream. It's all a bad dream," she assured herself.

A beastly chuckle boomed from the great beast. "No, it is not a dream, sorceress. Why have you summoned me?"

When she heard the beast speak her hands began shaking, her knees trembling. Never before had she been so scared. She had no response for the beast. Instead, she tried the brief rite again. This time with more will, focusing her energy through her body and to her hands where it released a sharp tingling feeling through her fingertips. Repeating the incantation, she pretended the beast was not there at all. Suddenly the wind rose and the air chilled. The hair on the back of her neck stiffened as large, angry waves bludgeoned the hull of the ship. Fierce clouds swept through the sky as if beckoned by the wind, churning black and heavy and bringing lightning in its wake.

Then unexpectedly, everything fell silent and the serpent retreated into the ocean beneath the darkened sky. There they sat inside the eye of a hurricane. They were straight in its center. On all sides, miles out, walls of clouds encompassed them. Tnasha looked up, seeing a break in the clouds directly above them. The clouds surrounding the opening swirled as if a reverse drain were pulling them into the cosmos.

"Oh, damn us to Arkeereon's pits! Another hurricane!" shouted Captain Vogman from behind her. The deck hands stood ready, pulling themselves from their stalemate and expecting the worst. Meanwhile, the serpent had descended far beneath the water and disappeared. The eye was shifting, and the storm moved closer toward them.

Then it came.

Waves of gray water smashed against the ship, throwing Tnasha back against a mast pole. Water poured from the sky as even larger waves bounded over the ship, covering her and descending. Tnasha grabbed onto some ropes tied around the mast and held on.

"What have I done?" she asked no one.

It seemed like the storm beat the ship forever, tossing it forward frantically until finally, hours later the storm subsided as quickly as it had come. Now tired and soaked to the bone, the crew breathed relief.

A loud cry pierced the strange silence. "There is a sorceress on this ship!"

With this new discovery, the weary crew assembled, whispering and pointing.

Tnasha rolled her eyes, noticing that still the ship moved onward, toward its original destination. Looking up at the stars in the now clear sky, she realized how far the storm had actually tossed them. They were getting closer to Zul.

Captain Vogman glared at her, visibly upset, yet he said nothing. Tnasha could sense his anger. After checking on her friends, bruised and soaked as she was, she went to Captain Vogman to express her apologies.

Vogman stood at the railing, looking down on the now calm water. He spoke to her as if he knew she was behind him. "Sorcery? On my ship?" He turned to her. "I do not allow sorcery on my ship!"

Tnasha looked down at her feet, wondering what to say. She then raised her eyes to meet his. "I am sorry. I didn't mean to scare you."

"It is not a matter of scaring people. I will not have sorcery on this ship!"

"I do not have a choice but to practice. Besides, there were no signs posted." Her head began throbbing.

"On my ship?"

"Wherever I happen to be."

Adarack turned away, then whirled about on his heel and stepped up to her. "You could have killed us! You could have ruined my precious cargo. For all I know, my crew could be planning to lynch you. Some of them are very superstitious. I was hoping they would not find out."

"You knew?"

"Of course I knew. Shadon told me after you came aboard. You could have killed us!"

"I believe 'could have' means I did not. Your ship and cargo are fine. No one died. And I didn't know that I needed to be discreet. Shadon knew. My friends knew. I assumed no one cared." Tnasha felt the aggression consume her in a flood of energy. It ran the length of her body from her toes all the way to the base of her skull, but she held it back.

"You are reckless and not a very good sorceress at that."

Tnasha lifted her eyebrows. "That's *exactly* why I have to practice. Imagine a world of feral sorcerers who have not been allowed to learn how to control their abilities."

A slow grin spread across Adarack's stern face. His expression softened. "You could have practiced someplace other than my ship. Though I do admit *you need* practice. A *lot* of practice."

Tnasha shrugged her shoulders. "Well, yeah, I suppose.

But I happened to be on your ship when the need for practice called."

Shadon let out a chuckle. "You are your father's daughter."

She turned to him, startled. "What's that suppose to mean?"

Shadon did not answer.

Adarack shook his head as a crewman approached, whispering something into his ear. He nodded and said, "Get one of the paddle boats ready. Our guests will have to leave us here."

"But we're in the middle of nowhere." Tnasha could scarcely believe her ears. One infraction of sorcery...

Adarack turned to her and leaned in. "Your little storm tossed us further out than you expected. Zul is two leagues to the north. This is as close as I will get to that damned place." He turned and shook his head at Shadon, leaving Tnasha agape.

She went to her friends. "Vogman is throwing us off the ship and it's my fault."

Shadon began laughing. "Adarack is not throwing you off. This really *is* as close to Zul as he wants to get. Trust me. Sorcery he can handle. Kersians, he cannot."

"We're not prepared." Kolgern said with obvious displeasure.

Shadon boasted a wide grin. "Well, let's hope Tnasha can work some of her flawed sorcery to our advantage when we get there. Natyis knows we'll need it."

"Oh wipe that stupid grin off your face," Alena said, stamping her small foot.

Shadon cleared his throat. "Let me gather some things. I'll get King Aragel."

Alena gasped. "We can't bring that boy with us. I don't want to be responsible for a Sherokean King. This is going to be a dangerous mission as it is."

"I will be responsible for the king. Besides, we don't have much of a choice, do we? Those raiders back at the port were not common barbarians. He has Kersians and Exavians after him. The last place they would expect to find him is on Zul." Shadon forced a grin.

Kolgern gave him a blank look. "Instinct?"

"You bet it's instinct." Shadon left to find Aragel.

Kolgern threw his hands up with a deep sigh. "Are we all following instinct?"

With a scowl, Alena shrugged.

Tnasha yawned. The sorcery made her tired. She thought of the ritual. She would have to remind herself to do another once they arrived on Zul. She needed strength now more than ever. Maintaining hope and confidence when she could scarcely cast a simple incantation was wearing enough. "Traveling on the left horse black," she said aloud.

"What?" Kolgern looked at her, puzzled.

Tnasha yawned again as Alena handed her a sword and dagger. She took them and ran her belt through the scabbard, then put the belt back on. "What will save us. *Instinct.*"

CHAPTER 26

Commander Corigerg found himself conveniently kept away from Princess Serena. The wedding moved along as planned. More quickly in fact. His only solace was in knowing that the princess had spoken with the tavern keeper about the tomatoes. She was certainly full of surprises. The counter-attack on the Exavian army was also proceeding as planned. All of Sherok stood afraid behind closed doors. Afraid enough to organize a resistance. Now that Serena knew the truth, he felt more comfortable about moving forward. Serena's knowledge was not obvious. She played Prince Hermond like a fine tuned instrument, using her womanly attributes as a weapon to keep Prince Hermond quiet and close. Unsuspecting. Smart girl. The commander had not given her enough credit.

He went about his daily duties, as if nothing had changed, under the watchful eyes of the general. A general with no name, he mused. For no one ever called the general anything more than the general. In Corigerg's eyes, it was akin to an executioner remaining anonymous. He brushed the thought from his mind and swallowed a mouthful of whisky.

"Another, Commander?"

"No. I'm fine. I must get back to the castle. I have security details to attend to."

The tavern keeper nodded.

Corigerg walked back to the castle deep in thought. Suppose the attack did not work? *Oh, come now*, he told himself. *Failure is something we will not even consider until it becomes the only option.* As he arrived at the castle, he looked up. Princess Serena stood at a window high above him looking out. He saluted her and entered the castle, heading straight to the command center. He reported to the general now.

•

Serena smiled when Corigerg saluted her. She sighed. Hermond was still speaking with a guard at the door. "Make sure no one bothers me for the next few hours," she heard him say.

She turned from the window. "Can we not have a moment's peace from all of these soldiers?"

He closed the door and turned to her with a sly grin. "Now we can. I have to make certain the kingdom's affairs are being handled, my dear."

She put on her own wily grin. "Have they found any marauders coming to kidnap me and whisk me away?"

"Now you're being sarcastic."

She smiled playfully at him. "Perhaps you can pretend you've kidnapped me."

Hermond licked his lips. "Do not tempt me to break with tradition."

"I think I want to take a nap." She jumped onto the bed.

"No you don't. Why don't we go for a ride?"

Serena smiled, pleased. It would be the first time she had been riding in a long time. With any luck, she could gauge the overall morale of the Sherokean people. Then again, she wondered if being seen in public with Hermond would make the people lose faith in her. They had to know she was on their side, didn't they? "Let us ride through the vineyards then. So we can have some privacy."

Hermond smiled. He took her hands in his and kissed each one lightly. "I shall see you at the stables shortly." He kissed her full on the lips, then left.

When he had gone, she wiped her mouth in disgust. She took her time putting on riding breeches, then, slowly made her way to the stables, stopping to idly chat with servants and unnerved Sherokean soldiers as she went. When she reached the stables, Hermond already had a horse saddled for her.

"This gelding should be gentle enough." Hermond handed her the reins. "Can you manage, or would you like a hand?"

Serena noticed his careful choice of words. She snickered silently to herself. "I can manage, thank you." She mounted.

He mounted his bay mare and turned her toward the vineyards. "Tomorrow we shall be married. Are you nervous?"

Serena stared off into the distance, feeling the horse's strong withers move beneath her. "A bit, I suppose. It is to be expected. I so want my wedding to go as planned." She closed her eyes for a moment, feeling the cool breeze on her cheeks, and inhaling the warm, late spring air. Her thoughts wandered to Aragel. With any luck, he had made it to Danaria safely. But what if he didn't make it...? She did not want to think about it.

Hermond broke the silence as they rode through well-manicured fields of grape vines. "The search parties went as far as Orana Tulk. They have not found Aragel yet."

"Perhaps he made it into Danaria."

"Serena, we must consider that perhaps Aragel has been assassinated."

"Why should we assume such things? And furthermore, by whom should we assume he was assassinated?"

"You never know. The Arkeeronish or the Cabalians. If they wanted to extend their territory, it would have been the perfect opportunity. When the search party docked at Orana Tulk they found the city burnt to the ground. There were no survivors."

Serena fought to keep the emotion out of her voice. "If that is the case, then *I* will rule Sherok as queen."

Hermond's smile was condescending. "Do you think your people will accept a matriarch ruler?"

Serena flicked back a lock of long, dark hair. "They will

not have much of a choice."

"Perhaps I should take the throne as king in the meantime. Just until we know what has happened to Aragel."

Serena smiled. "What's the difference? If I become queen, then you would naturally be my king. The balance of power would fall to both of us. Though my first order of business would be to send your troops back to Exavia. Their occupation of our city is making the people uneasy."

Hermond displayed a look of surprise. "Who told you that?"

Serena shook her head and gave him a knowing look. "No one had to tell me. You can see it in the eyes of every Sherokean in the castle. We are not a military people, Hermond. We are peaceful farmers and merchants."

"But Sherok could be so much more."

"Sherok does not want to be more. We enjoy our way of life."

"All things must change. We cannot resist change, Serena. We must embrace it and use it to our advantage to make things better."

She pursed her lips. "It's not a matter of resisting change. It's the way we choose to live. If the situation required such a drastic change, then so be it. But why change if what exists already suits our way of life?"

Hermond thought about this for a moment. She was becoming more difficult to keep in line. He tried to think of a way to convince her that the union of Sherok and Exavia was a good idea. "Change could mean larger profit margins, more lucrative trade agreements, and a stronger Sherokean economy. A strong military will ensure order, and would deter any other country from taking advantage of Sherok."

"You think other countries take advantage of us?"

He had her. "Certainly! Import and export taxes might be better negotiated if the other countries knew Sherok had a strong military. They would be less likely to cheat the Sherokeans and would pay a fair value for goods."

Serena narrowed her eyes. Hermond had outdone himself. "I hadn't looked at it that way. Perhaps you're right.

However, a change of that magnitude should happen over time. It will be easier for people to adapt if the change is gradual. We can discuss the formation of a full time military next week. After the wedding and once things have settled down. Coming up with the money to pay the soldiers is the biggest issue, I think."

Hermond had not thought that far ahead. Sherok was not a rich country. "I may have a few ideas for building resources for military funding. Sherok is in our care now. We will not let anything happen to her." Hermond smiled in triumph.

No, I will not allow anything to happen to Sherok. Little do you know that you will pay for my new military, but not through monetary means, Serena thought. She smiled back.

CHAPTER 27

It was daybreak when the Kersian ship reached Zul. Kalath and Rassia were immediately pulled from their dark prison and escorted to the ship's deck. Morvack stood in waiting. "As we go through the city, I expect both of you to mind your social graces."

Kalath almost burst out laughing. "We are hardly guests."

Morvack smiled. "Well then, consider yourselves guests. I would prefer to escort you to the palace in a civilized manner. Not kicking and screaming like captured ruffians."

Kalath and Rassia exchanged glances as Morvack tossed Rassia a plain, gray peasant's dress. She took it and slipped it over her tattered and dirt-laden clothing, grateful to have something warmer. The cool breeze from the ocean seemed to wash over them. She shivered.

Morvack held out his hand. "Come then. Welcome to Zul."

Kalath smirked and lifted an eyebrow. A group of soldiers surrounded them and escorted them ashore. The city itself did not seem as big as Kalath expected. By the disenchanted look adorning Rassia's face, he could tell it was not what she expected either. No more than five blocks of

222

buildings stood to the left serving as a merchant's pavillian with housing above, and to the right, stood eight blocks of houses. Undoubtedly there were other parts of the city hidden behind the temple and palace. Even so, the small city could not have been home to more than a thousand Kersians.

Reading their minds, Morvack spoke. "It is meager, but it is our home. The holy land of our temples."

Behind the small city loomed the palace of Gavgal to the left, and to the right a temple to the nameless god that stood well above any other building. Both buildings were made of rock and clay, but elegantly so. From where they stood, they could see intricate designed inlays of gold and silver reflecting the morning sun.

They went with the soldiers, Morvack leading them, through the city streets made of white sandstone to the arched entryways of the palace courtyards. It was there they saw him.

Gavgal, with graying hair, brilliant green mana, and eyes to match, emerged from the palace with outstretched, welcoming arms. "Brother. It is good to see you."

Morvack embraced him. Gavgal recoiled slightly, though Kalath was sure Morvack did not notice. To Morvack, Gavgal was the no-name god. Kalath did not hide the look of contempt he wore.

"It has been too long."

Wearing a fake smile, Gavgal's gaze traveled over his brother's shoulder to Kalath and Rassia. He examined them both, then his eyes fixed on Kalath, studying his mana. "What brings you here? With guests, I see."

"I have news. Let us go inside."

"Oh, forgive me. I am so rude. Please, please come in." Gavgal motioned them inside. His forced grin turned to a grimace as Kalath passed him. He held a rough, bony hand up to the guards. "Your presence will not be required. Stay here until you are summoned."

Gavgal joined them inside the vaulted entryway, then led them to a private study off the main corridor. Shelves filled with books lined the walls, and a large, oak desk ornate with gold stood near a large, stained glass window. He motioned

Rassia and Kalath to a polished mahogany bench with crimson velvet cushions.

"Please sit. Be comfortable." He led his brother from the room. Once the door was closed, he looked at Morvack expectantly. "Well?"

Morvack pulled the amulet from inside his tunic, and removed it from around his neck. He handed it to his brother, then tipped his head to show him the scar. "That amulet healed this fatal wound in a very short time."

Gavgal's green eyes examined the amulet with curiosity. "Where did you get it?"

"An anomalous fifth generation sorceress. She is on her way here to retrieve it as we speak."

"What about the old sorcerer and the girl?"

"The girl was a sacrifice. So was the sorceress before I knew she was a sorceress. The sorceress helped the girl escape, then her friends helped the sorceress escape. It was all quite confusing. Anyway, we found the sorcerer harboring the girl."

"Then why is he here?"

"He's a well known seer on the mainland. His name is Kalath. His ability for scrying is unmatched. I thought you might put him to good use. Or kill him, along with the girl. They would both make fitting sacrifices."

An appreciative smile slid over Gavgal's thin lips, and he slipped the amulet over his head. "You have done well. Tell me, is this sorceress of whom you speak trained?"

A smile came to Morvack's lips. "That's the best part. No. She's quite young and inexperienced."

Gavgal narrowed his green eyes. "Then how is it she got away from you?"

Morvack lowered his eyes and the smile vanished. "It was unexpected. She has resourceful friends."

"I see." Gavgal put his hand to his chin in thought. "Is she healthy?"

With a deep breath, Morvack tipped his head and met his brother's eyes. "It seemed so, aside from some injuries sustained during an attack on one of our encampments. Her mana is very strong. She could bear children with twice as much mana if she is not barren."

"Yes. If her mana is strong and she is untrained, how was she involved in an attack?" Gavgal's eyes widened with question.

"She is a Danarian soldier."

"How interesting. Perhaps other sorceresses will follow. They're very stubborn."

"That is what I was hoping for."

Gavgal gave his brother a pat on the back. "I promised you a family, dear brother. And when the other sorceresses come, you may have the next one."

Morvack bent his head. "Yes, thank you, Gavgal."

"You deserve such a reward. Now, shall we rejoin the prisoners?"

Morvack stopped him, pausing to take a deep breath. "There is one other thing. The sorceress is likely to have two friends with her. The ones who interrupted our ritual and who helped her escape from us the first time."

"Are they sorcerers?"

"Mere humans."

"Then we shall have nothing to worry about, shall we?" Gavgal put his hand on Morvack's shoulder. They returned to the study.

•

Kalath and Rassia sat quietly inside the room, patiently waiting for the Kersian sorcerers to come back. Kalath examined the titles of the books on the shelves. *"Basic Alchemy,"* he said aloud in disgust. *"The Grimoires of Early Kersian Sorcerers?* Hmmm. Perhaps family grimoires. They have not been read in some time. They're thick with dust."

Rassia said nothing. She glanced nervously from Kalath to the door.

Kalath cut his examination short when the door opened and the Kersian sorcerers entered the room. "You are very well read, Administrator Gavgal."

"Please, call me Your Eminence."

Kalath hid his amusement. "Of course, Your Eminence."

Gavgal wiped a thick layer of dust from one of the book spines. "Well, I would not be a
good host if I did not offer you food and something to drink. Please come with us and we shall take the morning meal together. Afterward, of course, I will have to send both of you to a holding cell until you are needed."

Rassia followed Gavgal, with Kalath close behind, Morvack at his side. They traversed the hallway of carved mahogany walls and marble tiled floors, to an arched doorway leading to the dining hall. There, vaulted, mural painted ceilings soared above them, making Kalath feel a bit uneasy. Paintings of their holy relics and temples covered the walls, along with tapestries depicting violent battles. Kalath's stomach turned.

Morvack led them to a long mahogany table surrounded by twenty chairs. He motioned them to the far end of the table. There were four place settings there. "Sit there."

They did as instructed. A door at the back of the room opened and servants, women clothed in white robes, entered carrying trays of meats and vegetables. They set the trays before the sorcerers and left. Kalath reached out and pulled an apple from one of the trays of fruit. "Ah. This is much more than I am accustomed to."

Gavgal smiled with genuine appreciation. "Help yourself."

Morvack narrowed his eyes and speared a sausage with his knife. He then took an orange and began pealing it.

"What would you like, Rassia?" Kalath took her plate to fill it for her.

Her answer was almost inaudible. "An apple and several sausages are fine."

Kalath leaned forward to gather her choices.

Sitting back in his chair, Gavgal crossed his arms over his chest. "Are you a virgin, Rassia?"

The question took Kalath by such surprise that he felt his face contort in disgust. He recoiled with the filled plate, slamming it down in front of Rassia. "I would think that is none of our business."

Morvack sneered, taking a bite of sliced orange. "Of course she is."

Rassia focused on her plate, but the crimson creeping into her cheeks made her anger, or embarrassment, obvious.

"Let me guess. You need a virgin for your sacrifice?" Kalath rolled the apple on his plate, searching Gavgal's face for a sign of compassion. He found none.

The elder Kersian Sorcerer leaned forward and took a peach, examining it. "No. I was merely curious."

"Because?"

A sly grin slid over Morvack's lips and he chuckled, spraying bits of orange onto the table.

Rassia lifted her eyes to meet Morvack's. "No. I am not."

Morvack's grin turned stony.

Kalath let out a sigh and without word, took a bite from the apple. He had a feeling Rassia was lying simply to be defiant.

Gavgal smiled and bit into the peach. "See? That is all I wanted to know."

Rassia lifted an eyebrow. "Well now you know. Do you plan to rape me?"

His eyes went wide. "No. What would make you think such a thing?"

She pushed the plate of food away from her. "Usually men don't ask those kinds of questions. I'm young, not stupid."

Gavgal jabbed his brother in the arm. "She's feisty."

"She's very…" Morvack paused. "Mature for her young age."

"Perhaps you should put us in a holding cell now. I see no need to continue this conversation." Kalath took another bite from the apple.

"You have not finished eating. This may be the only meal you have before tomorrow."

"Rassia and I have lost our appetites. We can take several pieces of fruit with us."

Gavgal nodded. "Fine. But Rassia will go alone. You will come with me. I want to speak with you."

Kalath ran his tongue over the roof of his mouth. "I don't know that I have anything to say."

"Nonsense." He nodded to his brother. "Take Rassia to the room below." Then to Rassia, "Kalath will join you in a short while."

Morvack stood and Rassia followed Morvack from the room with a nervous backward glance. Once they were alone, Gavgal leaned across the table. "I've been told you are a seer with some ability, old man."

"Indeed. And my name is Kalath."

"Of course. Well, Kalath, I am interested in the sorceress. Tell me about her." He pulled the amulet from the gray tunic he wore and rubbed a calloused finger over the sigil.

Kalath wiped his hands with the folded linen towel next to him. His eyes fell on Tnasha's amulet, wondering if he could grab it, but thought better of it. It wasn't the right time. "What is there to tell? I have already explained to Morvack that she will be here, and there will be a confrontation."

"And who will conquer?"

"That I did not see."

"Hmm. Of course not. Perhaps you could tell me more about *her*."

"What do you want to know? Whether or not she's a virgin?" His mind raced with all the possible questions the Kersian would ask.

Gavgal rested his head in his hand and leaned on the table. He shook his graying head of hair. "What does she like?"

"Easy. Horses and swords."

The Kersian sorcerer smiled. "It seems the Danarians breed stubborn, strong-willed women. What is her favorite food?"

"She's not picky. It has been my experience she will eat anything placed before her."

"And what about her favorite jewels?"

Kalath let out a chuckle. "She is not usually impressed with them. Most sorceresses do not wear fanciful jewelry. It hinders their mana. You should know that."

He pulled the amulet from where it hung around his

neck and examined it. "Yet she will come this far for a simple amulet."

"You know as well as I do it is not just a simple amulet."

"No. Of course it isn't. It's laden with her mana. Which means I could, if I chose, use it to bind her."

"You wouldn't dare..."

"Wouldn't I?" Gavgal stood, shoving the amulet beneath his tunic. "No, I wouldn't. I like strong women. Come."

Kalath stood with some reluctance. "You like them to react to you?"

"Why else would I ask a young girl if she were a virgin?"

"Because you're perverted, vile, course, foul mouthed, ill-bred, and ill-mannered." He shot the Kersian sorcerer a look of unrestrained contempt.

Gavgal smiled. "Come. You will show me what she looks like."

Kalath was led to another room. This room was draped in black velvet, with a black marble floor. In the room's center sat a small table with a scrying bowl on top of it. "I can scry all I wish, but I cannot make you see what you cannot."

They stepped up to bowl and Gavgal sighed. "Sorcerer Kalath. My brother may not be able to see, but I can as long as you conjure the image. That is where my talent lacks. I've only recently started my practice of scrying. I can bring forth the images, but I cannot yet keep them. Eventually I will be able to do it alone. Think of it as you teaching me."

"Very well." Kalath drew in a deep breath. The use of his abilities the night before had exhausted him. He was still somewhat tired. Once he closed his eyes, he summoned the image. There, in the black water, an image appeared. Tnasha stood at a ship railing looking out into the ocean.

"She is quite beautiful, and young."

Kalath could feel the Kersian sorcerer's hot breath over his shoulder. He took a step away. As he did, his mind conjured another image. The beast. Kalath fought the image back, as the bowl lifted from the table, overturned, and crashed to the floor, shattering.

"What was that?"

"I do not know," Kalath lied. "It frightened me. I couldn't hold it."

"It is the demon that possesses her," Gavgal said.

"How would you know?"

"My god has told me."

"Or was it your imagination telling you?"

Gavgal shook his head. "I have seen enough to know that the sorceress is as my brother described her."

It was then that Kalath understood the Kersian sorcerer's motives. "Would you kill her like you killed the others, even your own mother, if she cannot bear your children?"

"They were killed because our god wished it. It was not my decision." Gavgal's expression went cold.

Kalath narrowed his eyes. "How convenient to be able to blame one's own shortcomings on his god."

"I only do what the unnamed commands, whether I agree with it or not."

"Blind servitude?"

"I've had enough. I believe this conversation has ended. Guards?" Two armed men appeared in the doorway. "Take him to the prison cell below."

Obediently, the two Kersian soldiers led Kalath through the palace, down a set of stone staircases, through a long, dank corridor, and finally to a wooden doorway where they stopped. Upon opening the door, one of the soldiers shoved him in. Inside the cramped room stood two chairs, one occupied by Rassia. The door clanked shut behind him and the lock slid into place.

Rassia regarded him in the dim light seeping down from a high window. "Now what?"

"Did Morvack touch you?"

"No. He did not say or do anything. You didn't answer my question. Now what?"

Kalath sat in the wooden chair next to her, glancing at the door. "Now we sit and wait."

"Did he make you scry?"

He nodded.

"What did you see?" She leaned in closer to him.

He rubbed his eyes and took a deep breath. "I am unsure. The images were chaotic. Though I fear something terrible is going to happen."

Rassia grabbed his hand and held it. "I'm afraid."

Squeezing her hand, he looked into her eyes. "So am I, child." His gaze lifted to the window. "So am I."

CHAPTER 28

When Shadon returned to the deck with Aragel, he and Kolgern checked their supplies. The men had not yet made their plan known to the women or the young king.

Aragel remained quiet. Not because he had nothing to say, but rather the anxiety and uncertainty of the situation was overwhelming. He thought about Sherok. It made his heart ache to think about what could be happening. He prayed Serena and Corigerg were holding the throne and keeping Hermond and his Exavian brethren out of Sherok. Especially now that his uncle was dead. He had failed them. Now, Danaria and the hope of saving Sherok seemed further away than ever. He sighed and watched the sorceress, Tnasha. Her earlier weather working was such a breathtaking display of power that he felt in awe of her. In a strange way, he was still afraid of her. Not afraid that she would hurt him, but that her sorcery would get away from her. What would they do then?

With everything assembled, Shadon spoke briefly with Adarack. "Take care, my friend."

"Be safe, Shadon. I wish I could talk you out of this."

"It feels right. My intuition has not been wrong yet."

Adarack shook his head and forced a laugh. "I wish I had as much faith in my judgment as you do yours."

Shadon gave him a halfhearted smile and rejoined the others. "I know this seems sudden, but there is no time. Adarack does not wish to be here any longer than he has to, and we cannot delay this any longer even though we may want to."

Tnasha nodded in agreement.

Now that they were all assembled, each of them descended the rope ladder and stepped into the paddleboat. It was a tight squeeze for five people. The crew of the *Narassa* let the rope down, leaving the five travelers to fend for themselves in the midst of the West Ocean.

As the *Narassa* moved off in a faint voice they heard Adarack call, "Shadon, take care my friend. Be safe."

Only four paddles came equipped with the small boat. "So who will do the rowing?" Alena asked.

Shadon shook his head and took two of the paddles. "C'mon, Kolgern."

"What?" Kolgern pretended shock. "Just because I'm a man doesn't mean, theoretically, that *I* have to row. I mean, we have female soldiers who complain about equality and all that nonsense..."

"I never said anything about equality," Tnasha said with a laugh. "Did you, Alena?"

Alena snorted and shook her head. Her eyes searched the distance for any sign of land. "How do we know which way is north?"

"We watch where the sun goes down," Shadon said. Kolgern had since resigned to rowing. Together, he and Shadon heaved the small boat through the water, feeling as if they were not moving at all.

Aragel's thoughts wandered to Snowflake. He wondered then if his bird would be okay on the *Narassa*. Jerred would take good care of him. The *Narassa* was further away now. As he stared off into the distance, he could not help but continue contemplating the future of Sherok. His silence, weighed with the melancholy consuming him, hung thick in the air.

Tnasha sensed it. She reached out and put a hand on the boy's shoulder. "Hey. It's going to be all right."

Aragel pulled his knees to his chest. "How do you

know?"

"It's a feeling. I can't really explain it."

"Sorcery?" he asked.

"No. I prefer to call it heightened awareness." She smiled at him reassuringly.

Aragel let out a deep sigh and drifted back into his own personal fears.

Alena's eyes widened suddenly as if she had forgotten something. Really, she had an epiphany and just realized their situation. Her eyes bulged from her head. "You mean we're goin' to be out here at *night*?" She groaned with exaggeration. "We're gonna die."

"Don't say that. You'll scare the king," Tnasha whispered beneath her breath.

Kolgern heard her. "What?"

"Nothing. I heard somewhere that water is drawn toward land. Eventually we're bound to run aground somewhere," she said with confidence.

"That's a load of horse dung." Kolgern laughed. "If that were the case there wouldn't be any land."

"How do you figure?" Tnasha asked.

"If land attracted water and there is more water than land, wouldn't that mean that the water would cover the land?" He shrugged his shoulders noting that Tnasha failed to see his point.

Shadon closed his eyes and paused from rowing. "Just shut up. Both of you. Can I row in silence for awhile?"

Tnasha and Kolgern exchanged a brief glance and said nothing.

"What if we need to... you know. I'm not taking down my trousers in front of the likes of you two," Alena said suddenly, nodding at the men. She smiled at Aragel. "Or him."

"You should have thought of that before we left." Kolgern began laughing while Alena's cold gaze cut through him.

Throughout the remainder of the day, they headed north, mostly in silence. The waves were choppy, the current somewhat stronger than expected. Just before sunset, Shadon and Kolgern reached the brink of exhaustion. "You ladies are going to have to take over," Shadon announced with labored breath.

Kolgern gratefully passed his ores on to Alena. "Here you go."

Alena took them with some reserve. "What am I supposed to do with them?"

Kolgern raised an eyebrow. "You've never rowed before?"

"Oh yes. All the time. I'm a regular rowing fool! Of course I've never rowed before, you idiot!" she screamed.

"May I remind everyone that we need to work together here?" Shadon asked. Then to Alena, "We'll show you how to row."

"Can't we just stop rowing?" she whimpered.

Tnasha began rowing, feeling the strain in her forearms and shoulders. Her breathing became laborious almost immediately. "If we don't row we are at the mercy of the tide. And *that* could take us anywhere." She focused on taking even, measured breaths and smooth strokes with the oars.

With reluctance, Alena agreed.

Slowly, they moved on until night faded in on them, turning the world into a black, murky, watery abyss unlit by the moon, which hung high in the sky behind a dense layer of clouds. It was a frightening experience really. Tnasha did not recall having ever seen such blackness. Even the pinpoints of light from the few stars left uncovered by clouds did nothing to lesson the hollow feeling of the world. She could hear nothing around her except water and the occasional movement of something alongside the boat. She had to be brave. But it seemed her companions were braver than she. For no one, even Alena, said anything.

Then the fog began to roll in. A sure sign that land was near. However, they could not know it was Zul until they actually arrived. Tnasha held her breath for a moment as the fog swirled around and enveloped all of them. Where before she could at least distinguish the faint outlines of her friends in the blackness, now she was alone. Only inches apart and she could not see any of them. It really did put things into perspective.

Suddenly, she felt insignificant and lost to the world around her. That was until a thud jolted her from where she sat, throwing her backward into the side of the small, wooden boat. She lost one of the oars in the water and cried out.

"What in the name of Natyis?" came Kolgern's voice through the fog.

"I lost an oar," Tnasha said, annoyed. She clutched the remaining one and plunged her hand into the frigid water to find not only the oar, but earth as well.

She felt around a little more, letting the thick, wet sand ooze through her fingers; feeling its grainy texture on her palm. She sighed relief and softly giggled to herself. If it was Zul they had run aground on, she did not want to attract any attention from the island's residents just yet.

No response emerged out of the blackness from her friends. Nothing but waiting silence. "We've reached land," she finally said, delighted. Carefully feeling her way around, she slid over the side of the boat and into the shallow water with a small splash. Kolgern followed more clamorously. The thick fog made seeing anything almost impossible.

"I've never seen such fog," Shadon said.

"I'm glad I don't live on an island. This is frightening." Alena slipped out of the boat, feeling the cold water seep through her boots. It caused her more urgency in her quest for dry land.

"Move toward my voice and you'll find me. We can't see you." Tnasha carefully walked up the beach, careful to watch where she stepped.

Alena responded with a small "All right," and got out of the water with the rest of them. Together they pulled the small paddleboat ashore, hid it behind some trees, and made their way further ashore. Alena stood close to Kolgern, glancing around nervously.

"Watch out for snakes," Kolgern whispered.

Alena smacked his arm. "This is not a time to be cute."

"This could be one of those small islands with cannibal tribes living on it," Aragel said into the blackness. His imagination was at it again.

Tnasha stifled a giggle. "If that is the case, shouldn't there be poles with heads on them somewhere?"

Shadon snickered. "It is *not* a cannibal island."

Aragel envisioned a tribe of people with painted skin attacking them with hand-forged spears and arrows. "How do we know for sure?"

Shadon rolled his eyes. "It is *not*..." Just then, as they emerged from a grove of trees, it stood before them. A well-lit city. Its lights illuminated the fog. They had indeed landed on the Island of Zul. The temple rising high above the city offered proof enough.

Alena clutched Kolgern's tunic. "This looks like Zul all right."

Tnasha and Shadon took the lead and crept closer to the silent buildings. Aragel followed close behind Shadon, and Alena and Kolgern took up the rear. Everything was quiet as if the island had been deserted. There was something unsettling about it, but Tnasha could not place it. All for a simple amulet. Would any sorceress travel thousands or maybe just hundreds of miles to reclaim a magickal item? *Yes. Probably*, she quickly decided. Especially if it meant the end of the world as she knew it. It was almost too easy, though. Not a person around. No guards. No watchers. Nothing.

Gavgal and Morvack undoubtedly stood in waiting. Tnasha's dream about the horsemen upon the cliff came back to her. She immediately looked around for a cliff. From where they were, there was no way to tell. The question remained. Why had the Kersians made it so easy? They knew she was there. Tnasha could feel it. Sorcerers could sense one another. Aside from which, they were not stupid men.

A cool breeze swept over them. On a craggy knoll above the village stood the temple, menacing and glaring down on them like a cold tomb of mud and stone. Beside it stood the great palace of Gavgal, unguarded and open to the night as if some invisible barrier protected it. The torches at the arched entryway were lit which only meant one thing. They were expected.

Tnasha crouched behind a small grove of fruit trees and waited for everyone to catch up.

"Why are we stopping?" Kolgern asked. He looked at her warily.

Shadon said it before she had time to. "It's too easy. There are no guards. It has to be a trap. Otherwise, this city should have people wandering around. At least a few."

Kolgern shrugged his shoulders. "Maybe they thought we would come from the other end of the island."

"This whole island is covered with Kersians and not one is here to greet us? Not that I mind," she added thoughtfully. "But I would rather not walk into a trap. It's just too easy. This whole journey is beginning to remind me of one huge ambush. I don't like surprises!"

"Well there's no sense stopping now." Shadon moved ahead of her. "This confrontation will have to happen sooner or later. You have to get that amulet back. Aragel and I have to find out what Kersians and Exavians want with Sherok. Who knows what it would mean if Gavgal or Morvack figured out how to use the amulet?"

"I'm not even sure *I* know how to use it. Who's to say all of this is related to Sherok anyway? Maybe they're working two separate schemes at once." She moved in behind him.

"Come on, Tnasha. You know as well as I do that even if Sherok and Exavia have nothing to do with the amulet, that it all leads to the same end."

A sharp tinge of anxiety pierced her stomach. "Sure, perhaps they're trying to take over the world? With an amulet and a kingdom of farmers?"

Shadon looked at her. "Why not? That makes sense. If they have their people, Exavia and Sherok, they could easily take Cabalia and Carinth. Then Arkeereon and finally Danaria. The amulet could help them achieve that end if they learn how to use it for their purpose, which is undoubtedly something dangerous for the rest of us."

Tnasha felt the tension move up her shoulders. "So if they learn to use the amulet..."

"Exactly. The amulet and Exavia's plans to take Sherok may not have anything to do with one another now, but the amulet may make things easier. If they figure out how to use it."

Tnasha thought about it for a moment. "Not the amulet in and of itself. It's my mana. The amulet is saturated with my mana."

"So if they catch you, they have the source of that mana?" Shadon looked at her with a questioning glare.

"They're not going to catch me. I'll kill them first."

"How."

"I'll use sorcery. I have a plan. If I can raise lightening or something and use it to strike the sorcerers down, or raise a storm to hold off their soldiers…"

Shadon let out a fake laugh. "Ha! Or something? This coming from a woman who cannot remember the right incantation. Invoking serpents in place of wind? Then a hurricane?"

"Look, I may not be a perfect sorceress…" she paused with a heavy sigh. "But at least I am willing to try."

Kolgern cut her off. "Each minute we spend here wasting time talking about it is another minute they have to prepare their attack on us." Kolgern pushed them forward.

Tnasha rolled her eyes. "They've had plenty of time to plan. Who knows if all this hasn't been planned for months now? We don't know. What difference will a few more minutes make?"

"Yes, but how is it you think they know we're here?" Kolgern asked.

"Sorcerers can feel one another. I cannot explain how, I just know how it is. Does that make any sense? It's instinct." She drew her short sword and took another step forward.

"I say we find a way in where they won't expect us. We could find a window leading to the baths or a storage room." Shadon looked at Kolgern expectantly.

"Most storage rooms don't have windows. Kolgern? Do you know the design of the palace well enough?" Tnasha glanced around impatiently, waiting for an answer.

"I remember it. I retrieved the oracle, remember?"

"Wasn't that just a museum artifact?" Aragel had stepped up behind them, and poked his head over their shoulders.

Tnasha shook her head. "It really is an oracle. A magick crystal. For scrying."

Shadon nodded, and drew his own weapon.

Kolgern gave her a desultory grin. "Let's just go. We're already here and the Kersians are waiting. No sense delaying the inevitable."

"What should Alena and I do?" Aragel asked from the shadows behind them.

"Just stay close and keep your sword at hand." Shadon gave him a quick nod.

Tnasha held up a hand. "Wait. It's not that easy. I think we need to split up. If they can feel me, wouldn't it make sense if I created a diversion while two of you crept in and took my amulet? How about this? I'll go to the temple with Shadon and Aragel. I feel drawn to it somehow. You two go to the palace and see if you can find the amulet."

"Why do *we* have to search for the amulet?" Kolgern reasoned. "Wouldn't it make sense that if the amulet is here it would be with Gavgal? And if he can sense you that he'll be wherever you are?"

Alena cocked her head thoughtfully. "Not necessarily."

Shadon stretched his arm. "I don't like it. We should all check the palace first like Kolgern and I originally planned..."

But it was too late. Tnasha sprang up from where she crouched and made her way toward the steep stone steps of the temple. She turned back to them only once, motioning them to follow.

Kolgern shook his head and took Alena by the arm. "Let's just go. She has no idea what she's doing."

Reluctantly, Alena and Kolgern headed in the opposite direction toward the palace, while Aragel and Shadon hurried after Tnasha.

CHAPTER 29

Serena paced her quarters frantically, brushing off her maids as they fussed over her wedding gown.

"Princess Serena, you seem nervous," Carolyn said.

"Were the tomatoes delivered?" Serena could feel the tension make its way up her neck, through the back of her head, finally settling into her temples with a dull ache.

"Yes, My Lady." Carolyn let out an exasperated sigh.

Serena could not help it. She was nervous. What if the plan failed? She had not considered failure, probably because she did not want to imagine what would happen if they did fail. The insurrection had to happen before the wedding, and she would need to rightfully take her throne immediately afterward. She was counting on Commander Corigerg to survive. Without him, she would be a stranger in her own home. He was her last link between all that was familiar and safe.

While her maids kept themselves busy with last minute details, Serena turned from them. She was sure they were not looking in her direction, so she slipped the plain, wooden-handled dagger her father had given her into her garter belt. She let her skirts loose, allowing them to fall to the floor.

"Can I help you, My Lady?" Carolyn hurried to her side.

"Oh no, it was simply my garter belt. It was slipping. All

fine now." She patted her leg and smiled reassuringly at Carolyn. She wanted to make sure she was ready for anything. After all, the tomatoes had been delivered and likely stood in the castle even now.

Carolyn glanced at the other maids cautiously before speaking. "If the feast fails, no one would blame you anyway. After all, it was not you in the kitchens preparing the food."

Serena crinkled her nose. Then it dawned on her and made sense. So long as Serena feigned her lack of knowledge, things would be fine. Even if it did fail. But what would become of Commander Corigerg? "Any word about my cousin?"

Carolyn sighed mournfully. "My Lady, you did not know? I've heard rumor that prince Aragel succumbed to the attack on Orana Tulk."

The other maids looked on in silence. The pity displayed openly in their eyes.

Serena shook off their stares. "Yes, I have heard the same nonsense. Unless the body of my cousin is produced, I will not believe it." She looked around to gauge their reactions. "The same goes for my brother. Killed by assassins. Ha! He ran away, just like Aragel."

Many of the women cast their gazes down. Serena knew what they were thinking. They thought the princess suffered from denial. She shook her head and ignored them.

A stiff knock rocked the chamber door followed by a deep voice. "My Lady, they are ready for you."

Serena looked down at herself and smoothed her skirts. "I'm to have soldiers escort me to my own wedding. How quaint. I'll pretend I'm in Danaria." A tear fought its way to her eye. Her father should be escorting her. None of this should be happening. She fought it back and quickly wiped her eyes.

The maids looked on, surprised by her sudden outburst.

"Well, come on. Let's get on with it. I don't want to keep my prince and his military waiting."

The maids scurried in attendance to Serena, following her out.

The main hall of the Sherokean castle stood full of people. The King of Exavia had arrived quietly unannounced that morning. Among the wedding guests were the plethora of guards posted at every entrance and every corner of the main hall. Likewise, the dining hall, prepared and decorated for the reception, was well guarded. A Kersian priest stood at the front of the hall awaiting the bride and groom.

As Serena approached the entrance to the hall, she found King Agorak, Hermond's father, waiting for her. "You look lovely, my dear." He held out a thick, pale hand to her. "I hope it is not an imposition for me to escort you to the altar?"

Princess Serena fought the instinctive urge to roll her eyes. Instead, she curtsied politely and wrapped her small arm around his. "Of course, Your Majesty." Her gaze scanned the room to the lavish altar, and finally to the Kersian priest dressed in white silken robes embroidered with gold thread.

"It will be a few moments," the king said. He looked down at her, noting her expression had gone sour. "Is something wrong?"

"I was expecting a priestess, or a member of the high court to conduct the ceremony," she whispered.

"Our family, my dear, has recently seen the error of our ways. We have been purified. You and Hermond shall be married in the name of the god with no name according to my instruction."

Serena set her jaw. "Kersians?"

"You say that as if it leaves a bad taste in your mouth." He grasped her arm firmly.

"Kersians tried to destroy Sherok once. Why should I care for them?"

The king looked straight ahead. "That is all in the past. We cannot judge them for past transgressions."

"Is it all in the past or has it simply been forgotten?" Her own voice sounded foreign and far away. She could feel anger swell inside her. The crisp white gown she wore felt stiff and cumbersome. She hated it. The forced smiled caused pain in her cheeks. Pain so intense that she clamped her jaw. She wanted to reach down and pat the dagger, if only to reassure herself it was there. She knew it was. She took another deep breath and looked around. She could not tell the good tomatoes from the bad ones.

Serena began concentrating on the room then. The high ceilings and arched entryways, the deep purple and maroon tapestries hanging side by side of the Exavian seals of green and white with a silver scalloped shell at its center. The barrage of color looked terrible. Maroon, purple, and green did not go together. Serena found herself scrutinizing the attire of her guests as well. The male Exavian guests wore long tunics that hung to their knees. The Sherokean men wore practical clothing without all the embroidery done in lavish golden thread. Their tunics were cut waist length and dyed in earthen tones. There were only two Exavian women present. Both wore overly ornate dresses lavishly embroidered with enough golden thread to draw attention. The numerous Sherokean women present, however, wore more delicate gowns, subtly decorated with lace and pearls.

It was by this that Serena realized there were more Sherokeans than Exavians present. She stopped smiling. The king gripped her arm more tightly.

The herald took the crowd's attention by summoning the musicians to play. The crowd fell silent. Hermond stood next to the priest at the front of the room. He smiled at her. But Serena did not smile back. Instead, she shot him down with an icy glare.

"Smile," the king ordered, squeezing her arm.

"*You* smile," she said in a dry, dead voice. "I'll do as I please."

"Now is not the time for insolence, girl," he said through clenched teeth and smiling lips.

She could no longer resist. With all eyes upon her, she narrowed her eyes, pulled her arm away from the king and started down the isle alone, forcing him to follow behind.

"Presenting the Princess Serena of Sherok..." the voice of the herald dropped off into silence. With long strides, she made her way to the altar, fire burning in her dark eyes.

She faced Hermond in anger. "How dare you!" With that, her hand shot out, slapping the prince in full force on the cheek. She turned to the priest. "And you! How dare you people show your faces here?"

"Apprehend her!" came the king's order, which

resounded through the hall. In an onrush of voices, and the sound of steel meeting steel, the great hall became a sudden void of chaos.

All Serena could see were the eyes of the priest. She took a step toward him, pulled back her arm, and brought her small fist forward, meeting his abdomen with a thud. The priest fell back, grasping his stomach, a shocked look adorning his face. She faced Hermond again, who stood frozen, mouth agape. She felt her skirt for the dagger, oblivious to the chaos around her. She did not avert her eyes from her target.

Hermond could not shake the look of shock he wore. He grabbed her by the arm, his eyes wildly darting in every direction at the calamity around him.

You have no focus, you ass, Serena thought. Her hatred for him screamed from the well inside her. He killed her father. He was the reason Aragel ran away. Aragel knew. Whether her cousin lived or died she did not know. What she did know is Sherok could not fall to the Exavians. She would not let it happen.

How he could stand there and lie to her! Pretend he did nothing to her father! She would avenge her father's death. She slipped her hand up her skirt and retrieved the dagger. Hermond pulled her toward the door with force. She could feel her flesh bruising beneath his grip. The King of Exavia ran far ahead of them. He hurried as fast as he could, flanked by guards who fought off the oncoming Sherokeans.

Without hesitation, Serena lifted the dagger and plunged it into Hermond's back. A wail of wrath expelled from her throat.

He fell forward and she tripped over him. He grabbed her ankle. She pulled the dagger out of his back and slashed his arm deeply. He let go. She plunged it into his back a second time noticing the blood gurgling from Hermond's mouth as an Exavian guard brought his sword down heavily toward her.

A shrill clank sounded loud in her ears. Steel met steel, blocking the blow, and Serena was pulled to her feet by a strong arm. When she was able to focus, she realized Corigerg had lifted her from the ground. Beside him fought more Sherokean soldiers.

She and the commander rushed from the great hall to safety. Clearly outnumbered, the Exavians kept fighting their way through the continual onrush of Sherokeans.

CHAPTER 30

Alena and Kolgern made their way to the palace building without incident. Slinking their way around the building, they peered into each window as they came to it. As they approached a small, lit basement window, Alena saw them. An old man and a young woman faced away from the window. She tiptoed to the next window to see them better and gasped. "That's Kalath and Rassia! How did they get here?"

The sound of footfalls rounding the side of the building silenced her. Kolgern took Alena by the arm, pulling her back into the shadows. Two guards wearing golden-colored armor patrolled past.

Kolgern looked around, searching the blackness for signs of more patrols. "I hope the others have made it to the temple. All of this for an amulet."

"A magical amulet," Alena corrected.

Kolgern rolled his eyes. "Does it matter?"

Alena took a deep breath and crinkled her otherwise smooth forehead. "This puts us in a bad position."

"You think?" He looked toward the temple and squinted, as if squinting would bring it closer and into focus.

"Gavgal has Kalath and Rassia in that room!" Alena stamped one small foot impatiently. "Does that mean anything to you?"

Kolgern turned back to her, the defeat showing clearly on his face. "Of course it does. What are we going to do about it?"

"Well, we have to do something!"

"Why does it seem like everything is against us?"

"Everything is." She let out a sigh. "Come on, we're going to save them. We can't leave them here. Tnasha would kill us. Besides, I wouldn't be able to live with myself." She grabbed for his arm, caught his tunic instead, and pulled Kolgern back toward the dim-lit basement window.

He followed, knowing she would not change her mind. Alena rarely did.

When they returned to the side of the building, Rassia and Kalath still sat unmoving inside the small room. Alena lightly tapped on the grimy windowpane.

"There's someone out there." Rassia drew her chair beneath the high window and stood up on it, trying to see out. She saw nothing.

"Rassia," Alena whispered.

Rassia did not hear her. Kalath dragged forth his chair, joining her at the window, and pressed his forehead the thick glass.

"Can you see anything?" Rassia pressed her forehead against the window, too.

"No."

Kolgern reached forward and tapped the window where Kalath's forehead sat pressed against the pane of glass.

Kalath pulled back. "There *is* someone out there."

Alena and Kolgern began feeling around the window for loose mortar or any weakness about the tight iron frames in which the heavy panes of glass were securely lodged. There were none. The window might as well have been steel-barred. Only with a battering ram, and a shattering clamor of noise, could they smash their way through.

"We don't have the right tools. We'll have to go in," Kolgern said.

"What about a dagger?"

"If you want to break a dagger, go right ahead. It will

take hours. By then the guards will have come back around." Kolgern gave her a brief, sardonic smile and hurried around the other side of the palace wall. Alena followed. Very soon, they found an unguarded door.

Kolgern put his hand on the latch, pressed down, and it opened with ease. She put her hand over his before he pulled the door open.

"I know we've said it before, but this is too easy."

He shrugged. "Yes. It is. Let's go." Pulling the door open, he stepped inside. "This leads straight to the basement."

Again, Alena followed. This time with her heart in her throat. Kolgern was a risk-taker. She preferred planned measures. This situation, however, did not seem to allow for any. Instead, she placed her faith in Kolgern. Hoping he had a plan if they encountered any Kersian soldiers or sorcerers along the way.

Inside, the basement stood dark. With no light to lead them through the dank corridors lined by brick walls, they slowly made their way inside. The walls were wet to the touch and an inch of water covered the floor. Alena fought back a terrible thought. "Rats," she said aloud.

"What?"

"Rats."

"I know. Why are you *saying* rats?"

"What if there *are* rats?" The fear she felt rang clear in her voice.

"So what? They're just rats."

"*Where*?" She jumped.

Kolgern stopped and she bumped into him - hard. "Alena, I haven't seen a rat. Damn, woman. If I see a rat, I'll let you know. Come on."

They reached a main hallway. In the darkness, they could make out the faint outlines of doors. At the far end of the hall a thin line of light came from beneath one of them. Kolgern nodded and pointed. "Down there."

"Let me get ahead of you. I keep feeling like there's someone behind me." He stepped aside, allowing Alena to go first.

After a brief walk through the hallway, they reached the door. A simple iron bolt held it closed. Kolgern slid aside the bolt, opened the door, and stepped into the room. A candle provided the only light. "Happy to see us?"

Kalath smiled appreciatively. "I was wondering when you would get here."

"Sorry we weren't fast enough. We had a few snags along the way." Kolgern smiled. "Out we go." He turned toward Alena and jumped back.

Alena looked down and found herself confronted with a spider, the size of her palm, crawling up her chest. "Ah! Big, big spider!" She began jumping up and down, knocking it to the floor. She shuddered, her skin crawling.

Kalath stepped forward, crushing the spider beneath his boot. It made a crunching noise. "Well, if we didn't attract the Kersians before, that certainly did it."

Alena brushed herself off, still shuddering. "I hate spiders. Especially ones as big as my head!"

"It wasn't *that* big." Kolgern stepped past her back into the hallway. "Come on. Let's go."

Alena turned to follow, slapping his arm as she passed by him.

Rassia and Kalath followed close behind. Once again outside, Kolgern surveyed the courtyard, then turned to make sure they had everyone.

Alena lifted an eyebrow. She remembered something. "Weren't we supposed to find the amulet?"

"Don't bother. It's not here in the palace. It's in the temple with the high priest, Administrator Gavgal. He wears it around his neck." Kalath's expression changed and he nodded his head for Kolgern to look behind him.

Kolgern turned. Twelve Kersian soldiers surrounded them.

An armed guard took hold of each of them. Kalath glanced over his shoulder at the soldier holding him. "Let me guess, Tnasha is in the temple."

Kolgern struggled enough to warrant two guards holding him. "Are you surprised?"

"Not especially."

"Keep quiet, prisoners." One of the soldiers, apparently the leader, raised his palm to his men. He pulled off his helm and stepped up to Kolgern, grabbing him by the chin. "It seems I owe you an injury, infidel."

Kalath shook his head, noting the crimson mana surrounding the man.

Kolgern could not mask his surprise. Before him stood the Sorcerer Morvack. All that remained of the slit in his throat left by Kolgern's dagger was a thin scar.

Without warning, Morvack's fist met Kolgern's stomach, knocking the wind from him. Kolgern fell limp, coughing, feeling the pain blossom beneath his ribs. The soldiers hauled him back to his feet. Morvack pulled his dagger and put it to Kolgern's throat.

"Our god states that infidels should be cleansed and that we should treat infidels as they have treated us. The unnamed grants me revenge upon you."

"Your god is a farce." Kolgern gasped for air, but did not hide his distaste. "Kill me."

"Do not challenge *me*. I will kill you slowly as *I* see fit." With one swift motion, he stabbed Kolgern in the arm. Plunging the dagger deep and twisting it. He pulled it out just as quickly. Kolgern cried out in pain and fell to his knees.

The soldiers immediately brought him to his feet again. The blood poured from his arm in deep crimson streams, soaking his tunic through. Morvack handed one of the soldiers a rag. "Tie it off. I don't want him to bleed to death right away."

Tears of pain came to Kolgern's eyes as one of the men tied a thick strip of cloth tightly over the wound. His arm soon went numb. Though nausea filled his stomach and his head felt light, he attempted to maintain his defiant expression. "You don't scare me."

Morvack leaned in close. "I should. I'm your worst enemy, heathen."

"Leave him alone!" It was Alena. She twisted her way out of a soldier's grasp and sent her now freed elbow hard into the soldier's stomach, knocking him off balance. Another soldier grabbed her by the arm, twisting it behind her, subduing her.

Morvack stared at her with dead, cold eyes. "Shut up. Bind their hands and feet, then bring the prisoners to the temple. Lord Gavgal has demanded it." He hurried ahead.

Without delaying, the soldiers secured their hands and feet. When they were done the Kersian soldiers dragged them toward the temple.

As they reached the outer wall of the palace, there came a terrible noise. In a rush of voices, the guards stopped, watching as the beast rose from the ocean's edge and heaved its massive body ashore. Its weight proved clamorous, and each step shook the groung with a heavy thud.

It began to rain. With a thunderous crash and a harrowing growl, the serpent destroyed several small buildings on the outer edge of the city, as it made its way toward the temple. It did not avert its fierce, glaring red gaze from its objective.

All around them, soldiers loaded bows, shooting their arrows high and far. While some bolts managed to meet the beast, this did not deter it from continuing toward the temple. Several brave men, swords drawn, ran toward the beast's feet, only to be trampled.

A frantic man ran from the side of the temple, out of the beast's path. "It was conjured with diabolical sorcery."

"Indeed it was," Kalath said under his breath.

Rassia heard him. "Nasha?"

The old sorcerer merely smiled.

Kolgern winced in pain as the soldier grabbed his injured arm. "Maybe you should be more worried about that, rather than holding us," he said.

The soldier gaped at him, then at the beast. "Two of us will hold them here. You five, go and help the others destroy the beast." The soldier put his sword against Kolgern's throat. Kolgern clenched his jaw and closed his eyes. Alena stifled a gasp.

"If any of you move I'll kill him." Now, the soldier poised the short sword over Kolgern's heart.

"Don't anyone move," Kolgern said.

The soldier pushed the sword firmly against Kolgern's chest. "Shut up."

Alena held her breath.

CHAPTER 31

Aragel and Shadon followed Tnasha as she climbed the stone stairs leading to the temple's entrance. She moved quickly, her eyes searching her surroundings for hidden enemies. She found none. When she reached the doors of the temple she stopped and peered in. They stood wide open. Perhaps it was an invitation? She took a deep breath. "I should have done the ritual back on the beach." She could have kicked herself. With an absence of confidence she looked back over her shoulder to make sure Aragel and Shadon were still with her. Right now, she needed their strength.

With Aragel and Shadon beside her, she stepped inside the large building and took it in. Years of marauding and pillaging had built it. Marble floors and gold plated embellishments decorated the temple. Ghastly paintings of war and death adorned the vaulted ceilings. A red carpet led between the pews to a raised altar.

The temple stood empty, yet the voices of men carried from a room somewhere beyond the hall to the left of the altar and pulpit. "Your Eminence, if the sorcerer will not tell us the outcome, we should kill him. For being one with such powers of foreseeing, he certainly knows very little. I believe he is not telling you what you want to know. The only way to make him talk is through persuasive measures."

"We will not torture him. I have no need for him now. We will kill him, and the girl, later," came a strong, resolute voice, thick with a strange accent.

"Yes, Your Eminence."

Aragel's deep brown skin seemed to turn a shade paler and he felt dizzy. He bolted forward. "That's him!"

Tnasha grabbed the young king, holding him firm. "You can't charge in there."

Aragel tried to say something, but nothing came out except a wheezing gasp for air.

Tnasha swung around, her eyes pleading for Shadon's help.

Aragel leaned in to her, still wheezing. "That's the voice. Assassin. Your Eminence," he managed in a whisper. Then he collapsed with a dull thud to the marble floor beneath him. Shadon dropped beside him to feel his pulse.

"Is he alive?" Tnasha glanced nervously toward the sound of the voices, then back to Shadon.

Shadon nodded. "Yes." His eyes narrowed as his gaze followed the voices. His hand went instinctively to his sword. "That man killed my father."

Tnasha widened her eyes in surprise. "And that's the sorcerer who has my amulet. From their conversation it sounds as though he is also holding some friends of mine." She paused and looked around. Her gaze fell back to the steps leading to the temple. She leaned down to Aragel and patted his cheek. "Wake up, Aragel. Come on. Aragel, wake up."

Shadon lifted his cousin to a sitting position and shook him gently. "Aragel."

Aragel's eyes opened in dazed slits. "What," he said breathlessly. "What happened?"

"Come on." Shadon lifted Aragel to his feet, helping him forward. They began making their way toward the hallway. Tnasha did not bother hiding her mana. Not this time. If it was war the Kersians wanted, that is exactly what she would give them. She was in no mood for casual negotiation.

Just before they started down the hallway, two men

emerged from the room. "Welcome Tnasha."

Tnasha stopped dead in her tracks as Shadon helped Aragel behind a pillar and peered around it.

"I see you have brought friends," came the voice again. A tall, well-muscled man with graying hair and deep green mana appeared from the darkened hallway. He stepped to the side of the altar. "I have been expecting you. Though I must admit I expected you to come alone."

"I know," Tnasha said, biting her lip. He was the man in her last dream aboard Adarack's ship. The sorcerer. She wanted to kill him where he stood.

Gavgal's green eyes, the same color of his mana, bore into her. "Do you know why I have conveniently led you here?"

Tnasha looked toward Shadon and Aragel, then back at Morvack.

"Hmm. I have no interest in your little friends, my dear. No, I am interested in you."

"For sacrifice?" She held her ground. "Because I think that whole thing about drinking blood of other sorcerers to retrieve their mana is a myth."

Gavgal laughed. "By the grace of the unnamed, no. You have an interesting imagination. No, I would not sacrifice you. You are a precious resource. Your friends, however, may well suit that purpose. Though you might enjoy your wedding more surrounded by those you care about. Yes? We can sacrifice them in a celebration afterwards."

A mask of disdain slipped over her face. "You want me to marry you?"

Gavgal smiled. "With you as my consort, you will give me sons. With our combined mana, our children will make up an army of invincible soldiers. Think of it. Once I take more sorceresses from Danaria, with your help, our children, and my brothers' children will be infallible." He came forward a step, lifting his fist and shaking it for emphasis. "We will crush the world and bring the Kersian Empire to its long awaited glory! Our god has ordained it!" Gavgal's eyes went wild with the zeal of a fanatic. He took another step toward her and narrowed them, the pupils becoming mere slits. "It is already started. I have Sherok and Exavia within my grasp. Yes, you and your friends were almost quite right. My brother reads minds, you see. Arkeereon and Cabalia *will* be next. I shall save Danaria and Carinth for last. When their cities fall and we take them over one by one, we will add more sorceresses with powerful mana to our breeding stock. We will be unstoppable. First the West Ocean Mainlands and then the world."

"You're insane!" Tnasha felt her stomach churn. "I'd rather be sacrificed."

"Well," Gavgal cocked his head to one side. "If you do not come willingly, I will have no choice but to take you by force. That is your choice." He turned to his minion. "Bring me the prisoners and her other companions. Perhaps I can make this choice easier for her."

Tnasha stood there, unable to speak. Shadon approached her side and grabbed her arm. "Do something."

For a moment, his voice seemed distant, but she pulled herself from her shock and looked at him—through him rather than at him.

"Do something," Shadon commanded again, turning to Gavgal. He lifted his sword and charged Gavgal. "You won't get away with this."

With a simple flick of his wrist, a stream of mana shot Shadon twenty paces into a pew where his body fell limp in unconsciousness.

Tnasha's cold gaze met Gavgal's. She grasped her sword firmly, feeling her palms seeping sweat. "By Natyis…"

"Do not utter the name of demons in this holy place. Come to him and be cleansed."

"Ha. Cleansed?" Tnasha set her jaw, feeling her teeth grinding against one another in sheer rage. Her voice issued from her throat almost a hiss. "Cleansed! As if you were pure? You kill women and children in the name of your god. You speak of demons? *Your* god is the *true* demon."

Gavgal curled his lip in a sneer. "Heathen! You will do as I say."

Tnasha looked back at Shadon who was still recovering from the blate of mana that struck him down.

A voice from her left side pulled her attention from behind her. It was Aragel. "Perhaps you need to do as *she* says."

"I see Hermond failed in killing you. Though he succeeded in killing your trusting uncle. I should not have left an aristocrat to do a warrior's job."

"Assassination is a coward's job. Unfortunately, your coward was unable to anticipate my way of thinking. I am *not* my trusting uncle." Aragel stood solid, with his sword drawn, defiant in the face of Gavgal.

Aragel's bravery inspired her, giving her a renewed sense of hope. The insecure boy prince was gone. In his place stood a young man. A king.

"Young Prince Aragel. When will you learn? I am an adept sorcerer. You are a mere mortal."

Tnasha snorted. "Sorcerers are not immortal."

"You do not seem to understand either. My god has granted me everlasting life." Gavgal lifted his hands into the air for emphasis.

"You have completely lost your mind." Tnasha could feel the disbelief on her face. She had heard the Kersians were fanatical, but she had not known the full extent until now.

"No. You, my dear, are naïve."

"You won't get Sherok, and you won't get her." Aragel stepped up beside Tnasha, then stepped in front of her as if to shield her from the Kersian sorcerer.

"Such chivalry from such a foolish boy. Sherok is already mine. Hermond may have not gotten rid of you, but he managed to rid me of your uncle, and he's taken your cousin for his wife. Hermond is easily led. Now, all that must be done is I shall kill you myself." He poised his hand at Aragel.

"Sorcery against common men is coward's play, Gavgal." Tnasha pulled Aragel back. "If you want to throw mana blates, throw them at me. At least I can throw them back."

Gavgal narrowed his eyes. From that short distance, by the dim light of torches and candles, they looked almost black. He said nothing. Instead, he watched her as if trying to figure out what she intended to do.

"You do not know who I am. You do not know what I

can do."

"Nonsense. You are a fifth generation sorceress. I think I know better than you what you are capable of. You are also untrained. An untrained sorceress is something of a prize. Without training, you cannot even begin to compete with my power."

Tnasha took a deep breath, noting Aragel kneeling at Shadon's side, helping him to his feet. Turning back to Gavgal, shre realized talking to the Kersian sorcerer was like arguing with a stone wall. But she continued talking as she moved toward the center isle leading between the pews and to the entrance doors. "You will never get enough sorceresses for your forced breeding program. What will you do then?"

"I have other means. Magickal weapons, not nearly as effective as an army of sorcerers, but effective all the same."

"Oh? Then why haven't you used them?"

Gavgal frowned. "I will. In time."

Tnasha forced a laugh. "You lie."

The Sorcerer Morvack entered from a side door and moved to stand at Gavgal's side. "You remember my brother, High Priest Morvack?"

"Of course. My memory is not that short."

Gavgal held out his hand. "You should come with me now. Morvack will see to your friends."

Tnasha stared straight ahead. "No." In her mind, she prayed to Liale, god of earth and steel. She imagined the granules of earth dissolving in her mouth into pure strength. She allowed the imaginary soil to slide down the back of her throat. Taking even, deep breaths, she allowed another vision into her mind. A serpent. She summoned it. Beckoning it to come forth. The force of the ocean. It was instinct. *Dagon, lord of water. Aithian, lord of the seas and oceans. Hear this and come forth.* She looked around expectantly.

"Why do you hold back?" Gavgal asked. He seemed amused and took two steps toward her. "I am offering you a cared-for life. Children. A home. A god who loves you."

"I do not want you or your no-name god." Tnasha's eyes turned violet, matching her mana. *Do what comes naturally, and do not fight it*, her reason told her. She stretched forth her hand and a violet blaze of light came forth, striking Gavgal in the chest, merely throwing him off balance. He regained his footing easily and moved toward her. Morvack smiled in amusement. His eyes seethed an angry red like his own mana.

Tnasha stepped away trying to remember the words to raise a tempest. Gavgal had asked why she held back. She would not this time. It would destroy everything on Zul. She held up a hand to Aragel and Shadon. "Stay back." She turned back to Gavgal and Morvack. "Serpentis veneficium!"

A bolt of lightening stretched through the sky with a rumble of thunder. It began to rain. Morvack and Gavgal exchanged glances and laughed. "Is *that the best* you can do? Rain?" Morvack smiled.

Relax, she told herself. *Let it come naturally.* "Yedan tasa hoet naca, Leviathan!" She raised her arms above her feeling the mana run through her body and out from her fingertips. The ground began to shake.

Gavgal's gaze went beyond her, outside past the open temple doors. "What have you done? You witch! Morvack, see what it is."

Morvack hurried past her with a growl, making his way to the temple's entrance.

"You told me not to hold back. I am simply an untrained sorceress," she hissed.

"She has called forth a serpent!" Morvack yelled to Gavgal.

She turned to survey her work. Her jaw dropped when she saw it. With each thud of the shaking earth, something big and black moved from the edge of the ocean inland. A horrible growl bellowed through the night. The hair on her arm stood on end.

Gavgal ran forward and grabbed her arm tightly, his fingernails biting into her skin. He scowled and growled deeply, "Get rid of it."

Tnasha eye him coldly. "I don't know how."

Gavgal leaned in close. "Do not lie to me. Get rid of it."

With a wide grin, she lifted her free arm and shooed at

it. "Go away, uh, Leviathan away? Hmmm. I'm afraid I'm stumped."

The beast continued toward the temple still, leaving the far edge of the city of Zul in ruins in its wake.

Gavgal kept a firm hold of her arm, pulling her toward the beast. All the while, he became more insistent. "Send it away, witch!"

Morvack stood in front of her, glaring at her. "I'll make her send it away." He drew his sword.

"Killing me is not likely to help you get rid of it," she paused, noting the fear in their eyes. "Ah, I get it now." Laughter tumbled from the back of her throat. "You are a fire element, and you are an earth element. Neither of you knows a thing about water sorcery." The exertion of so much mana strained her and she felt weak. She held on to Gavgal to steady her legs, feeling they would give out from beneath her at any moment.

That is when she caught a glimpse of something glowing violet from beneath the Kersian sorcerer's tunic. Her amulet hung around Gavgal's fat neck.

She reached around with one hand, grasped it, and shoved herself back with one hand while pulling with the other.

As it came loose, both she and Gavgal tumbled to the floor. Morvack hurried to help Gavgal to his feet. Once he succeeded, the Kersian sorcerers ran toward the altar for safety.

The beast clawed at the stairs now, clamorously tearing its way into the temple. Shouting and screaming echoed through the city behind it. Tnasha got to her feet and moved toward the altar and the Kersian sorcerers cowering before it.

The ceiling of the temple entrance crumbled with an explosion of concrete blocks that crashed to the floor sending dust and shards of rock into the air.

"What is your command, sorceress," a voice hissed from above her.

Tnasha looked up and recognized the serpent. Hot fishy breath assaulted her nose. Clutching her amulet, she coughed and gagged. "Destroy the Kersian sorcerers."

Aragel helped Shadon, who still sat dazed from the blast of mana. Aragel called out to her in a frantic voice, "Tnasha, get him! He can disappear!"

"Who?"

Aragel pointed at the sorcerers. "Gavgal!"

Swiftly, Tnasha turned in a swirl of pulsing energy, throwing a blate of searing violet mana at the sorcerers, striking Gavgal in the chest knocking him into his brother, who held onto him.

"You have not seen the last of us, heathen sorceress," Morvack said. With those final words, Gavgal and Morvack dissipated into the air. Vanishing like a mist.

The serpent reared its head back, its eyes searching for the sorcerers.

"By Natyis, how?" Tnasha looked around, then turned to the serpent. Like a military commander, she barked the order. "Keep the Kersians occupied while we find our friends and get out of here. Do not destroy the city until we are gone. You could inadvertently kill us."

Shadon and Aragel came up beside her, keeping distance from the serpent. Aragel ran ahead of them. "Side door," he called over his shoulder.

They followed. Outside they traversed the dark alley between the half destroyed temple and the wall of the palace. The serpent stepped out of the hole it made in the temple's entryway and stood there like a giant stone guardian, allowing the soldiers to shoot their arrows and throw their spears. Tnasha, Aragel and Shadon slipped by, spotting Kolgern and Alena, held at sword-point just outside the palace entrance.

"By Natyis, now we have to save them!" Aragel threw his hands up.

Still feeling a bit dazed, Shadon shook his head and, with swords drawn, the three ran toward their friends. As they got closer, they noticed two more prisoners. Rassia and Kalath. Tnasha stopped short.

Aragel had since decided he had a wonderful plan. He ran up to the guards frantically. Upon his approach, he adopted the a less than perfect Kersian dialect. "Hurry, the commander needs you at the front to kill the beast. We are supposed to take the prisoners around the other side of the island until the beast is defeated."

Without question, the soldiers hurried off.

Shadon almost laughted aloud as he began to unbind their friends' hands and feet. Herding the group toward the docks, Shadon smacked Aragel's arm. "Come on, let's get out of here now before they realize they were fooled. Either they're stupid, or you are not as daft as I thought. How did you know it would work?"

Aragel ran beside him. "I didn't. I was hoping they were nervous and distracted enough to fall for it."

For being quite elderly, Kalath was spry and able to keep up with them. He turned to them briefly as they ran. "Who cares why it worked. It did. Let's concentrate on getting out of here."

"I think we're going to need some weapons," Alena yelled above the cacophony.

"There is no time!" Kalath hurried them forward, shoving with his hands, herding them toward the docks. "We must make haste to where the boats are moored. We will find a ship there. Don't stop!"

The seven ran without looking back. On their approach, they spied a large fishing boat, which they took, leaving the Kersians to the serpent – and their deaths.

CHAPTER 32

Serena stood in the main hall facing the crowd of men and women before her. Commander Corigerg, with his arm nestled in a white linen sling, stood beside her. "You all have done more than I could have alone. For this I am forever grateful." Tears of joy came to her eyes. "From this day forward, any man who wishes to fight for Sherok is welcome to enlist in our permanent military. Without all of you…" she paused, sweeping the crowd with her gaze to include every last one. "Sherok would not be. My father would be so proud."

The soldiers of Sherok cheered and clapped.

Commander Corigerg lifted his good hand to her shoulder, giving it a reassuring squeeze. "Dismissed!"

Joyous comrades-at-arms filed from the room. Serena smiled at Corigerg. "I never lost faith in you." Tears poured freely down her cheeks.

"You were very brave, My Queen."

"At least Hermond is dead, but his father escaped." She pursed her lips and set her jaw, wiping the tears from her face with a silk kerchief.

"He may come back with more war ships. If he does, he is in for a fight. I think he knows better, though." Corigerg closed his eyes and rubbed his forehead.

Serena looked toward the main entrance of the hall. "Any word from the Danarians?"

"Reports from Orana Tulk suggested Aragel escaped on a ship before the raid. The Danarians have sent war ships to Zul."

"What would Aragel be doing on Zul?" Serena gave the commander a disapproving look.

"I'm sure he had reason."

"Nonsense. When he gets back here, I'm in my right mind to take him across my knee!"

Commander Corigerg smiled. "He's not a child anymore, My Queen. As a matter of fact, when he gets back, he may want his throne."

She smiled. "Well, he had better come back to me safe. If he does, I will *gladly* remain a princess."

"We all pray he returns safe."

"I need some rest. It has been one eventful week." Serena forced a smile and turned to leave.

"My Queen?"

She turned back to Corigerg.

"Don't worry. Aragel is an intelligent young man and a competent swordsman. He was in good company. Your brother will have kept him safe."

Elation washed over Serena, her smile no longer forced, but genuine. "Thank you, Corigerg. May the gods always bless and keep you." She strode from the main hall, feeling for the first time in weeks that everything would turn out fine.

●

The Danarian warships moved quickly. Lord Termark and Lord Kyran stood at the helm, passing the spyglass between them.

Kyran forced a laugh, but his eyes told a different story. The dark circles beneath them gave away his exhaustion. "What are we expecting to see again?"

"Some small measure of hope, my friend. Hope." Termark squinted through the lens searching the early morning horizon. Even though there was barely enough light, he persisted. Suddenly, he caught glimpse of what looked like a small fishing boat and his heart leapt into his throat. "How far would you expect a small fishing boat to stray from shore?"

Kyran yawned with a shrug, but ventured a guess anyway. "A few miles perhaps. Rhetorical question?"

"There is nothing rhetorical about it. Look." He handed the glass to Kyran, pointing. "Look there."

Kyran saw it. His stomach jumped. "There isn't land anywhere near here except Zul. The boat, if my eyes do not deceive me, is moving away from Zul."

"Zul is twenty-five miles due northeast of here." A broad smile appeared on Termark's lips.

"Maybe the fishing is better?" Kyran suggested. He did not want to get his hopes up.

"We should be coming upon a Kersian fishing boat in the next hour," Termark shouted over his shoulder. "Due east."

The Danarian's fleet of warships pressed on, the morning wind kind in urging their ships forward at a good clip. As the water and wind carried them closer to the fishing boat, the sun began its ascent, lifting the first rays of golden light above the watery horizon. Termark put the glass to his eye again. Another broad smile extended across his lips. He handed the glass to Kyran. "The gods have looked upon us kindly this day. There will be no battle." He gave Kyran a stiff pat on the back.

Kyran lifted the glass to his eye and saw her. He felt a tear of joy escape the corner of his eye.

●

Adarack stared into the water, his aging eyes laden with worry. He turned to his first mate with a sigh of resignation. "Turn the ship about."

The man gave him a puzzled look, but did as he was told.

Jerred, the young deck hand, approached the captain with the cage. Inside, Snowflake, squawked noisily. "Cap'n, we's turnin' about?"

The captain put his hand on Jerred's shoulder. "There are some things in this world, lad, which we must do, even when it goes against our better judgment. Leave the bird here. Go below to my cabin, and bring me my sword."

Jerred set the bird's cage down and hurried to do as instructed. He returned quickly with the sword, handing it to the captain warily. "What's ya gonna do with 'is, Cap'n?"

Adarack gathered his men around him. "Arm yourselves and ready the harpoons. If necessary we shall fight the Kersians."

His first mate twisted his thin mouth in protest. "You expect us to fight Kersians for the wages we're paid? I will not risk my life for fools."

Several other men mumbled in agreement.

"Is this more dangerous than battling a hurricane?"

The men fell silent, awkwardly attentive.

Adarak felt his expression turn sour with disgust at their cowardice. "You risk your lives every day aboard this ship. The Kersians have killed people you knew and loved. Well," he paused, meeting each startled gaze directly. "I have left a dear friend. Someone I care about. I will not *run* while he stands and fights those people who would destroy all of us if they had the opportunity!"

A wave of murmuring passed over the men crowded around him.

Adarack turned to his first officer. "Are you such a coward that you fear death?"

The man's gaze fell to his feet in shame.

"Now – arm yourselves and prepare to fight!"

The men, still startled by the captain's orders, obeyed them willingly. The ship came alive with the bustle of practiced, synchronized activity.

"I'm coming for you, my friend," Adarack whispered into the wind. He looked west, staring into the gray water. Something moved. He picked up his spyglass and searched the horizon. He smiled, bent down, and lifted Snowflake's cage to the railing. Upon opening it, the raven flew out, toward the west.

●

Morvack and Gavgal found themselves standing on a cliff on the opposite end of Zul, looking out over the ocean. Gavgal fell forward, feeling sharp pain in his chest. Morvack steadied him.

"How badly are you injured?" Morvack leaned around to inspect the wound left by the sorceress' mana blate.

"I will be fine once I go into the temple to regenerate and rebalance. Help me." He directed his brother away from the cliff's edge, inland toward the entrance of a small, weathered stone temple. He hobbled toward it, hanging on to Morvack's arm for support. Once they reached the entryway, Gavgal started forward. "Stay here."

Morvack obeyed.

Upon entering the meager temple, Gavgal made his way across the barren floor to the stone altar and knelt in front of it. "Unnamed one, I ask for your help and direction," he whispered, trying to ignore the pain.

The blate wound in his chest began burning. From within, a deep blue light surged forth, healing the wound.

"You already know what to do," came a hollow voice from the other side of the altar.

Gavgal looked up. A dark figure stood there. Never before had the unnamed appeared before him and spoken to him directly. "I praise you, Lord."

"I need no praise. Now stand."

He did as he was told, averting his gaze from the dark figure, not wanting to look upon the unnamed for fear of retribution. "What shall I do?"

"Find the ancient artifact and use it as you intended," the voice, void of emotion told him. "Now go."

The Kersian Administrator bowed and left the temple just as he was told to. When he emerged from the temple he found Morvack waiting patiently, wearing an eager expression.

"How did you heal so quickly?" Morvack seemed surprised.

"I spoke with the unnamed and he told me what we must do." Gavgal's gaze turned seaward. "It is time for our alternative plan, dear brother. We will be given everything we desire, and the sorceress has sealed her own fate. I will deal with her myself."

Morvack's gaze followed his brother's. Both men looked out over the water seeing a prosperous future on the horizon.

•

"The serpent wise deals death to lies." Rassia was the first to break the silence.

Kalath merely nodded. The others said nothing.

Tnasha held her amulet in front of her, watching it swing on the broken silver chain. "I'm going to have to cleanse this amulet. It has Gavgal stench on it." Her statement was met with several snickers and forced laughter.

Alena was not so easily amused. Afraid and irritated, she kicked the deck. "We're completely defenseless if they come after us."

Kolgern snorted, wincing as the pain shot through his arm. "Tnasha, Shadon, and Aragel still have weapons. You can use that pole net over there."

She stamped her foot and glared at him. "Great. A pole net."

Rassia hid an amused smile as she and Kalath inspected Kolgern's wound.

"Calm down, Alena. I doubt the Kersians will be coming after us. They were preoccupied with my serpent friend. I'm pretty sure I hurt Gavgal, too. I hurt him good. And I doubt Morvack will give us any trouble with Gavgal out of the way. He was merely a pawn in his brother's grand delusion." Tnasha gripped the amulet in her hand and inspected the broken chain. The link where the chain was broke, was missing.

"I think you killed him. That disappearing act probably didn't help the injury," Shadon agreed. "As a matter of fact, couldn't that, alone, have killed him?"

Kalath nodded. "If it didn't kill him, it gave him a terrible imbalance, which could eventually kill him. He has no sorceresses or healers to help regenerate his flesh." Kalath's gaze went distant. He added hopefully, "I believe that's the last of him."

Aragel sat back against the bulwark below the railing. "But Morvack is still alive and well. What if he decides to avenge his brother?"

Tnasha shook her head. "He won't. People like him are easily led. I wouldn't be surprised if he and his other brothers simply disappear."

"How can you be so sure? You act as though this is the end of the Kersians." Alena's voice rang crisp on the cool morning air.

"There is only one thing for sure, Alena," Shadon asserted. "There will always be men like Gavgal and Morvack. Just as there will always be people like us who will fight against them. There is no escaping that and no guaranteeing that we are rid of madmen forever."

Alena forced a weak smile. "I suppose so."

"The knife does not appear to have hit an artery." The old sorcerer patted Kolgern on the back.

"Can't you use sorcery to heal it?" Aragel asked.

"Kolgern is not a sorcerer."

"So sorcerers can only heal sorcerers?" Aragel looked perplexed.

"Uh huh." Kalath stood. "Healers, like me, are rare. The females of our race do have the ability to heal through regeneration. But that's a different type of healing."

"It's just a painful flesh wound then?" Shadon gave Kolgern a weak grin.

Kolgern curled his lip. "It throbs."

Rassia put her hands on her hips. "Of course it does. You have a hole in your arm."

"So he's not going to bleed to death?" Tnasha asked, prodding them for an answer to Shadon's question.

"Not today, though I doubt he could handle a sword right now." Kalath stood, allowing Rassia to bandage the wound.

Aragel rubbed his eyes. "I'm such an idiot."

All eyes focused on him.

"Why is that?" Kalath lifted an eyebrow.

"I suppose I figured all sorcerers could heal people. I was wrong."

Tnasha laughed. "We can all do different things. Evidently my ability is conjuring serpents." She put on a crooked grin. "Now I know why you were inching away from me in the galley back on the ship."

"I was not," Aragel protested weakly.

Kolgern snickered. "With your lousy sorcery, Tnasha, I'd inch away from you, too. But since you're my friend..."

She shot him a playful warning glance. "Watch it or I'll injure that other arm."

They all laughed. But under the surface, discomfort lingered.

Tnasha took a ragged, shallow breath. "So what will you do now, Aragel?"

Aragel tipped his head. "I guess I'll go to Danaria to get reinforcements, then go back to Sherok, take back my throne and learn to be a king." He gazed off into the water. "I hope Serena is all right."

Shadon placed an arm over Aragel's shoulders. "Serena is more stubborn than you know. By the time we arrive with the Danarian legions, I'm sure she'll have Hermond in a cage. Women have a way with that sort of thing. Besides, she has Corigerg there to protect her."

Kalath interrupted. "Shadon, be a good man and steer this boat in a westerly direction, please."

High above a bird squawked. Aragel looked up, feeling the hair on his arms stand on end. A black raven circled high above them. He pointed skyward. "It's Snowflake!" His attention turned east. "And Adarack."

From the west, three Danarian warships sped their way to meet the fishing boat. From the east, Adarack's ship hurried to greet them.

Tnasha stood up. Excitement and warmth shot through her. It was the feeling of finally being safe, and she had instinct to thank.   "Traveling on the left horse black. Tell it again, Kolgern."

Kolgern leaned against the mast of the small fishing boat and ran a hand through his knotted and tangled blond hair. He smiled appreciatively. His voice, a bit weak, broke the stillness. "Before the world split, all horses were black…"   ∎

Watch for the following Darkerwood Publishing titles also
by *S. J. Reisner*

Sorcerers' Twilight Series
- Warrior's Blood Red - *Book Two* (Fall/Winter 2006)
- Eagle's Talon Gray - *Book Three* (Fall 2007)

www.ingramcontent.com/pod-product-compliance
Lightning Source LLC
Chambersburg PA
CBHW071249250626
47163CB00002B/395